LEXIA

The *Deadwood Hunter* Series

Rachel M Raithby

COPYRIGHT

First published 2013
4th Edition June 2017

Cover Design by Rob Smith of www.creationinspire.com
Interior Design by Kat Smith of www.creationinspire.com

Dedication

For my Gram, Dot.

For always being there, no matter the miles between us.
For always knowing the right words to say.

I love you.

Books by Rachel M Raithby

The Deadwood Hunter Series

Lexia

Whispers of Darkness

Holocaust

Box Set – Bonus Alice story

The New Dawn Novels

Winter Wolf

Wolf Dancer

Wolf Sight

Novellas

The Beast Within – Woodland Creek Series

Deaths Echo – The Complex Series

ACKNOWLEDGEMENTS

A huge thank you...

To my beautiful children for putting up with average meals and days of watching movies whilst I sat lost in the worlds I created in my head, to my mum for the hours you spent reading draft after draft of "Lexia." For always answering a facebook message no matter the time of night and your support in this crazy adventure.

To Dad for putting up with all the hours I stole mum and making such awesome covers and book trailers.

To all my friends who put up with me, grumpy and tired from all the late nights I've spent writing, and to all my followers on FB and Twitter, you've kept me going on days I've wanted to cry!

Prologue

The panther prowled the night drawn to something he didn't understand; leaping from rooftop to rooftop, he heard a soft cry. Looking down he saw a young woman being attacked by vampires. As his lean panther body tensed to jump, she let out a wild cry, throwing them off herself. He froze, transfixed, as she ripped them apart with her bare hands, like a wild, crazed animal. Moving with a cat-like grace, she spun around to face the last vampire. Brilliant gold streaks run through crystal blue eyes; lighting the dark night.

That's what you are, Little Wildcat, he thought, moving back into the shadows, as her screams rang out into the night.

CHAPTER 1

Her feet pounded on the pavement as she raced down the dirty backstreets of Deadwood. The night cool, it turned each heavy breath into a misty opaque vapor.

They're so fast, she thought, *why didn't I stay in tonight? Just for some stupid party…Now I'm being chased by these... these... things. What are they?*

Turning the corner, Lexia stumbled on the uneven curb. Regaining her balance she gasped, pulse freezing as came to a dead end. Whirling around, she faced the three creatures circling her, fear closed her throat like icy fingers, strangling the scream desperate to escape. Her eyes widened in fright as they flashed their razor sharp teeth at her. *Vampires?*

Blood-red eyes, full of the intent to kill, their pale ghostly skin stretched tight over the hard angular bones of their faces; these creature looked like they'd walked off the set of a horror movie.

Back flat against the wall, Lexia's hands grazed the rough surface, wishing she could somehow melt into it. Her body shook in terror as tears silently rolled down her face. *I'm sorry, Dad,* she thought as they leapt at once.

Whimpering, she curled into a ball, their nails slashed at her skin, gouging into flesh. Fear clawed her mind, blackness taking over, when...

Mind suddenly blank, pain rippled through her. It was torture as adrenaline rushed through her veins, charging her muscles with a strength, which took over her body.

Screaming she stood, throwing the vampires to the ground. Her next moves were not her own; she tore them limb from limb, until there was nothing left but her quivering body, soaked in blood. Smell; metallic and bitter, filled her nostrils. With heavy breaths, Lexia turned slowly, looking at the scene, seeing blood, death, and a never ending darkness.

For what felt like hours, Lexia gazed upon the hell before her. The torn bodies rotted before her eyes, then turned to dust and blew away.

Panic bubbled like acid, coating her tongue as voice came back with a vengeance, she screamed. Screamed so hard her throat burned. Tears ran down her blood-stained face. She'd created this darkness. She'd caused their deaths.

Hearing distant footfalls, Lexia looked one last time, before running mindlessly into the night. Concentrating only on putting one foot in front of the other, of feeling the vibrations travelling up each leg as she raced away.

Opening her eyes slowly, Lexia frowned at the leaves blocking her vision. Brushing them away from her face, her gaze zeroed in on the fine cracks forming in the dried blood coating her hands. *Dried blood?* Memories from the previous night suddenly bombarded her mind. Jumping to her feet, Lexia braced to attack, only to find herself alone, surrounded by tall pine trees, their needles littered the ground, and stuck to her clothes.

Why she'd ended in this location she wasn't sure. Deep in the forest that surround her home, she saw no one as she scanned the dense trees. Deciding she was definitely alone, Lexia ran in the direction she hoped was home.

Dad's going to freak if he finds me missing–He was due to take her to school that morning.

Finding some hidden energy, she pushed for more speed, soon arriving at the edge of the trees lining her garden. There were no signs of life inside the old wooden house. Running across the grass to the trellis below her window, climbing with an ease she'd not had before, Lexia landed in her room, slipping under the duvet as her dads head poked around the door

"Time to get up Lex, sweetie," he said.

Lexia's dad, Mike, raised her on his own, since her mother, Lucy, had walked out when Lexia was five months old. Lexia had only one picture of her mother, taken when she had been born; Lucy looked down at her baby, her pale blond hair covering her face. Lexia didn't know what she looked like but sometimes she would dream of a woman with blond hair singing to her.

She'd asked her dad if her mother had sung to her as a child but he'd never answer her questions. Always closing up, he'd snap at her, as if the mere thought of Lucy caused him pain. Lexia had tried to come to terms with the fact that she would never know her mother, and the reason she'd been left behind. Sometimes, though, no matter how hard Lexia tried, she long to meet her mother.

As her dad walked down the stairs, Lexia climbed from under the duvet, looking at herself in the full-length mirror, hung on the back of the door.

Her long boots were torn, the leather stained with blood. Running her hands over her shredded jeans, she turned slightly so the back of her blouse was in sight; it to was ripped. Pulling the shirt off, to inspect her torn skin, Lexia realized some of her wounds were already healing.

Stripping, Lexia looked at herself, dressed in only her panties and bra; even with all the muck and blood staining her skin, she couldn't miss the subtle changes to her body. Her stomach just that tiny bit tighter, the slightest hints of a six pack showing. Her whole body had become more refined; as she moved, muscle shifted beneath her skin.

Leaning toward the mirror, gazing closely at a slash across her cheek, Lexia watched in horror as the flesh knitted together, felt the tingling, stabbing sensation. Running a finger across the red scar line, it then disappeared leaving behind unblemished skin, vanishing as if she'd just imagined the whole thing.

"What has happened to me?" she whispered against her

fingers, looking at eyes gone wide with fright. No longer were they a clear, crystal blue but lined by a fine rim of gold.

She wanted to hide, to run, to cry, but there was no hiding from this; there was something wrong with her, the evidence staring back, every time she looked in a mirror.

Backing away from her reflection, unable to tear her eyes away from the stranger staring back at her, Lexia's heart galloped in her chest, emotions bombarded her, her mind in chaos. Stumbling into the back of the bed, she gasped, "What am I?"

"Lexia, everything alright?" her Dad called up the stairs.

She didn't answer at first. Not knowing the answer.

"Lex?"

"Yeah...fine, Dad. I just tripped," she answered. Her eyes hardened, she could never tell a soul.

Dashing across the hall Lexia locked herself in the bathroom, and stepped into the tub, turning on the shower. The near-scalding water skimmed her body and turned red at her feet. Fixated on the swirl of reddish, pink water around her feet, Lexia played the night before over in her wind. She wondered whether she had gone mad, whether everything had just been a dream. But it was hard to ignore the blood washing down the drain; it wasn't make-believe, and the cuts and scrapes covering her skin had been made by the sharp nails of vampires. Yet the scariest thing of all—magically watching her skin heal. What am I?

Chapter 2

School moved at a snail's pace and Lexia struggled to listen to anything in class that day. *Thank god school's nearly over.*

Walking through the bustling school, Lexia's friend, Alice talked a mile a minute over the sound of banging lockers, and shouts of the other students.

Alice was unaware Lexia was finding it hard to pay attention. Looking at her friend, Lexia thought how quickly things had changed; in a single moment her life had taken a three hundred and sixty degree turn.

Alice carried on babbling about some boy, but her voice blurred into background noise as Lexia turned her thoughts to more serious subjects. *What's happened to my eyes, and how did I kill those vampires? Vampires existed - how is that possible?*

"Lex, are you even listening to me? Lexia!"

Focusing on Alice's petite freckled face, her big brown eyes glaring at her in frustration, she'd tied her blond hair into a ponytail. Alice always dressed up-to-date with the latest fashion, spending most her time worrying over her looks and the latest boy she liked. They had an easy friendship, one with no secrets or lies. *Until now; why can't I just go back to worrying about boys and which parties I should attend? God why do I have to keep replaying last night? Their blood red eyes, the feeling of power...*

"Lexia!"

"Sorry, Alice, can't do the party, I'm working."

She had a shift at the local diner that night. It didn't pay much, but she was saving for college, so she could escape the small town.

"Oh, that's crap, I'm not going to the party alone."

"You could always come keep me company?" Lexia asked, already knowing her answer.

"No, thank you, I am not sitting there bored all night."

Lexia smiled to herself, Alice was allergic to hard work, or being anywhere near it. Walking out of the school, Lexia heard Alice this time. "Got time for a quick coffee before work?"

"It will have to be quick," she smiled at Alice. How hard she had it, having to spend a night alone.

They walked the short distance to the local coffee shop all the students used, door chiming as they walked in, Lexia rushed for the last two remaining sofa chairs in the corner.

"Grab me a sandwich, and cake too, please, Alice."

Watching her friend impatiently tapping her foot on the wooden floors as she waited in line, made Lexia giggle to herself;

they were complete opposites. Lexia laid back and breezy, and Alice impatient and fiery, yet they complemented each other perfectly, had been best friends since the moment they met on the first day of school. Alice was the only one of Lexia's friends who knew about her mother leaving. The only one who knew Lexia was older than all the other students in her year. Lexia told her everything and for the first time in her life she had something that not even Alice could know.

Alice put down their food and then plonked herself in the chair opposite, sighing dramatically. She looked at Lexia, frowning. "Hey, Lex."

"Yeah?"

"Are you alright? I mean, you seem really distant; you'd tell me if something was wrong?"

Should I tell her the truth? "I'm fine, honestly," she said, plastering a smile on her face.

Lexia spent the next thirty minutes forcing herself to pay attention to every word Alice said. Fortunately Alice was the talkative one out of the duo, as long as Lexia added a comment or two, Alice was happy. When they parted ways, Lexia thought she'd done a good job convincing Alice she was okay.

Arriving at her house, Lexia walked down the long driveway leading to her house. Stopping she looked into the forest, feeling as if someone was watching her, but could see no one. Rushing away just in case, Lexia bolted the door behind her. The strangest feeling had come over her; the hairs on the back of her neck stood on end, and every nerve in her body felt like it was electrified. Peering out through the closed door, Lexia watched for movement in the trees but nothing stirred, she ran up the stairs and threw herself on the bed with a sigh. "I'm losing my mind," she muttered.

She'd never been one to be afraid of being alone, but right now Lexia jumped at every shadow. She felt as if her body was on high alert, ready and willing to attack at a moment's notice. If she wasn't mad, then the world of the supernatural was real, and Lexia couldn't decide which was more frightening.

Three hours later, Lexia looked at herself in the mirror. She was hiding out in the bathroom at Lucky's Diner. Everyone kept mentioning her eyes; she'd tried to avoid eye contact with people but that proved hard when she had to serve them. Taking a deep breath she stepped back out into the diner, chanting the lie she'd been telling everyone all night: *it's just a play of the light, it's just a play of the light. Who the fuck am I kidding? You're a freak, Lex.*

The night turned out to be pretty busy, keeping Lexia from dwelling on her worries. Twenty minutes before closing, the door chimed; Lexia stiffened as a chill slivered over her skin. A man took a seat in front of her, he was tall and well-built, the kind of man she and Alice would drool over, and his eyes were so light brown they could have been gold. He smiled but there was nothing friendly about it; the kind of smile that whispered of danger and excitement. Lexia gulped, the hairs on the back of her neck bristling.

"What can I get you?" She smiled back, squaring her shoulders.

"Just a coffee, black." His voice was a rough caress against her skin.

Turning to fetch his coffee, she felt his eyes on her as a lion would stalk its prey. There was definitely something about this guy, but she couldn't quite put her finger on it. He felt off but not in a run for your life way. He was dangerous, but enticingly so.

Shaking her head to clear her thoughts, she returned with his coffee. He reached out for his drink, his finger brushed hers sending a jolt of heat up her arm. Gasping she lost hold of the mug. She saw nothing more than a blur, as he reached out to catch it, not spilling a drop of the liquid within.

Chuckling, he said, "Careful now, love."

"S-Sorry." Lexia turned to head for the back, needing some distance between herself and this man.

"What's your name?" he asked.

Lexia froze not sure whether to tell him her name. *Argh, stop being so paranoid, he's probably just being polite.*

Turning back around, his eyes twinkled in mischief as she looked at him. He slowly brought the mug to his lips, holding her gaze, Lexia felt trapped; unable to drop the eye contact, it was like looking into the stare of a hunter before he made his kill. She was a helpless rabbit caught in headlights; she had no choice but to answer his earlier question, "Lexia, but most people call me, Lex."

He snorted sending coffee splattering all over the counter. "You're joking?"

Temper rising, Lexia walked towards him, her fists clenched and her face harden. "No, I am not joking. Why is that so funny?" She glared at him, her eyes ablaze with anger.

He paused for a second, his smile faltering, "Lexia means 'Man's Defender,'" he answered. Looking at her as if that explained everything.

"And that's funny because? Actually don't bother answering, finish your coffee and get out." Lexia never saw his reaction; she turned and strode out back. When she'd returned five minutes later, he'd left, and the diner was empty.

"Do you wanna head off, Lexia? I'll finish up," Jan said, coming out of the kitchen door.

"Hey, are you all right?" Asked the small plump woman, her brown eyes scrunching up with concern.

"Yeah, just some jerk who was in here before, got under my skin."

"Will you be okay getting home?"

"Yeah, thanks Jan, I'll see you Friday," she called, heading for the door. All she wanted to do was crawl under her covers and hide.

Walking along Main Street away from Lucky's Diner, Lexia headed home. Her house was built on the edge of town, about a fifteen minute walk from the diner, it was set back off the Street, with a long driveway enclosed by tall pine trees, hiding the house from view.

As she turned up the drive a sickening chill set in the pit of her stomach. Lengthening her strides, each crunch of gravel made her cringe. There was movement up ahead in the shadows, stopping, her eyes adjusted to the dark. Taking a step back, her breath caught in her throat as she saw what waited her.

A woman stood ten yards ahead blocking her path to safety, only she wasn't a human woman; she had blood red eyes that glowed in the darkness, and white skin pulled sharp over her bony face. Her clothes were torn and dirty, clinging tight to bones that jutted from her skin. Standing with her feet apart, her arms hung loosely by her side, each long finger was curled, ready to strike.

"What do you want?" Lexia called, surprised how strong her voice sounded even though she was shaking with fear.

"You killed my man, bitch!" the woman spat, jumping with lightning-fast speed. She'd closed the space between them in seconds, leaving Lexia had no time to think, or draw breath to scream.

Cold, hard, steel gripped Lexia's arms, throwing her; cool air rushed past her face, before Lexia collided with a tree. Pain exploded throughout her body, gasping as she connected with the hard, unforgiving surface, the air rushed from her lungs.

For a second Lexia laid there, stunned, unable to move; tears pricked at her eyes as she tried to deal with the pain. A voice screamed in her head, '*get up*'. It told her. '*You can't just lay here and be killed! FIGHT.*' Scrambling to her feet Lexia mentally shook herself, *I've killed three of these things before, I can do this.*

Peering out into the darkness to find the vampire woman. A ghostly fist appeared before her, Lexia attempted to dodge it, but wasn't quick enough. The fist caught the side of her face; it slid off her cheekbone and past her ear as Lexia moved her head. She'd missed the full force of the punch, but still felt dazed. Aiming hits blindly, hoping the vampire would back off while her head stopped spinning.

By sheer luck her fist connected with the vampire, yet she never flinched. Each blow felt like hitting concrete, with each wave of pain up her arms, Lexia's spirit dropped. Panting furiously she tried again to cause the vampire injury, but she was formidable and soon Lexia grew tired. The energy and strength she'd had, drained away with each punch, or block Lexia made.

Knocked to the ground, the vampire's teeth snapped near her throat. Lexia brought her knees up as a barrier, desperately trying to keep the vampire from her neck, but her muscles ached; a dark gloom clouded her mind. *There's no point*, Lexia wanted it to be over; the fight, the fear, the madness she'd felt gripping at her all day. Looking up into the savage face of the woman above her, the woman who would bring death. She no longer had any resemblance to a human, she snapped and snarled like a savage beast, her blood-red eyes bulged from their sockets.

Closing her eyes, feeling oddly calm she prepared for the pain that would surely come with death. But when her eyes closed she didn't see darkness, but the face of her dad. Sadness enveloped her as she thought of how he would be alone if she died.

Picturing her dad gave her power; it raged through her worn-out muscles, pleasure and pain erupting throughout her body, giving her the strength to throw the vampire off. Lexia felt around on the ground desperately searching for some kind of weapon, as her fingers brushed across a sharp branch, she felt a surge of hope fill her. She was strong, she was invincible, and as the branch sank through the vampire's heart Lexia smiled, feeling elated. The vampire woman slumped to the floor, the branch still protruding from her chest, her blood-red eyes widened in disbelief, looking at Lexia stood above her. The adrenaline, the ecstasy, rippled through Lexia, and for just a moment Lexia felt like a god; alive, powerful, her prey dead at her feet.

The body rotted away, panic replaced the endorphins. Like a tsunami Lexia had no hope at stopping it. She ran towards the house as her chest constricted, her stomach twisting in revulsion.

Inside the dark, quiet hall, Lexia took huge breaths before collapsing to the floor; a trembling, frightened mess, lost in the dark.

Crawling up the stairs, careful not to wake her dad, Lexia stripped off her clothes, climbed between cool sheets and closed her eyes. Curled into a tight ball, gripping her knees, small tremors travelled down her body. She willed herself to sleep, hoping to shut out the horrifying images, hoping that maybe she would wake tomorrow, and the past two days would have been only a nightmare

CHAPTER 3

Her dad left early for work the next morning. Lexia listened to him leave normally she would still be asleep, but she'd tossed and turned all night; vampires and death haunting her dreams. With no one home it made it easy to skip school; pulling the duvet over her head, she planned to stay in bed for most of the day; she wanted to wallow.

When she finally crawled from her pit of despair, Lexia had made the decision to no longer hide from her problems. Grabbing her laptop, Lexia brought up a search engine, and typed in 'Vampire.' She sat for hours filling her head with information. Most of it seemed to be fantasy, but she was beginning to believe not everything was as it seemed. By late afternoon she'd ordered herself a stake, and a silver knife from a site she'd found - they did next day delivery, too - she hoped nothing would attack her before then.

"I cannot believe they sell this stuff on the internet!" she muttered to herself.

Her phone vibrated, Lexia looked down to see ten texts from Alice, the latest read:

Why aren't you at school & why are you ignoring me? Up for going out later?

Lexia didn't reply, she had no idea what to say; she never missed school, and she always kept in touch with Alice.

Suddenly her room felt too small; the walls seemed to be closing around her. Vampires and the supernatural buzzed through her mind.

"I've got to get out of here." Lexia pulled off her pajamas as if they were suffocating her. Changing into running clothes, she dashed from the house onto the trail near her home; she'd run this path so many times it felt like a second home.

Watching her feet move steadily over the forest, she fell into a steady rhythm. Relaxing, she inhaled and exhaled with the thud of her steps.

As a sheen of sweat covered her skin, and her breathing grew heavy, Lexia turned for home.

Jogging slower, her senses alert as she felt eyes on her. Her chest tightened, her heart rate doubled, as she glanced around, her mind racing. *It's not night time. Vampires can't go out in the sun? What else was out there if vampires were real?*

Catching movement to the right, Lexia picked up her pace, cursing herself for tiring herself out. Lexia pushed herself to the limit; her heart threatened to beat right out of her chest. She glanced back… *What the fuck!* Risking another glance, she saw a sleek, black, panther prowling through the trees.

The panther was closing the gap between them. Lexia's breathing labored with each hard footfall. The exit was nearing. *I'm gonna make it... I am going to make it!* She chanted in her mind. Yet Lexia was growing tired, she couldn't keep up her pace for long; her lungs burned with fiery strain.

But you're not just anyone, a voice whispered in her mind. Pushing past the burn, increasing her speed, tapping into power, which had always been there, hidden away deep inside. *No, I'm not just anyone, not anymore.*

With the exit just yards away, a surge of hope filled her, but her foot caught, twisting on a rut, pitching her forward. Her hands reached out as she hit the ground, the air rushed out of her body, on impact. A car screeched, stopping centimeters from Lexia, and scattered gravel into her face. Scrambling back, rubbing at her eyes, she looked for the panther. In the trees she saw a blur of midnight black, its gold eyes seemed to glow, before it turned, and vanished back into the undergrowth.

"Lex! Lexia! Oh my God, are you alright?" her dad shouted running to her side, shaking her lightly, "Lexia, what were you doing?"

Dragging her eyes from the forest, she focused on his distraught face. "I...I...I thought I saw something, chasing me, a-an animal."

Lines of confusion marked his face. "What kind of animal?"

Looking into her dad's face Lexia thought she might tell him everything. *He's always been there for me...* But as he looked at her; as if she'd lost her mind. Lexia realized, this was a secret she could never tell.

"Lexia, are you sure you're—look at your eyes, they're…?"

Lexia tore her gaze away from her dad, his last question lingered in the air. Panic twisted her gut, jumping to her feet, Lexia was afraid of the way he was looking at her. "Yes, yes, I'm fine, must have been running too long." Turning, she dashed to the house, heading for the bathroom, leaving her dad staring at the spot she just ran from.

He didn't bother her after that. Feeling lost and confused, his face replayed across her mind. She couldn't quite grasp his expression, he'd looked at her like she was a stranger, or his worst nightmare come to life. He felt miles away from her, even though in reality he was down the hall. She couldn't shake the feeling, in that moment, as he had stared into her new eyes, she had lost him forever. The feeling settled heavy in her stomach, twisting at her insides.

She had to get out of the house; there were too many thoughts and feelings inside of her, slowly growing and twisting, threatening to consume her. She needed a distraction.

Looking at herself in the mirror an hour later; she'd dressed into a short, tight dress that clung to her every curve, it was made in a soft grey material. The color seemed to make her eyes sparkle even brighter, the new ring of gold muted against the crystal blue; she smiled, feeling more like her old self.

Tying her long, wavy brown hair over one shoulder, ringlets

curling together over her breast, and a few escaped curls framed her face. Pairing the dress with long leather boots that stopped just below her knees, Lexia stared at the person before her, the person she used to be. This person in the mirror looking back at her was her old self; she didn't understand what death was, or what it felt like to be utterly lost. She was young, and free; her only worry - to get out of Deadwood.

For a brief moment Lexia wondered if she could pull it off, whether she could climb out of her window like she'd done so many nights before, meeting Alice and being an ordinary teenage girl. *Fuck it! I can't sit around here with all my thoughts.*

Slipping her fake ID into her purse, she sent a quick text to Alice, asking her to meet her, and then pulled up the window, climbing down. Leaving her worries and troubles behind her, she felt her gut unravel as she landed softly on the ground and raced away.

Alice turned up an hour after Lexia, she'd already had a few drinks, and different men kept coming up to buy her more, hoping they would get lucky.

"Jeez, Lex, what are you wearing?"

"It's new, you like?" She smiled sweetly.

"Well, I see plenty who do," Alice said, glancing around and glaring at the men who were openly drooling over her exposed thighs.

"You okay, Lex? You've not been with it lately. And since

when did you dress like a slut?"

"Hey, enough abuse! I just want to have fun! Isn't that why we came?"

"Ok, I suppose, get us a drink then."

For the next hour they chatted about boys and school. Lexia felt herself relaxing, the crazy events from the last few days a distant memory. Alice mentioned the amount of drinks she was throwing back a few times, but Lexia brushed her off insisting everything was fine.

"Let's dance!" She pulled Alice up, dragging her toward the dance floor.

"Lexia, it's eleven, maybe we should head back?"

"I climbed out the window, Dad thinks I'm in bed," she giggled, "Come on, one dance. Please?" Lexia smiled, the kind of goofy smile you smile when on a happy high from too many drinks.

"O-kay."

Lexia sauntered onto the dance floor wiggling her hips, she turned around to face Alice. Alice swayed stiffly in front of her. "Come on, Alice, loosen up!" She grasped her hand making her twirl around.

"Stop it," Alice said.

"Fine." Lexia dropped Alice's hand. Turning dramatically she wiggled off into the crowd of bodies until she reached the middle of the dance floor. When she looked back, Alice was walking out the door, Alice paused for a second, giving Lexia a pleading look that said 'come home with me' and then disappeared into the night.

For a split second Lexia felt bad, but then her happy drunken haze banished the thought and she stomped over to the bar. She didn't want to think about the fact that Alice was normally the silly one out of the two of them, or about the look she'd given her, instead Lexia ordered another drink, and washed Alice from her mind with the sharp taste of vodka.

Many drinks later, Lexia was well aware she'd had too much to drink but the alcohol had numbed her brain just like she had intended it to. The pounding beat jerked at her body as she swayed to the music. She felt like a puppet being controlled by an invisible master; her hips moved on their own accord, under the spell of the music that swirled around her.

Twisting around, she noticed strange brown-gold eyes watching her from the bar. He smiled, noticing her gaze. As walked toward her, a warning whispered in a distant part of her brain, but before she could think of what it meant, his warm hands touched her hips, sending sparks across her skin. Drowning in sensation Lexia twirled around, hands in the air, moving along to the hypnotic music, his body pressed along the length of hers, making every nerve come to life. The lights and sounds blurred together, bodies brushing by hers as they swayed and danced around her. Their energy crackled in the air, making Lexia's skin tingle; it was a heady feeling and for once Lexia let go.

His hands trailed up and down her body leaving a scorching mark. He spun her around, pulling her close, their bodies touched, her breasts rubbed against his chest. His eyes widened as she gave a slow seductive twist of her hips, she smiled, taunting him; it was so unlike her, yet she felt as if someone had taken over her body. It felt good, empowering, to feel how she affected him, to see his eyes focus on only her. In that moment as they both swayed and twisted as if one, she felt spellbound, lost in the fever of lust that spun around them like a magical web.

Someone bumped into Lexia, a jolt of dread ran through her body. Spinning around she looked for the person who'd knocked her, yet everyone was dancing lost in their own secret worlds. Hands skim over the curve of her hips, wrapping themselves around her waist, and pulling her close. Lexia pulled away, the spell had been broken, and as her vision cleared, shivers, having nothing to do with arousal crawled down her spine. Looking up into his eyes, they seemed so familiar, but there was something not quite right about her mystery dancer. Stumbling back, Lexia staggered to the exit; he held out his hand, a questioning look in those golden-brown eyes but didn't follow.

Cold air hit her as she stepped outside. Wrapping her arms around herself, Lexia headed for home, feeling stupid for how she'd acted tonight; getting so drunk when danger seemed to be following her around every corner. She knew she had to do more than just type 'vampire' into a search engine; she'd changed, and now she was seeing the world for how it was. Had there always been darkness around her, and she'd only just noticed it? She couldn't carry on being so reckless, otherwise she may wind up dead.

Lexia managed to walk home without seeing anyone and

as she snuggled into bed she felt as if she was finally coming to terms with the events of the past few days. Suddenly exhausted, sleep claimed her almost straight away, she drifted off dreaming of a golden-eyed stranger drawing tingling trails across her skin.

CHAPTER 4

Lexia woke the next morning feeling well-rested and ready to take on the world. She dressed quickly, almost skipping down the stairs to find her dad, but found the kitchen empty. She looked around the old kitchen and noticed a plate and coffee mug sat on the countertop. Glancing at the clock, it read just after 7.30 am so he shouldn't have left for work yet. "Dad?" she called, heading back into the hall in search of life.

A note sat on the hall table, the single line looking as lonely as she felt: *Lexia, I had to work early.* Dropping the note she watched as it floated to the floor. With each flutter towards the ground, her stomach followed and when it lightly came to rest, Lexia realized there was more than just the unordinary troubling her life. She could feel the distance growing between her, and her father as if it was a physical thing.

Walking back into the kitchen Lexia felt angry at her dad; he had no right to avoid her. He was her dad, he had to stand by her always. Her anger increased turning into a torrent of rage. Balling her hands into fists she fought the urge to hit something. It churned and built within until she needed to scream. Storming across the room, Lexia caught a glimpse of her reflection. Freezing, terror replaced her anger; her eyes had changed to completely, the cold hardness within them startling.

A knock at the door caused Lexia to jump. Taking a deep, calming breath, she watched her eyes change from gold to blue, then the knock came again. "Just a minute," she called, her voice breaking. *Oh God what is happening to me? I feel so out of control.*

Opening the door Lexia found a delivery guy holding a package. Signing quickly she took the package, barely registering the man as she slammed the door in his face.

Ripping open the package with her hands, she didn't pause until her fingers brushed smooth silver. Taking the slick, sliver knife in her hand, she twisted it around watching the early morning light glint off the metal. Smiling she felt strangely powerful. *God I wish there was something around I could kill!*

Startled by the strange direction her thoughts had taken she dropped the knife back into its box. Next picking up the stake; the smooth silky wood felt cool against her skin. Excited, Lexia decided to try out her new toys. Heading out to the old shed outback, Lexia pulled the creaky wooden doors open and amongst the old boxes, and cobwebs, found her dad's punching bag, a film of dust covering its surface, hung in the back.

Having cleared the junk to the side, Lexia stood staring at the bag, stake in hand. *Well now or never, Lexia; time to die, punch bag!* She jabbed the stake forward, a cloud of dust puffed into the air but the stake didn't pierce the fabric. She tried again putting all her body weight into the thrust, but still the stake only just cut through. *God, Lexia, you can't even kill a bag.* Frustrated she put all she had into the jab; hitting the bag the stake slid in an inch, and she stumbled forward. "Stupid thing! How am I supposed to stake a vampire if I can't even stake a bag?"

Lexia punched the bag, repeatedly, as he rage and fear from the past few days built within her. She channeled it into her strikes, jolts of shock ran up her arms, and a sheen of sweat broke out across her skin. With fury flowing through her veins the stake this time slid through the fabric, and into the bag with ease. Pulling the stake back, Lexia inspected the hole. *God that felt good.*

Hearing a rustle behind her, Lexia stilled, slowly she looked around, seeing a reflection on the dusty surface of an old cracked mirror. The black panther, reflected back, crouched low to strike. Looking at the knife laid on the table besides her, Lexia made a split second decision. She spun with the grace of a ballerina, taking the knife in her hand as it brushed past. The knife left her hand, flying true, turning over in the air before sinking into the ground where the cat had been seconds ago. Running forward, Lexia bent to retrieve the knife, catching a glimpse of the panther retreating into the green depths of the forest.

For a second, Lexia felt overwhelmed with the urge to hunt down the panther. She stepped forward, gripping the knife tight in her hand, feeling the impulse take hold, she imagined sinking the sharp blade into the smooth, velvet fur of the cat... Sucking in a breath she mentally shook herself; *where did that come from? I need to get my emotions in check.*

Lexia returned to the shed feeling a little troubled by the

overpowering anger she'd been feeling on and off since the day of the vampire attack. Needing a distraction she practiced for the rest of the day, and when she closed the wooden doors later, all her troubling thoughts had been forgotten, replaced with tired, aching muscles, and an odd excitement.

Using the weapons felt like second nature now. At first Lexia was startled by the strength she had and how natural it felt to hold a weapon, yet somewhere deep inside, she knew she'd be needing these skills.

CHAPTER 5

Lexia headed inside to shower and change, deciding she would cook her dad supper; they hadn't sat down together in a few days, and she missed him. She hoped the simple act of sharing a meal together would fix the problems between them.

Gathering the ingredients to make lasagna, she got to work on the task at hand: thinly slicing onions and garlic, putting them in the pan to fry, next she added the ground beef, stirring until it browned. Canned tomatoes bubbled away, the smell of basil filling the kitchen. Lexia loved cooking, it had always made her relax and since she had never had a mom growing up, the job quite often fell to her if her dad had to work late.

Lexia's dad walked through the door just as she pulled the lasagna out of the oven. He walked towards the kitchen smelling the air. "Smells good, Lex." He smiled, sitting at the table.

They ate in silence but Lexia didn't mind; it was good to be with her dad, and doing something normal. "How was work?" she asked, clearing the plates.

"Good, you know, just the same. How was school?"

Turning to the sink, feeling guilty, she began to wash the plates avoiding his face as she answered, "Yeah, good."

"That's funny, because I had a visit today asking why you were missing another day of school. Honestly, Lex, I work there."

Lexia stiffened, keeping her back to him. "Erm...Well, I was going to tell you—"

His frosty voice cut her off, "I don't want to hear your lies, Lexia. Make sure you are there for the rest of term, do you understand? Don't disappoint me again." He got up and walked from the kitchen, his final words like a brick wall between them.

She finished the dishes, walking straight out the back door and headed deeper into town, deciding some retail therapy was in order. She sent a text to Alice, asking her if she'd like to meet up.

Alice didn't ask why she had been skipping school and for that she was grateful. They chatted and laughed whilst trying on clothes and looking in the gift shops. Lexia slowly began to slip back into her old life, the more bags she carried the happier she felt, things *would* go back to normal, and her dad couldn't stay angry forever. She *would* finish school, go to college, and when she looked back years later, she would laugh at the crazy, insane things she'd done.

Lexia realized too late that Alice had been asking her a question.

"Earth to, Lexia!"

"Sorry, Alice, what did you say?"

"Just that that dress would look like a million dollars with your legs."

Laughing she took the dress into the changing room. "It's short."

"Didn't stop you last night!" she laughed.

"Hey, I'm sorry for being such a bitch last night."

"No probs, come on, let's see it."

Lexia pulled back the curtain and walked out doing a little twirl. "What do you think?"

"I think it's shorter than last night's dress and I wish I had your legs!"

Both girls laughed, and Lexia did another twirl. "You're right, too short even for your standards."

"I think it's perfect," said a deep, rough voice from the doorway.

Lexia froze, she knew that voice. Turning slowly around she sucked in a breath. She recognized his eyes straight away; they were so unusual.

"Get lost, creep," Alice snapped.

"Now, now, Lexia, and I are friends." He smiled that smart, confident smile that sent shivers down Lexia's spine.

Alice spun around, glaring at Lexia with her hands on her hips. "What is he talking about?"

Lexia ignored Alice. Looking straight at him she said, "One dance does not make us friends! Get lost."

He chuckled. "You're more fun drunk. Such a tease, made me rock hard then left." He laughed again as Alice gasped, glaring at Lexia. "Later, ladies," he drawled, turning to leave.

As soon as the door shut Alice began her lecture, Lexia wasn't listening though. She was remembering dancing with him, remembering every touch he'd placed on her body, and the way he made her feel; each caress over her hips a scorching brand.

"Lexia!" Alice yelled.

Shaking off the memories Lexia looked at Alice's enraged face. "Look, I'm sorry. I was drunk, alright? You know I'm not normally like that but come on, Alice, you can't blame me, that guy is seriously hot!" Walking into the cubicle she felt angry and embarrassed.

"I have no idea what's going on with you, Lex, but you obviously don't want to tell me. If you ever need to talk, you know where I am," Alice said sadly, before leaving.

"Alice," Lexia called to her retreating figure as she poked her head back out of the curtain.

Closing the curtain again, with a huff, Lexia took off the too-short dress and dragged on her jeans and shirt. Leaving the store, her earlier good mood had vanished, she was lying to her best friend, and her dad; Lexia didn't recognize the person she was anymore.

But what would she tell them? *Well, I kinda have eyes that glow gold, I've been killing vampires, and, oh yeah, a black panther and a stunning but scary ass guy are stalking me, too!*

*B*usy dwelling on her problems Lexia almost missed the tall man on the opposite side of the road, following her. He didn't take his eyes off her, even as she looked straight into his arctic, blue, eyes; he wore an old, torn checked shirt with faded jeans, his scruffy blond-white hair hung to his shoulders.

The shops were closing for the night, and Lexia was around ten minutes from home. The longer she walked down Upper Main Street the fewer people she would meet, but still she couldn't risk fighting him on the streets. *Think, Lexia, think! Okay, up ahead is a path to the forest that will have to do... Oh God, can I do this? Am I really ready to fight?*

Lexia walked faster catching up to a bunch of girls chatting away; she slipped into the middle of them and dashed into an alley as they passed by. Quickly putting her bags down, Lexia ran to the end of the alley. Pulling her knife from her leg strap, she broke through the trees as heavy footsteps sounded behind her.

There was a slight clearing amongst the trees. Waiting for the man to arrive anxiety a tight ball in her chest, Lexia was determined to be strong; she couldn't hide anymore, it was time for her to face her problems head on.

He walked through the trees at an arrogant pace, pausing as he saw the knife in her hand. Looking at Lexia with a twisted smile, he laughed, "You want to play, little girl?" *Fuck, what am I doing?*

A sudden bright light, made of silver strands, sparked out from the center of him, they brightened, and grew until he was nothing but light. The light cleared as suddenly as it had appeared, revealing a white wolf.

Lexia was astounded; she couldn't quite grasp what she was seeing. *Men turning into animals, what's next?* She would have said that the wolf was beautiful, if he wasn't intending to kill her. The wolf snapped and snarled, before he lunged toward her throat.

Lexia couldn't hold back her ear-piercing scream. The fight seemed to unfold in slow motion, her heart boomed in her ears, her chest rose and fell with each slow breath. A strange emptiness filled her, as instincts kicked in, Lexia twisted to the side, slicing her knife across the wolf's body. A deadly silence filled the air, only her slow, calm, breaths and the boom-boom, boom-boom, of her heart broke it.

She blinked, and the wolf was on her; blinked again, and the knife gouged into the wolf. Spinning her body, Lexia slammed her foot into the wolf sending him sliding across the ground. With her hands hung at her sides, Lexia looked at the wolf already recovered, and in front of her, red slashes of blood broke its snow white fur, its ice blue eyes staring with hatred.

Boom-boom, boom-boom.

She blinked, and his paws slammed her to the ground. Gasping Lexia allowed her body to fall backwards, and brought her knife up, slicing into his gut. As her back hit the ground she rolled quickly to the side, jumping to her feet. Standing over the wolf, slumped on the ground; it twitched once and then changed back into human form.

All at once sound rushed to her ears, she breathed panicked, ragged breaths. Stepping back, horrified at what she'd done, Lexia ran from the forest, grabbing her bags, and pulled off her blood-soaked clothes. Replacing it with the long maxi dress she'd bought earlier, Lexia then rubbed furiously at the blood on her hands and arms, and put the blood soaked clothes in the bag.

Walking with long, quick, strides towards home, Lexia worked over what the creature could be. *Holy shit… what the?* More research was needed. *If vampires exist then maybe werewolves do, too?*

Stepping up onto her porch ten minutes later, Lexia's emotions were barely contained, her hands shook as she attempted to open the door. *Keep it together, you're nearly alone,* Lexia chanted over, but as her key slid into the lock, and slowly turned with a click, a low growl rumbled from behind her. Spinning quickly, heart in her throat, Lexia clamped her hands over her mouth to keep from screaming as she saw the black panther prowling down the side of the shed, its golden eyes lit the darkness.

With her back pressed against the door Lexia begged, "Not tonight, please, I've had enough... This is all just too much."

The panther surprised her by freezing; it cocked its beautiful head to the side in a very human gesture. In the split second the panther hesitated, Lexia forced her scrambled brain to work, and dashed into the house closing the door as the panther landed lightly on the porch. She froze, holding her breath, and watched out the small square window as the panther rubbed its long, sleek body against the door, then disappeared into the darkness.

She slid to the floor and let out her breath. Pulling up her knees, Lexia wrapped her arms around them and rested her head forward as tears spilled down her face.

She didn't recognize herself anymore; she'd killed again and it almost felt natural. She was lying to everyone that cared about her, doing things that she never even imagined she was capable of. Lexia sat for a long time, tears rolling down her cheeks, and when they finally stopped, she dragged herself to bed, falling into a restless sleep.

CHAPTER 6

Lexia woke early the next morning and headed outside before her dad woke. Tossing some rubbish and the clothes she'd worn yesterday into a barrel, Lexia poured over some lighter fuel and flicked in a match.

An early morning mist lingered over the front lawn, dew drops glistening in the morning sun, and the air filled with birdsong. Walking away as the smoke twisted into the sky, Lexia paused as she passed the entrance into the forest, deciding to stick to the streets. Though the forest was one of her favorite places, she knew it would be silly to go into the forest after everything that had happened lately. Lexia always felt as if she'd entered another world, a world full of simple beauty, when she was inside the forest, though today that world would have to wait.

Falling into an easy rhythm, the sound of her footfalls a peaceful tempo. She ran at a steady pace and zoned out, the houses around her becoming a blur. As she turned onto the street to take her home she could have sworn she saw a glimpse of black velvet amongst the houses. Slowing her pace, Lexia listened with her senses, but nothing warned her of danger so she carried on a little quicker. Twenty minutes later she slowed to a walk, and turned onto her drive. Walking towards the house Lexia froze; on the edge of the trees near the old shed crouched the black panther. The cat watched her with his beautiful golden eyes, as Lexia walked slowly towards the door never dropping her gaze. As she neared the porch the cat became hidden by the shed wall, running the last leg, Lexia turned at the last minute to see it had moved from behind the shed was only a few yards away. She was certain the panther could cover the distance between them in seconds, but it never moved, instead watching her with its far-too-intelligent eyes, as if waiting for something.

"What do you want?" she whispered.

The cat returned a low growl creeping slowly forward.

"Go away, I don't want to hurt you." Lexia slowly bent to retrieve the knife she now always carried strapped to her leg. She'd killed a wolf last night, she was certain she could defend herself against this large cat. Yet for some reason she was inclined not to harm it. The panther didn't feel evil in the way the wolf had, and it was so beautiful, so sleek, and graceful; its black velvet coat shimmered in the sun, and those eyes seemed to see, far too much to belong to an animal.

The panther moved closer; if Lexia stretched out her hand she'd be able to run her fingers through its fur. The need to touch the wild, dangerous animal creeping up the steps of the porch, its head low, eyes gleaming, was a strong one; nothing else mattered but to run her fingers through its coat.

She never heard her dad approach the front door from

inside, and as her hand stretch out to touch, to feel, he opened it, knocking her forward. The panther snarled, lashing out with its paw, slashing its claws through her skin. She heard her father yell as he tried to pull her inside, but the need to touch the cat, had her struggling. The panther held her gaze intensely, as if calling her, then disappeared into the trees, and the spell broke.

Shaking her head she looked at her dad, his face a mixture of anger, and worry. Glancing back to the forest, Lexia saw the cat vanish into the trees. Lexia's knife lay on the porch floor, Lexia snatched it up quickly, sliding it into the back of her jeans as she stood.

"What the hell were you doing, Lexia? It's a wild animal, a panther," he told her in disbelief.

"I—I don't know." *What had I been doing? The panther has been following me, it tried to kill me and I wanted to stroke it!* She got up, walking into the house, ignoring her dad's harsh words. He stormed in after her, but noticed the claw marks. "Oh god, Lexia, you'll need stitches? You must be in agony."

Lexia looked down at her arm, noticing the pain from the deep slash marks.

"Its fine, dad, not that deep," she answered vaguely.

Retrieving some medical supplies, Lexia began to wrap a bandage around her arm.

"What are you doing? Let me see," her father said, reaching for her.

Lexia sighed, pulling out a chair, she sat at the table.

"I cannot believe that was a black panther; you realize you could have been killed. I'm going to have to call someone about it; we can't have that animal running around attacking people."

"Dad, no! Please just leave it alone, I would have been fine if you hadn't knocked me over."

"Honestly, Lex! What has gotten into you lately? I... I can't believe you have only a few cuts, I mean that animal can kill someone with a single swipe."

Her dad grew silent. Lexia worried about the train his thoughts had taken; had he noticed how quickly her arm was healing? It had already stopped hurting, and as he finished, her skin tingled as if knitting back together.

If she was honest, the fact that she now healed at an incredible rate was freaking her out big time, and she was also beginning to panic at the way her dad was now looking at her. He saw far more than they should. Lexia stood quickly knocking the bowl full of the dirty clothes stained blood onto the floor.

"Shit," she muttered, bending to retrieve them. Walking to the trash can, her dad blocked her way. Lexia had a sudden urge to defend herself. She could feel her mind going into defense mode, preparing to attack, and it took all her resolve to rein herself in. "Excuse me," Lexia snapped.

"Just leave it, Lex, let me cleanup," he replied just as sharply.

"Dad, I have it in my hands." She stepped around him towards the trash can and then felt the sting of her dad's hand clasping her arm.

"I said I would clean it up."

Lexia gasped, stunned at his sudden anger. "Dad, you're hurting me!" She could feel the power slowly pulsating through her, every instinct told her to attack, he was hurting her, being aggressive, and this new side of Lexia hated it.

He looked down at his hand gripping her bandaged arm and snapped back to his normal self. "Oh God, sweetie, I'm so sorry."

Lexia squeezed the bowl in her hand as she tried to get her anger under control, it cracked, falling to the floor, smashing into pieces. Turning abruptly, Lexia ran from the room.

Taking the stairs two at a time, Lexia slammed the bathroom door shut. Standing at the sink she splashed cold water over her face, then looked at the mirror, seeing gold eyes staring back.

"Oh God," she whispered, sinking to the floor crying. *Was I really going to attack my dad?*

CHAPTER 7

Morning classes dragged, Lexia didn't listen to anything the teacher said, her thoughts switching between her dad's weird behavior, and the panther.

She'd decided the panther a he now, the more she thought about him, the more she was certain the panther was male. He had a cocky masculine air about him.

The bell rang; Lexia pushed her thoughts away into the corner of her mind, and tried to concentrate on Alice as they walked into the cafeteria.

"He's going to ask you out! He's so hot, Lex. Jealous!"

"What! Who?" Lexia asked stunned.

"Seriously, Lex, what's with you lately? Dan is…" Alice waited for a reply but got nothing. "Lexia! Are you listening? Dan wants to go out with you! What you going to say?"

"Erm ... I'm not sure, I suppose."

"God, what is wrong with you? For months you've been obsessing over him, and now he has finally dumped Alicia and you're not sure!?"

Yeah, what is wrong with me? Why aren't I squealing and excited? Lexia felt confused by her response. When she first heard Alice say Dan's name she immediately thought of the panther. She needed to do something about the cat; he was definitely not normal, and obviously doing something to her.

Alice's excited voice broke through her thoughts; Lexia snapped her head up just in time to see Dan crossing the cafeteria towards them. *Shit, what do I say?*

Dan sat across from the girls and Lexia smiled at him taking in his features; he was good-looking, a pretty boy, she thought. With his refined features, and pale blue eyes, his blond hair hung in soft waves to his jaw line giving him a surfer-boy look. Dan was always polite and friendly; the kind of guy to look after a girl. She should say yes, but her life was kind of crazy right now.

"So, Lexia, can I take you out for a drink later?" Dan had a soft, warm voice and Lexia found herself thinking how it would be nice to spend an evening with a *nice* guy who wasn't planning on killing her.

"I'd love to, Dan, but I have to work tonight, sorry." And she really was sorry.

"Well, what time do you start? We could grab a quick drink before your shift?" he asked hopefully.

"Six."

"I have to look after my sister till five, but I could meet you there about five thirty?"

"Ok, that'll be great."

When Dan left a little while later, Lexia felt quite excited about seeing Dan later, and the panther, and her new abilities were at the back of her mind.

"Oh my God, Lexia! Everyone is going to be so jealous of you!"

"It's coffee, Alice. Chill."

"Come on, Lex, seriously what's wrong with you? You always liked Dan, and now you're not interested?"

Lexia looked at her friend's concerned face. She was right, they always talked about boys and she'd never been shy about liking Dan. Lexia knew she had to tell Alice something or she'd never stop asking what was wrong. However she just wasn't certain the best way to explain all that was wrong.

"Yeah, it's just... I have a lot on my mind at the moment and I'm not sure I have time for him."

"Bullshit, Lexia."

"Okay! Dad's fighting with me; we've hardly spoken lately and this morning he went mental at me over something silly. I am not quite sure what I've done wrong and why he's acting so weird."

"Aww, babe, why didn't you just say so? You two never fight, but really don't worry, normal people fight with their, parents, all the time."

"So I'm not normal now? Thanks," she laughed.

“Ha, in all the time I’ve known your, dad, I don’t think I’ve ever heard him angry. That’s not normal; how many times you heard, my parents, yelling at me?”

“Too many to count, but maybe I’m just an angel,” Lexia countered, trying to hide her grin.

“Yeah, yeah, those puppy dog eyes may work on, Mike, but not me! You were definitely not channeling your good side the other night.”

“Shut up! I’m trying to block that from my memory!” Lexia moaned, cringing.

“Oh yeah? And that sexy-ass bad boy, too?”

“Alice!”

The girls were laughing as they took their seats for English. Lexia wiped the tears from her eyes as she tried to control herself. Her gaze passed Dan for a second a few rows in front and she smiled to herself, *maybe things will be okay after all.*

The day passed quickly after lunch and before she knew it five thirty had arrived. Lexia hadn’t gotten too dressed up because she had to work after but she’d put on her best skin tight jeans that enhanced her every curve and a top that hung low framing her cleavage. Her hair hung loose, her natural curls cascading loosely over her breasts and she’d just applied a bit of lip gloss to finish her natural look.

Dan seemed pleased to see her when he walked in. They ordered drinks and chatted about finishing school and college.

Lexia liked Dan; he was nice and listened to everything she said with great interest yet after a while Lexia became bored. Dan was good-looking and nice, but he didn't make her heart race, reaching out, Dan clasped her hand and…she felt nothing.

Her thoughts started to wander; she remembered the night she'd been drunk and danced with a stranger, she remembered his wicked smile when he'd followed her into the clothes shop. He wasn't as sweet as Dan or as polite, yes when they touched; every one of her nerves came to life, just the thought of him made her heart race.

By six she was ready to say goodbye. Dan kissed her on the cheek and…still nothing.

Lexia said her goodbyes and started to serve customers. Jan usually worked with her but she ended up calling in sick so Lexia found the night flying by as she rushed around serving everyone. At ten thirty Lexia collapsed in a booth with a cup of coffee; her feet throbbed from all the walking she'd done. *Roll on eleven!*

The door chimed and Lexia sighed, getting up when a familiar voice said, "Don't get up, love, I'll get it."

Before she could protest he'd poured his coffee, and slid into the seat opposite her.

"What are you doing here?" Lexia snapped, though secretly she was excited to see him.

"Having a coffee with you." He smiled sweetly at her, his eyes alight with mischief.

"Really? Just like you happened to be to be in a women's clothes shop?" Sarcasm dripped off her every word.

He laughed, his golden-brown eyes sparkling in a way that made her heart skip a beat.

"Well, if you're going to keep stalking me you might as well tell me your name," Lexia said, her tone softening.

"Stalking. Really, you don't think highly of me, do you? It's your dance moves, you got me hooked," He grinned, "It's Lincoln, or Linc, whichever you prefer," he drawled. The corner of his lip lifted up, looking bitable.

"Do you really think talking to me like that will get you anywhere?" she asked, sternly, while her thoughts wandered to places they shouldn't go.

"Probably not but I'm sure my amazing good looks will."

How does he say that with a straight face?

"What do you want?" she snapped, because the alternative was to melt and smile dreamily.

"Just a coffee with you"—His eyes said more, yet she found herself smiling at his attempt to keep an innocent face—"Well okay, maybe another dance, but come on, Lexia, can't blame a man for wanting another feel of your sexy body," Lincoln continued, clearly enjoying himself.

"Enough! You want to have a coffee with me? Stop reminding me of how stupidly drunk I was. And in my defense it had been a bad day."

"Really, want to share?"

"Nope," she smiled back.

Lincoln held his hands over his heart with a hurt look on his face. She couldn't stop the laugh that escaped her lips.

Lincoln cocked his head to the side slightly, and she suddenly had sense of déjà vu; an image of a black panther tilting its head to the side floated across her mind. Lexia shook her head to clear her mind of the panther. It worried her how much she was drawn to the beautiful cat, the way he stared at her with his golden cat eyes like he was calling to her soul.

Lexia realized too late that Lincoln had asked her something. "Sorry?"

"I said what are you thinking about?"

"Erm, nothing important."

"Come on, Lex, give a bloke a chance," he said with a smile.

Lexia felt her anger grow at this man whom she hardly knew; why did he think a simple smile would have her spilling her every secret? He was so sure of himself, yet if Lexia was honest she'd admit that she was angry at herself for wanting to fall for his charms. He was nothing like Dan, and that was the appeal. Though she snapped anyway, "I don't even know you, why would I tell you my problems?"

For a second she thought she saw a glimpse of hurt flitter across his eyes. “Fair enough, love, but maybe you should get to know me?”

Lexia looked at him and wondered if there was really more to this stunning, arrogant guy. She should tell him she wasn’t interested but he made her forget all the crazy. He made her heart race with just a charming smile…And those eyes, at first glance they looked light brown but when she really looked, Lexia noticed gold through them; it circled his pupil, bleeding out to the edges. His eyes were so striking and unusual, yet…familiar.

“I wish I could read your mind,” he laughed.

“Sorry I keep spacing out on you, don’t I? I was just admiring your features.” She smiled, surprised at her flirting.

“So I take it you’re giving me a chance?”

“For now,” she murmured, glancing at her watch, “Shit, I should have locked up twenty minutes ago! You’re such a bad influence.”

To Lexia’s surprise he helped, ten minutes later Lexia locked the doors and turned to walk home. “Bye, and thanks for the help,” she called over her shoulder; not wanting any awkward goodbyes or worse still…Lincoln trying to kiss her, but much to her dismay, he caught up easily.

“What are you doing?” she asked, risking a quick glance at him.

“Walking,” he laughed.

“You live this way?”

“Could do,” he said, his grin wicked.

“I don’t need walking home, I can protect myself.” The comment earned her a snort, Lexia picked up her pace deciding to ignore him.

After a few minutes of silence he asked, “So your parents don’t mind you walking home alone?”

“Parent, and no, I’m not a child.”

“Just you, and your mom?”

“No, just me, and my dad. How about you?” Lexia didn’t like been questioned. Questions led to her mom, and they lead to her story of abandonment.

“Just me. I was passing through.”

“Passing through, so when do you leave?”

“So keen to get rid of me, Lex, I’m hurt.” Lincoln put on his best puppy dog expression.

Lexia laughed; how was it he managed to cut straight through all her defenses? He might look harmless with his sweet smile and charming words, but Lexia could feel the power rolling of him.

“So Lexia, are you in your last year of school?”

“Yep, finish in two weeks,” she replied, happily. Only two weeks and she’d be free.

“You’re eighteen then? What are your plans?”

“Nineteen and yes, I have plans,” she smiled sweetly, daring him to bite.

He didn’t, but smiled back with a glint in his eyes, “I’m twenty-three, and have no plans as of yet. I could tell you were dying to know.”

Lexia stopped walking as they reach the end of her drive. She turned to face him trying to keep the smile from her face. “This is me. I started school a year late, travelled a lot when I was young. I could tell you were dying to know.” She couldn’t keep the smile off her face. Walking away she called, “Bye.”

“Wait....I should walk you to your door,” he told her casually.

“Goodbye, Lincoln.” Lexia didn’t look back, striding down the dark driveway with a huge grin on her face; she couldn’t help it, he made her heart pound, and blood bubble with excitement.

“How about a goodnight kiss,” He whispered in her ear.

Lexia let out a gasp as his voice came out of nowhere. She twisted on instinct, elbowing him in gut.

Lincoln doubled over with a grunt. “Bloody hell! That hurt,” he coughed, holding his side.

“Shouldn’t sneak up on a girl, then.” Lexia felt a little guilty, she’d reacted on instinct and he’d not fought back. It surprised her, deep down she’d thought he was up to no good.

"Won't make that mistake again, and you certainly don't need walking to your door…but how about that kiss?" His words ended with a killer smile, and she almost kissed him…Almost.

"See you around, Linc." A few steps away from Lincoln, Lexia's phone rang; she jumped in surprise. The number was unknown. She turned, smiling at Lincoln, and waving 'bye' then walked a few long strides before answering her phone.

"Hello?"

"Hi, Lex, its Dan, just wanted to make sure you got home okay?" he asked, sounding a little nervous.

"Yes, I'm walking up the driveway now, and I'm perfectly capable of making it home alone."

He laughed in return, moving on to questioning her about her shift.

Lexia relaxed, talking easily to him. She was shocked Dan had even thought to make sure she was home okay and she enjoyed talking to him but he was more a friend than anything else. Dan didn't make her feel like she did with Lincoln; he was too safe, too predictable. She smiled at the thought of how opposite Lincoln and Dan, were.

Lincoln said bye to Lexia and turned to leave. He didn't

know what he was doing openly flirting with her; using all his manly charm to cut through the thick wall of defense she had around herself. She was supposed to be the enemy and here he was thinking of ways he could get her into bed, instead of how to kill her.

Her phone rang seconds after she'd turned away with a glint in her eye. He found himself turning back around, but she'd smiled and waved him off so he carried on, until his keen hearing picked up the sound of a male voice on the phone. Lincoln slowed his pace, listening; from what he could hear some guy was making sure she'd made it home, they carried on talking and Lexia laugh at something he said. He felt suddenly jealous; he wanted to make her laugh like that. Taking a step into the trees, Lincoln stopped. What was he doing? He'd only just met this girl, and he had only bad intentions in store for her; jealously had not place here.

Lincoln turned to leave, confused by Lexia's ability to get under his skin, to affect him in a way no other woman had.

She laughed again, flirting with the boy on the phone. Lincoln to pause, his skin bristling in anger. *Get a grip, Linc, she's the enemy.*

Lexia was on the porch, laughing at his jokes. Focused on their conversation, Lexia wasn't watching out for danger. For a moment she was like every other girl laughing with a friend; life was easy, simple.

Lexia hung up, laughing hard; Dan had been persistent in his desire to bring her coffee Monday morning. She'd surprised herself by flirting with him. Distracted, she reached to open the door, never noticing the tingle of power in the air, the way her hairs had all stood on end.

She saw the sharp claws sailing towards her, too late. Pain burst through her skin as the panther's claws connected with her shoulders, piercing her skin. His mouth closed around her neck, his sharp teeth sinking into her flesh. She let out a strangled cry as she fell hard onto the porch, the air leaving her lungs, in a rush.

Tensed, waiting for him to bite further, waiting for the moment he'd end her life, Lexia was shocked when he paused. Her instincts kicked in immediately, legs tucking up, she kicked out, flinging the cat away. He hissed, leaping again, but Lexia was prepared this time. As he neared her body, she spun to the side, bringing her leg around and slamming it into him. The panther fell back, sliding across the ground, coming to a stop, he jumped up, and prowled towards her with a gleam in his eyes.

Lexia had her knife strapped to her leg yet for some reason she couldn't bring herself to cut his beautiful, black, velvet fur. *What is wrong with me?* The panther was obviously not friendly and yet she had an almost uncontrollable urge to not hurt him.

He leapt, she didn't move as quick and his claws ripped her side. Crimson seeped from the wound, ignoring the pain, because she had no choice, it was either fight, or die. Lexia went for the cat, knocking him to the ground, she kicked him while he was still down.

The panther laid momentarily stunned, giving Lexia the chance to dash into the house. He jumped up, letting out a low, deadly growl. Goose bumps broke out across her skin, then he turned, and disappeared into the night.

"Fuck," she muttered to herself in the dark, her side and neck throbbed in pain. Blood trickled down her shoulder, collecting in the crease of her breast and seeped into her clothes. Walking quietly, into the kitchen, Lexia switched on the light, finding medical supplies and sat at the table, feeling dizzy as she patched herself up. *I've not been hurt like this before, I wonder how fast I'll heal.*

CHAPTER 8

When Lexia woke the next morning she hurt everywhere; the wound on her stomach had closed, but dark purple bruises covered most of her side. This was easily hidden but the nasty holes on her neck stood out, a stark contrast to her milky skin. Each hole from the panther's sharp teeth had nearly closed but the skin on her neck was dappled red and purple.

Not only did Lexia feel sore and bruised from her fight, but mentally bruised also. Too much had happened over the last week, and everything was catching up to her. When she finally dragged herself out of bed, Lexia took great care in wrapping a scarf around her neck; she couldn't risk her dad seeing the marks.

Lexia entered the kitchen in search of food, and her dad was nowhere in sight. No note lay on the table to inform her when she would see him again. Lexia tried to not let this hurt her, but that little voice in her head wouldn't be quiet. Something was wrong; they'd always been close, and ever since she'd fallen in front of his car, he'd been distant. *Does he know I've changed? How can he?*

Lexia knew she had to find more information on the supernatural world. She wasn't sure what was real or fiction on the internet but it was all she had right now. Her Saturday flew by in a blur of words and images; the wolf man could be a werewolf, or even a shape-shifter. On the TV werewolves changed forms during the full moon, but it hadn't been when she was attacked, so the information wasn't of much help.

From what she found on shape-shifters, they could either turn into any form they imprinted on, or they could only turn into one animal. She found so much information about different legends and myths, yet had no way to know what was real, and what wasn't.

There was a bang at the door. For a second she felt like hiding, but the banging grew louder. Jumping off her bed, Lexia hurried down the stairs, opening the door to find Alice, tears streaming down her face.

"Oh my God, Alice, what's wrong?"

"Alec dumped me!" she sobbed.

"Oh babe, come here." Alice barreled into Lexia, squeezing her tight; she winced as Alice pressed against her side.

"He said he just wasn't feeling it anymore... I gave up my virginity for that guy, I hate him!" Alice's voice turned into huge, heaving sobs.

"Come on, let's go upstairs."

Lexia left Alice crying under her covers, and went in search of junk food. As she stretched to reach the top shelf, a sharp pain shot through her side.

“Ouch.” Lexia lifted her top, the claw marks had torn open and were bleeding.

“Shit,” she mumbled, heading for the first aid kit. *I really need to replace this stuff before Dad notices.*

By the time Lexia returned upstairs, Alice had stopped crying and was sat up, the duvet up to her chin. Lexia’s laptop sat open next to her, displaying her research.

“Took you long enough,” Alice moaned.

“Sorry, Dad had hidden the junk food,” she lied.

“What’s this you’ve been looking at?” Alice asked, reaching for the laptop.

Lexia dashed forward, snatching it away before Alice’s fingers brushed it. “Nothing,” she said, snapping it shut.

“Jeez, Lex, chill.”

“How about you sleep over and we can have a girly night?” Lexia asked, hoping to distract her, “And look what I found in my dad’s liquor cabinet!” Lexia continued, waving a bottle of whiskey in front of Alice’s face.

“He’ll kill you when he finds out you’ve taken that.”

“So what? You’re worth it,” Lexia smiled.

“Well, when you put it like that, give me the bottle. Let’s get wasted! Where is Mike anyway?” Alice asked, taking a glug of whiskey, and shivering as the sharp liquid went down.

"No idea, he was gone when I woke up."

"You two still fighting?"

"Mmm but let's not talk about me...What do you want to watch?"

"No lovey dovey crap! Too depressing; give me blood and gore!" Alice laughed, swallowing more whiskey.

"Blood and gore coming up."

Two movies and half a bottle of whiskey later, Lexia and Alice were feeling pretty drunk. They were giggling and stumbling around Lexia's bedroom when her dad walked in. Thankfully Lexia had a few brain cells left to hide the bottle of whiskey she had in her hand.

"Dad, hi!" His brows creased for a second, then he noticed Alice and smiled.

"Hey Mike," Alice said with a small wave.

"What are you girls up to?"

"Oh, Lex here is cheering me up, you see my ass of a boyfriend dumped me, and I was just so sad, and well, if it wasn't for Lex..." Alice broke off into huge pretend sobs.

"Babe," Lexia whispered, then glared at her dad.

"Oh erm, well, Alice, I...Well..." Mike turned, and half ran from the room, slamming the door behind him.

Lexia looked back over at Alice who'd began laughing.

"Alice!"

"What? Did you want to get busted for drinking? Dads can't handle tears," she giggled.

Lexia took another swig of whiskey then burst out laughing, too. "Here, drink up you crazy woman."

They finished off the bottle and eventually passed out. When Lexia woke next, the night was pitch black. She turned her head and looked out the window, they'd never closed the curtains before falling asleep. From her position on the floor Lexia could see the moon, bright and full in the night sky. She moaned quietly as her head pounded. *What woke me?*

Listening to the world around her, Lexia couldn't hear a sound. The night was quiet, *too* quiet. Sitting up, Lexia clambered to her feet, waiting for the world to right itself, she then staggered over to the window.

There he was; the reason why the night had grown deadly quiet, and the reason why she'd woken. Quietly opening the window, Lexia whispered, "Hello, pretty panther," as she sat on window seat.

The cat looked up and slowly prowled towards the house. His golden cat eyes glowed in the dark, the bright full moon reflected off his soft fur.

"I'm not coming out, I've drank too much. I wouldn't be much of a fight, and there'd be no fun in that, huh?"

He stopped and growled, twisting sharply around. Lexia

gasped as he leapt onto the shed roof, his light paws barely made a sound on the tin. Lexia's numb brain thought she should probably be frightened by the cat's power, and speed. Yet she saw beauty; the way his lean, muscled, body moved and those eyes, the way he looked at her. "What are you?" she whispered, resting her head on her elbow as she leaned on the window sill.

He cocked his head then sprawled out on the shed roof, his paws hanging over the edge, and tail wrapping his hind legs. Looking up, the panther roared, the sound sending birds into the sky.

Lexia jumped, "Ssh!" she hissed, glancing at Alice.

Laying his head between his paws, he closed his eyes. Lexia watched him for a while longer, until sleep beckoned her. "Good night, pretty panther," she whispered, drifting off her, head rested on the sill.

Waking with a clear head, Lexia quietly went through her drawers for running clothes, then slipped out the house, careful not to wake anyone. It was early; the sun hadn't quite risen passed the tree tops, and morning dew still covered the ground.

She paused as she walked past the shed, wondering if she'd dreamt seeing the panther last night; he wasn't there anymore.

Jogging into the forest Lexia took a deep breath releasing her tension with a sigh. She knew she shouldn't run in the forest but jogging on the streets just didn't clear her head the same.

The sun streamed through the edge of the trees, shards of

light casting them into silhouette, dust particles danced in the light and an eerie orange haze covered the forest before her.

She was in a fairy tale. Out here, alone in the forest, Lexia imagined she could be anyone. If she only listened to the sound of her breaths and the music of her feet, she could imagine no one hunted her, that she hadn't changed at all. Within the magical walls of the forest she could imagine anything...

Lexia smiled to herself. When she finally escaped to a big city, this would be the one thing she'd miss, stepping out into another world, one filled with life and freedom. Out in the forest she was free.

"What ya smiling at?"

Lexia screamed, jumping away from the rough whisper on her neck. Stumbling, her feet tangling around each other pitching her toward the uneven ground. "Lincoln, you asshole!" She felt her anger flare as she looked into his amused golden eyes.

"Sorry, I'm surprised you didn't hear me coming." The laugh lines around his twinkling eyes contradicted his statement.

Lexia breathed out, dispelling her anger before it took hold. "I was too lost in...Ouch," Lexia pulled up her knee and looked at the deep cut she'd received from falling.

"Sorry. Will you be alright?" Lincoln held out his hand for her.

Lexia looked at his hand, then his face, there within the infinite depths of his eyes, she saw concern. Clasping his hand she let him pull her up. "I'm fine, I've—"

"Lex, your neck," he interrupted.

Lifting her hand to her neck, Lexia absently rubbed it. "I forgot to cover that up," she murmured.

"Cover it up, Lexia, who did that to you?"

"You wouldn't believe me, if I told you. Leave it, I'm fine." She searched for a change in subject. "What are you doing out here, scaring me to death, anyway?"

"I was out for a run like you, and saw you smiling. It suits you, you know, smiling... So what were you smiling at?"

Lexia couldn't answer that question while looking at him. Seeing this side of him, so charming and sweet, it chipped away at her defenses, made her question her reasons for not trusting him. She began to jog, slower than before, glancing at Lincoln by her side, Lexia thought over his question. *Why was I smiling?* "I was smiling because I was happy. I get lost out here, it makes me feel free."

"Oh...I can run on ahead if you don't want company?"

She looked at him, into his golden-brown eyes and felt her heart race. "No, it's fine."

"So I'm good company then?" he asked, with a glint in his eyes.

"Don't push it."

Pushing her worn muscles harder, determined not to have

Lincoln holding back because of her, they ran in silence, only the rhythm of their feet could be heard. It echoed off the densely packed trees as they climbed higher into the hills. Lexia noticed the birds had grown silent, and small animals no longer scurried out of her way, yet she wasn't afraid; Lincoln made her feel safe. *Safe with Lincoln, I'm such an idiot!*

By the time they'd finished and reached the end of Lexia's drive, she was bent over panting hard, sweat dripped off her face splattering onto gravel at her feet, her clothes stuck to her skin as if painted to her body.

"Wow, I'm done in."

"I'm actually surprised you ran so long with me," he chuckled, "I don't normally run that far."

"God, I bet I look a right state," she wheezed, pulling up her tank and wiping the sweat from her face. Glancing at her watch, she said, "I've been gone for two hours, I hope Alice hasn't woken yet."

"Who?"

"Alice. She's my friend. We kind of got wasted last night on my dad's whiskey; she'd been dumped so she needed some consoling. I bet she has a wicked hangover this morning."

"But not you?"

"No, I seem to have developed a high tolerance to alcohol. Not sure that's a good thing, but anyway, I need to go die somewhere."

"Not going to invite me in?" he asked, his smile cheeky.

"Ha! I'm sure my dad would really approve, seeing me walk in the house with a grown man covered in sweat."

"I can pull off harmless," he said, seriously.

Laughing as she walked away, Lexia replied, "Sure you can. Later, Linc."

"Later, Lex."

Lexia walked away from Lincoln. Despite the fact she'd put her legs through a small marathon, and they throbbed with every step, she felt great. Being with Lincoln made her feel good; they'd hardly spoken, but being in his presence was enough to make her feel alive.

Opening the door, her dad was in the kitchen making breakfast, the smell of waffles, and maple syrup filled the air.

"Hey, Dad," she called from the hall, careful to keep her neck angled away from him.

"Lex, there you are. Alice has just been down looking for you. She didn't look too well, poor girl must be taking the break-up hard, huh?"

"Yeah, she is, bless her. I was out for a run." *She's really hung over from your whiskey!*

"I said I'd bring her up some breakfast, do you want some, too?"

"Please."

"Strawberries, coffee?"

"You're the best."

She turned to go but her dad called her back, "Lex?"

"Yeah?" Her stomach rolled. Dreading what he'd asked.

"You'd tell me if something was going on with you, right?"

Lexia stared in silence for a moment; panic gripped her like a steel vise, constricting her chest. *Does he know?* He looked up from the pan, concern on his face. *Should I tell him?*

"Everything's fine, Dad, don't worry." Lexia hurried up the stairs before he asked her anything else.

She found Alice passed out in bed; she stirred as Lexia entered the room. Rolling over with a moan, her eyes cracked open slightly.

"I feel like crap, how are you even walking?"

"High tolerance. Dad will be up soon with food, you'd best look less hung-over. He thinks you're feeling emotionally unwell from the break-up."

"This is from the break-up, and since when did you have such a tolerance for alcohol?"

"I think you must have hogged the bottle. Anyway, I need to shower," Lexia picked up a t-shirt and hung it around her neck to hide the mark on her neck.

Alice sat up, looking at her properly for the first time since walking in. “Hey, Lex, what have you been doing? Your knee?”

Lexia looked down having forgotten about tripping over. The cut on her knee had gone, but dried blood clung to her skin. “Oh, I tripped out running.”

“Jeez, Lex, what’s with you lately? All you do is run, you’re making me look so lazy!”

“I love running. It clears my head, and I’ve had a lot to sort out lately.”

“Dan?”

“And other things.”

“Need to talk?”

“I do actually, but first let me shower, I’m gross.”

“Mmm, not got the brain power yet anyway. Maybe after waffles?” Alice didn’t wait for Lexia’s answer, she pulled the duvet over her head, and promptly fell to sleep.

After breakfast in bed, Lexia and Alice put on another movie. They both laid out on the double bed pretending to the watch the film when both of their minds were really far off, thinking about boys.

“Hey, Lex,” Alice said, rolling onto her side, to look at Lexia.

“Yeah?” Lexia replied, looking at Alice suspiciously.

“Are you going to get with, Dan?”

"I don't know, I mean he's nice and all, and cute but..."

"But what? What's wrong with a nice guy?"

"Nothing, I…" Lexia had no idea how to explain her feelings for Lincoln, it's not like she even knew if he was interested in her.

"Come on, Lex, I'm not stupid. You were constantly going on about, Dan."

"It's just, I kinda like someone else," Lexia admitted, wincing as she waited for Alice's reaction.

"And nice guys are only good enough when there's not a sexy bad boy hanging around, huh?"

Lexia laughed. "I'm stupid, aren't I? I should just go out with, Dan."

"Well, I am not going to judge."

"Come on, Alice, you always judge, and I need you to now. Set me straight."

"Well, you asked for it. This guy, Lincoln, I've only met him once when he was being a total creep, but I can see the appeal. He's movie star hot and has the whole bad boy charm going on, but is that really what you want?"

"He's not always like that. Sometimes when he drops his guard he's so sweet - and the way he makes me feel, Alice, just one smile, a slight touch and I'm lost in him." Lexia forced her face to drop the dreamy, faraway look, currently on her face as she pictured

Lincoln.

"God, Lex, you have it bad! But he's going to break your heart; if you carry on seeing him, and things get more heated, imagine how you will feel then...He might leave town, or get bored with you."

"But he might not."

"Lexia, what's this town got to offer a hot twenty-something-year old?"

"Me?"

"Aww, babe, come on. I love you, but really, wake up."

"Alice!"

"Okay, say I'm wrong and he stays for you but if I'm right... Is he really worth the risk?"

"I don't know, I think so."

"Well, only you can decide, and I am always here for you. I'll pick up the pieces."

"Aren't I supposed to be picking up your pieces?"

"You did last night. I'm over him now, and on to my next target."

"And who's this target?"

"Not decided yet, but I'll tell you when I do."

"Are you planning on going home today?"

"Yes, I best do soon. My head's stopped pounding but do you think, Mike, might feed me first?" she asked, smiling sweetly.

"I'll go ask," Lexia answered, laughing.

CHAPTER 9

Fidgeting with the scarf, she'd wrapped around her neck to cover the nearly healed bite mark, Lexia walked down her driveway, freezing as her hairs stuck on end, her body tingling in warning. She'd planned to meet Dan this morning after his insistence to walk her to school, yet Dan definitely didn't give off that kind of vibe. Having the sudden thought, Dan was at the bottom of the drive, and in trouble, Lexia began to walk again, this time though, her body moved quietly, her feet steady and light, her every sense searching for danger. Yet as she approached she recognized the energy lingering in the air, and sure enough Lincoln's smooth voice reached her.

"Are you planning to take forever to reach me?" He laughed softly, almost a rumble, and the sound made her heart skip a beat, her legs stretch farther in anticipation.

"What are you doing here?" she asked, her smile bright.

"Bringing you coffee - three sugars, and lots of milk?"

She smiled. *When did he noticed how I took my coffee?* "Thanks, but I'm supposed to be meeting a friend this morning, we were going to walk to school together."

"Really?" From the mischievous smile, and the knowing glint in his eye Lexia could have sworn he knew she was meeting Dan, and that was exactly why he was here. Before she had chance to question him further, Dan came into view. A wide smile spread on Dan's face, but dropped as he saw Lincoln.

"This your friend?" Lincoln asked, giving her his 'I'm-just-a-sweet-puppy-dog,' smile.

"Hi, Dan," Lexia said, smiling reassuringly as his steps faltered.

"Hi, Lex." He walked up and kissed her on the lips. "You ready to walk to school?"

Lexia was stunned into silence. She glanced at Lincoln, who wore a look of hatred, and then Dan, looking smug. *And I thought you were a nice guy.* "Erm...this is, Lincoln, he's...he's new to town. We met at the diner."

Lincoln laughed at her, replying, "come now, love, I'd say we were good friends."

Lexia glared at him in response, wishing she had the power to vanish into thin air. An awkward silence followed.

"Right, time for school," Lexia announced, walking away with long determined strides, she didn't look back.

Soon two sets of footfalls came up behind her, Lincoln reaching her first, followed by Dan seconds later; slightly out of breath. She laughed softly to herself thinking he must have jogged to keep up with Lincoln's big strides.

"Did you want your coffee, Lex?" Dan asked, a nervous smile on his face. "I didn't know how you took it; I got it with lots of milk?" He said, holding the cup out.

Lincoln jumped in before she could answer. "You remember the three sugars, Kid?"

To give Dan credit he didn't react to the *kid* remark, but Lexia saw his expression change to one of anger before he regained control a few seconds later. "I figured she was sweet enough," was his reply, looking straight into Lexia's eyes, giving her his sweet, boyish smile.

"That she is, but I already brought her a coffee, just the way she likes it." Lincoln smiled with victory.

Dan gulped, but he didn't back down. "How old are you? Like 30?"

That was it, she'd had enough. *How have I ended up with two guys fighting over me?* She was not a piece of meat, for them to snarl over.

"Tell you what, Linc, here's your coffee." She thrust it into his hand, splashing coffee on his white T-Shirt. Turning her attention to Dan, Lexia continued with a glare, "And he's right, I take it with three sugars. See you in class."

Sprinting away, Lexia steadied her pace when they didn't follow. A few minutes from the school gates she slowed to a walk, taking deep calming breaths as she regained her composure. By the time she met Alice, you'd have never known she'd been stuck between two males with testosterone issues.

They walked up toward the school's entrance chatting when Lexia froze. Feeling a tingle of power in the air, she turned, searching for the source. The black panther's head peered out from behind a wall, they locked eyes before he disappeared. *I am going to have to do something about you, pretty panther.*

"Lex. Lexia!" Alice said, waving her hand in front of her face.

"Sorry, thought I saw someone."

"What, like a miserable-looking, Dan, walking towards us?"

"Shit, let's move," Lexia gasped, pushing through the double doors, and hurrying towards class.

Alice ran to catch up. "Tell me now!" she demanded, jumping into her path.

"Later, ok?" Lexia begged, glancing nervously for Dan.

"Fine, but don't think I'll forget!"

Oh, if only you would forget, she thought, walking into first period.

The rest of the morning went smoothly. Dan smiled at her when he came into class, so he can't have been too upset.

When the bell rang for lunch she shot out of the classroom hoping to avoid him. Alice had a different subject to her that morning so they met in the hall. She seemed excited about something, she had a massive smile on her face.

"Have you found your next target?" Lexia asked, wondering what her happy smile was for.

"What? Oh yes, but that's not why I'm smiling."

"Why then?" she asked, dreading the answer; Alice had that look in her eye that singled trouble.

"First tell me about this morning," Alice demanded as they walked into the cafeteria.

"Fine…Dan, met me this morning to walk to school, only Lincoln was the one waiting for me. Then Dan turns up, I'm lost as to what to say, when Dan walks up and kisses me on the lips like we're already together!"

"Aren't you?" Alice asked, sitting at a free table.

"No, why would you think that?" Lexia asked, joining her.

"Too late, you'll find out in a second," she smiled.

"What do y…" Lexia never finished her question; she spotted Dan and as she looked up to see what he wanted, he pressed his lips against hers. Too stunned to react, Lexia sat speechless as he slid into the space besides her, wrapping his arm around her shoulder.

"Hey, babe," he said.

"Hey, Dan!" Alice said, jumping in, she flashed a wicked grin at Lexia, then began rambling. Lexia sat in silence, bending awkwardly from Dan having his arm around her.

Throughout lunch Alice talked, leaving Lexia no chance to question Dan's actions.

Where has this bold behavior come from? Dan was a nice guy, and here he was acting like they were already together. She replayed over the times they'd spent together, and was certain she'd never agreed they were going out.

The bell rang for afternoon class, Lexia breathed a sigh of relief, whispering to Alice about killing her later.

They walked out of the cafeteria together but thankfully Lexia and Dan needed to go separate ways. "Come on, Alice, we're this way," she said, clasping Alice's elbow roughly, "See you, Dan."

Dragging Alice down the hall, Lexia paused as Dan called, "Hey Lex?"

Lexia breathed in a deep breath, and squeezed Alice's arm as she giggled. "Yes?" she asked, turning around.

"Where's my kiss?"

"Yeah Lex, where's his kiss?" Alice laughed, "Ouch!" She whined as Lexia gave her a kick.

"I'm going to kill you later for this," Lexia whispered to Alice.

Looking at Dan's expectant face, she thought; *what do I say?* Slowly she walked back to him. *Am I really just going to kiss him? Why not just tell him to get lost? What am I doing?* Her lips brushed his, and Dan wrapped his hands around her waist pulling her close. Lexia gasped and bit her lip so she didn't shout at him.

"God, you're sexy," he whispered, before he turned and left.

Lexia stared after him, students walked past, staring and whistling. She couldn't decide whether she was angry, shocked, or turned on. *Where had this Dan come from?*

"Fucking hell, Dan's possessed," said Alice, slipping her arm back through Lexia's, and dragging her off to class.

"I'm going to kill you for that!"

"Hey, I didn't tell him you two were going out."

"Neither did I!"

"Well, then, Dan, grew some balls," she laughed, enjoying the situation far too much.

"He sure did," Lexia replied in wonder.

"You like it don't you!"

"Alice, shut up," Lexia giggled. *Maybe just a little.*

"Girls, settle down."

"Sorry, Mr. Peterman," they said in unison.

Lexia and Alice walked into the center of town after school. They sat in silence, each eating the slices of chocolate cake they'd ordered. Alice opened her mouth; she'd never been good at keeping quiet. "Spill, Lexia, what the hell's going on with you?"

Lexia looked at her stern face; she and Alice had been friends since she'd first started school, and they'd been inseparable ever since. "I already told you about, Dad, then there's, Lincoln, and now, Dan's, acting insane, too!"

"Well I think you've brought out, Dan's, competitive side and really, can you blame him?"

"But he's just acting like we're together." She'd still not decided what she thought of that.

"Babe, you didn't stop him," Alice pointed out, "Didn't you feel anything when he kissed?"

"I don't know, maybe... I was just so shocked, and pissed off, but then... Well, I kind of like his bold side."

"God you have to like the bad side don't you."

"But what about, Lincoln?" Lexia asked, mostly to herself.

"Lex, maybe you should give, Dan, a chance. I mean, he lives here, and he isn't as scary as, Lincoln."

"He isn't scary, and he just keeps showing up, like this morning, then both he and Dan were acting like cavemen."

Alice laughed. "Well, what did you expect? You're gorgeous. But seriously, Lexia, be careful around him."

"I can take care of myself, don't worry."

“Really? Because Lincoln looked like a well-built man, and you don’t exactly work out.”

They both burst out laughing. *If only you knew the things I could do, Alice.*

Walking together as they headed home after coffee and cake, Lexia felt better having talked with Alice, yet she still didn’t know what to do. Aware they were being followed, Lexia kept her focus on the panther popping from between buildings every so often, he would disappear as soon as he caught her looking. The closer the panther got, the more on edge she felt; her skin prickled, and she had to suppress the urge to turn and fight.

Relived when Alice left in the direction of her house. Lexia felt the panther stalking closely from the shadows, he made no attempt to hide his presence. Determined not to play his cat games, Lexia kept her pace steady and looked straight ahead, ignoring him. If he wanted her, she was ready; all he had to do was make a move, but she’d decided he was toying with her right now.

As Lexia turned down her drive, fear flooded her, she bit her lip to stop herself from yelping in fright. There he was in the middle of the drive between her, and the house. She forced her fear deep in her mind, and carried on walking. She had killed three vampires at once and taken down a nasty wolf-man, she would not back down to this cat, even if a small part of her still thought the panther was good.

The panther vanished into the trees, she moved to follow but heard the reason for his departure.

"Lex, wait," Dan called running after her.

"Later, Kitty Cat" she murmured, hearing a low growl as her reply. *Yes you are defiantly more than just a cat.* "Hi Dan," Lexia said, turning around, but keeping her senses focused on the woods.

"I'm really sorry about today, I was an idiot." He smiled shyly.

Lexia pushed her anger down. "Its fine, Dan, but I don't appreciate being fought over, and you assuming we were together." Walking back toward the house, he followed.

"You noticed that, huh?"

"Bit hard to miss you kissing me, Dan," she snapped.

"But you kissed me back! It's not like you to just go along with something."

"I think I was just shocked at seeing that side of you," Lexia answered, glancing at him.

"Really?"

"Don't push your luck, Dan." The smile fell from his face.

"Hey, that guy, you know him well?"

"Not really." She didn't like the way this conversation was going.

"He seems a bit sketchy. I mean, I can see the appeal but he's a lot older then you."

Anger renewed, Lexia paused, hands resting on her hips.

"Not that it's any of your business, Dan, but he's twenty-three and in a few months I will be twenty." She hated being told what to do.

"What?" Dan gasped in surprise.

"Dan, this has nothing to do with you," she said, a little softer. Wishing she'd not told him that snippet of information.

His face fell further. "I was kind of hoping after that kiss, it would be my business."

Lexia looked at him with his sad eyes and his cute surfer-boy looks; she could be happy with him. There might not be the same fire between them that she felt with Lincoln, but Alice was right; there was no guarantee he'd stay in town. Then she remembered the vampires, and the panther probably watching her right now, and realized, it didn't matter either way; her life was too messed up for a new relationship.

"I did feel something, Dan. But I have a few things going on at the minute...I'm sorry I just...Can we be friends?"

"Friends? Sure" he smiled, but Lexia could see the hurt in his eyes.

Lexia closed the distance between them, and hugged him, whispering in his ear, "I really am sorry, Dan, if only you'd found me a few months ago"

He pulled away his eyes creasing. "What do you mean, Lex?"

"Nothing, it doesn't matter," she told him vaguely.

"Bye, then." Dan walked back down her drive towards the road.

She watched him go, taking in his wide, well-muscled form from all the sports he played, and his messy hair blowing in the breeze. As he turned the corner he looked back one last time with a cheeky, cocky grin.

For a moment Lexia felt sad at turning him away, she could have been happy with him, only a few months ago she'd stared at him and daydreamed about the day he'd be interested, but now...

A low growl snapped Lexia out of her trance, she whipped around seeing gold eyes peering from the forest. It took her a split second to decide what to do, she ran towards the house as fast as she could, her feet crunching and sliding on the gravel. She could hear his light foot falls as he closed the distance between them. Her heart beat in her throat; was this it? Were they finally going to finish their game?

Lexia raced across the grass, she felt like her lungs were on fire, adrenaline course through her veins forcing her on. The porch was up ahead. *How am I going to get the door open before the panther gets me?*

His paw caught the back of her leg. Lexia screamed, stumbling, but managed to right herself. Noticing the open window to her bedroom, Lexia jumped as high as she could, her hands gripped tightly onto the wooden slats of the trellis. Crying out as her body slammed into the house, momentarily knocking the wind out of her, she scrambled up, her knees banging and scraping against wood.

Sharp teeth sank into her ankle as she neared the top, pulling her down, Lexia screamed, desperately reaching out something to hold onto. Regaining her hold, Lexia kicked out with her foot, pulling with all her strength in an effort to escape the panther's jaws. Her foot hit his head but his grip never faltered.

"Get off, get off!" she screamed, kicking out again but he wouldn't let go. A blood-thirsty look gleamed in his eyes, and the more she kicked the further his teeth sank into her ankle.

The sound of a car made Lexia glance up, its horn sounded over and over momentarily distracting the panther, and as Lexia slammed her foot into his jaw; he let go, falling to into a heap below.

Lexia sighed in relief but it soon vanished as her dad's car sped up towards the panther. The cat froze, still in a jumbled heap as the car raced towards him. He scrambled to his paws trying to avoid being run over but he'd hesitated too long.

Lexia screamed as the car hit the cat. "No!" she cried, scrambling into her bedroom. Lexia stared down at the panther unmoving on the ground, her heart hurt, as she looked at this beautiful animal hurt and broken before her.

"What have you done?" she screamed at her dad in the car, tears welling in her eyes. She didn't care how irrational she was being, or how it may look being so upset by the panther being hurt; she couldn't control her feelings. Lexia felt as if she'd been split in two, one half of her wanted to jump from her window, and make sure the panther was dead. The other felt heartbroken, as if her best friend lay below. She didn't understand her feelings but then she didn't understand much anymore, so she cried. Cried for the panther, and for the loss of her old life; she stopped holding all of her feelings inside, and let them out.

The panther slowly lifted his head, for a second the world froze as he stared into her eyes, yet they weren't the eyes of a panther anymore; she was looking into the eyes of a man. For that split second everything felt right in the world, then she blinked, and he was gone.

Her dad scrambled out of the car. "Lex, Lex! Are you okay?"

Lexia couldn't speak, she felt too shaken; she nodded to him, smiling weakly.

"I'm coming now, don't move."

As he ran in the house Lexia looked down at her ankle in panic, the holes were deep, and blood poured from them, but already she could feel the power in her blood fixing it. The blood was slowly stopping. Glancing up Lexia saw her reflection in the mirror on the back of the door, a strangled cry left her throat as she looked into the bright gold eyes staring back at her.

Her dad's feet pounded up the stairs. "Oh God, oh God," she said to the girl in the mirror, Please stop, oh God please, he can't see."

The floor boards squeaked as he walked across the landing,

her heart hammered in her chest, as her hands began to shake. "Go away, turn blue," she pleaded to the mirror, but as the door opened they were still gold. Lexia closed her eyes, tears slowly rolling down her cheeks.

"Lex? Lex, honey, its okay, open your eyes, I'm here."

But she couldn't, if he saw her eyes, he'd never be there again. He'd already pulled away, and she didn't think she could handle losing him for good. She slowly turned her head from side to side, her tears still falling. "I can't," she sobbed.

"Lexia, look at me, you're okay now. The panther's gone, you're safe."

Lexia slowly opened her eyes, bracing herself for the moment he realized her eyes weren't blue anymore. But he didn't gasp in horror, he took her head in his hands and then wrapped his arms around her. Lexia sobbed as she looked at the mirror, into her blue eyes.

"Oh Lex, its okay I'm here, I'm going to call the ranger straight away, sit down let me see your foot."

Panic set in again as she remembered her injury.

"Dad, don't fuss. I'm fine, it's not too bad."

He sucked in a breath when he knelt on the floor. "Lex!"

"Dad seriously, it looks worse than it is. See I can walk on it just fine."

"Lex, I think we need to take you to hospital…"

"No," she snapped.

Startled he looked up.

"Dad, I don't like hospitals, and really its fine, can't you just clean it up? Please Dad? All I want to do is curl up in bed," Lexia pleaded.

He looked at her for a few moments longer seeming to work out the battle in his head. "Alright, let's get you downstairs and clean it up, then I'll decide if we need to take you or not."

Downstairs in the kitchen Lexia sat on a chair. Her jeans leg had been cut off, and discarded next to the pile of blood-red cloths.

"I don't understand how there was so much blood, I really thought we'd find your ankle shredded. You were so lucky, Lex."

"So I don't have to go to hospital?"

"Well I don't know, some of these teeth marks are quite deep and I think you could do with some antibiotic, and a tetanus shot."

"Dad please, can't we just see how it is tomorrow? I'm so tired, and we'd be sat in the ER all night."

"Hmm, I suppose you're right, but I don't want you walking to school tomorrow, if you even go at all."

She finally managed to get her dad to leave. Her ankle throbbed as she lay in bed, and as she drifted off to sleep, she wondered how long her leg would take to heal. *I'll get to see how good my super powers really are.*

CHAPTER 10

Lexia woke before her dad the next morning and unwrapped the bandage around her ankle. What she found shocked her, the shallowest scratches had healed leaving behind a faint red line and the worst bites; where she'd had deep holes in her tissue, had filled out. It still looked bad, and hurt to move but she was healing at an incredible rate. If her dad saw it, he'd know there was something different about her.

Lexia covered her ankle again. Pulling on a pair of loose linen trousers, which she paired with a shirt, Lexia fixed her hair, and makeup. At seven she heard water being run, and twenty minutes later her dad walked down the stairs.

As she thought he'd left her in bed, most likely he planned on making breakfast, and bringing it to her. So now all she needed to do was walk downstairs with enough of a limp that he wouldn't think anything was suspicious, but not too much of one that he'd want to look. "Simple, Lex, fucking simple!"

Carefully she got up, walking across the landing, and down stairs, it still hurt, and she had the slightest of limps but as she pushed the kitchen door open, Lexia exaggerated it further.

“Lex, I was going to bring you your breakfast in bed; really you shouldn’t have walked until I’d had a look.”

Pulling out a chair, Lexia took a seat and answered without looking her dad in the eye; she hated lying to him. “Please don’t fuss, it hurts a little but really I’m fine to go to school, I think you must have over-reacted last night.”

“Let me see.”

This is what she’d dreaded, he couldn’t look. To Lexia it felt like her whole life depended on this moment, she had to convince him everything was okay, or there’d be no going back. She was on the edge of the cliff; everything had been compounding together bringing her to this moment, but she wasn’t ready; Lexia was too afraid to jump, she wasn’t strong enough to lose her Dad.

“No,” she snapped, “Don’t touch me.”

“Lexia?” he gasped, shocked.

“Dad I... I’m sorry I didn’t mean to snap, it’s just I’ve read somewhere taking off the bandage can pull off all the new skin cells.”

He looked at her, puzzled. *Please buy it, please, Dad.*

“Okay, if you’re sure. We’ll need to be going soon. I have an early morning meeting at school.” He got up and retrieved the plate of food he’d prepared.

Lexia sat in silence eating, her dad placed a drink and some pills next to her but never said a word. Staring into space as her dad wandered around the kitchen, when she finished Lexia got up and slowly limped over to the sink with her plates. As she turned back around her dad was bent over the trash can. Her heart lurched as she saw what he was doing, in his hand he held a Ziploc bag, and he was retrieving the stained cloths he'd used to clean the blood off her skin. She watched in horror as he closed the Ziploc then slid it into his bag.

"Dad, what are you doing?" His eyes locked with hers. She held her breath waiting for his reasonable explanation.

"Well…I…"

Her heart thundered, her head swam. *He knows, oh God he knows.*

"The ranger called, they want a sample to… see if the panther had any diseases."

"From my blood?"

"Yes, hopefully there will be saliva from the panther."

"Dad?" she question, knowing he was lying.

"Enough. Get ready we are leaving."

Lexia felt like he'd slapped her, in all her life she couldn't remember a single moment where he'd spoken to her in that tone.

Alone in the cafeteria, after her dad had left for his early meeting, Lexia got out her phone and began to text.

Lexia -I really need 2 talk babe, can U come 2 school now?

Alice - School now! Ur crazy!

Lexia - I need u A

Alice - C U Soon XXX

It felt like an eternity waiting for Alice to arrive, she'd been so afraid of jumping off the cliff she'd been walking along the past few weeks, it never occurred to Lexia that she could be pushed. She felt like she was falling and she had no idea if she'd survive. Had she just lost her dad forever this morning or was he telling the truth?

"Lex! I just ran into Mike! He said you'd been attacked by a panther!"

Lexia couldn't stop the tears as they sprang from her eyes.

"Fuck, babe, come here"—Alice hugged her—"It's ok babe, I text Dan, he's coming now, we'll take care of you."

"What? Alice—God-why?"

"Well, I just thought you were going to give him a chance? I'm sorry babe, shouldn't I have?"

"You knew we weren't going out! Alice!"

"Sorry I just thought."

"That you'd interfere, like always?"

"That's not fair, Lex"

"Argh! Look it doesn't matter but I really need to speak with you before he arrives."

"Okay, I'm listening."

"My dad has been acting so weird and he wouldn't stop going on about how lucky I was not to be badly injured and well, this morning my leg's not so bad but he didn't believe me and we ended up snapping at each other..."

"Lex, I think he was just worried about you, I'm sure he was pretty shook up. You could have been killed."

"That's not all though, I saw him put the cloths with my blood into a Ziploc bag."

Alice frowned. "Did you ask why?"

"Yes and he said the ranger wanted to test my blood to see if there was any saliva from the panther."

"But that sounds reasonable."

"You didn't see the way he looked at me and he got so mad."

"Babe, I think you're just reading too much into this. What else would he need your blood for?"

Lexia opened her mouth with the intention of telling Alice the whole truth, when Dan burst through the doors. "Lex. Are you alright?"

Lexia looked into Alice's eyes, pleading.

Lexia looked up at Dan and wished she could disappear. He climbed into the seat next to her, giving her a hug, Lexia stared at Alice over his shoulder, glaring.

"Lex, you're overreacting, okay? Mike loves you."

Dan pulled away looking between the two girls, "I know we aren't together, but you said we were friends right?"

Lexia sighed nodding.

"Don't worry; I'll take good care of you. From now on I'll be your slave."

Lexia couldn't help laughing at that. "Help me to class then before this place is crawling with people staring at me."

Dan put his arm around her waist and lifted her slightly, Lexia pulled away, "Dan, I'm not an invalid."

As she slowly made her way to first period, Alice and Dan rambled on about the panther and how she could have been killed. By the end of the day the whole school was talking about how a panther was terrorizing the forests; wherever she walked they stared and whispered. And she was also completely over Dan fussing over her. She was about ready to retract their friendship; did he think he could get her to reconsider her decision to not go out with him?

Wandering down the school corridor, the teacher having

let her out early to avoid the stampede of students. Lexia's foot hardly hurt, she'd taken pain killers at lunch to help with the pain. Yet she still limped just in case someone saw her.

As she reached the steps she stopped; she'd told Alice she would meet her there after school. Staring into space Lexia waited for the bell to ring. Students piled out the doors and whispered as they went past. She leant against the wall, looking at her phone, drowning out the noisy chatter of the students around her.

A group of girls walked past, overhearing some of their conversation, Lexia looked up from her phone, they were practically jumping up and down about something, and it wasn't her and the panther attack.

Her heart stopped, at the gates was Lincoln, he had on his usual faded denim jeans, and white T-Shirt but he'd put on a leather jacket, too. He seemed completely unfazed by the hordes of teenage girls drooling over him. Catching her gaze, she felt like a rabbit caught in headlights. Making out the amused look on his face even from her position, she had to go to him or he'd think she was crazy.

"Shit," she muttered, and looked behind her. Alice was walking towards her, her head bent texting, and Dan was running to catch up with Alice.

God why does Lincoln have to keep showing up unannounced?

She glanced back at Alice and Dan, they would see her any minute. Then back at Lincoln, now walking down the school drive. *Arrrh! Screw it! I can't be doing with Dan anyway.*

Lexia dashed down the school steps, completely forgetting she was supposed to be injured, texting Alice at the same time: *had 2 run*. She heard someone say, "Isn't she supposed to be injured?"

Oops, Lexia began to limp again as she rushed up to Lincoln. He was laughing as she approached, ignoring him, Lexia grabbed his hand, and hauled him after her. Risking a glance back at school; Alice had paused on the steps reading the text, and Dan was looking over her shoulder. She felt her phone vibrate before they continued on their way out. All they had to do was look her way and they'd be seen.

"Lexia?"

Lexia ignored Lincoln, pulling him along, glancing around for an escape. *That will do.* Dragging Lincoln between two buildings, Lexia stopped, and glared at him. "What the hell are you doing?"

He didn't snap, just chuckled at her like her being crazy was highly amusing. "I could ask you the same thing." He smiled looking down at her hand still clasped with his.

Lexia dropped his hand immediately, stepping back. *I've finally lost it,* she thought. "Lincoln, you can't just turn up at school; someone could see, Alice could see, and my Dad works there."

A group of girls walked past laughing, Lexia turned, walking towards the end of the alley. The last thing she needed was Alice spotting her in a dank, dark alley with him.

"I'm not a criminal, Lex. I just wanted to see you, besides

you sprinted to me like I was a long lost lover," he laughed.

"God, Lincoln, how can you laugh at everything? Alice was about to meet me and I really don't want a lecture from her and oh God, I was running in front of everyone." Lexia paced backwards and forwards completely forgetting Lincoln. "He's going to go nuts if he finds out, I'm going to be in a padded cell before I know it. God, Lex, you're such an idiot!" she chided herself.

"Wow Lex, hold on a minute, what's wrong?"

"I... I can't tell you."

"Why?"

"Please Lincoln, I like to be around you because you don't ask questions, I don't have to explain everything to you."

He looked at her for a minute. "Okay Lex, but if you ever want to talk..." He walked further down the alley, away from the street.

"Where are you going?" she asked, frustrated.

"Well, I didn't really plan on spending my time with you in an alley." He hopped over a fence, which bordered the forest.

"Lincoln, wait, we'll get lost."

"Chicken," he called.

Lexia paused at the fence, she could just leave him and walk back to the street, but really she wanted to spend more time with him. What she didn't understand was why he wanted to spend time with her. She was just a school girl, and right now she was acting crazy. He was a sexy man that could have any woman he wanted.

"Don't have all day, Lex."

"Coming," she sighed. Putting her foot onto the mesh fence, she winced as she put her weight onto her ankle.

She felt quite pleased with herself as she climbed to the top of the fence without much effort, but as her foot swung over the top it got caught. Twisting painfully, Lexia lost her grip, falling towards the ground. She braced for the impact but it never came, landing instead into Lincoln's strong arms.

"Got ya," he whispered, his eyes burning with hunger. Lexia eyes dropped to his parted mouth, she licked her bottom lip, biting it slightly as an image of him kissing her popped into her head. Her heart beat faster as his head lowered towards her; she held her breath waiting for the moment his lips would touch hers. Her whole body tingled with anticipation, then it dawned on her what she was doing. This was Lincoln - this was stupid - they'd never work.

She looked one last time into his eyes and pulled back, his lips millimeters from hers. Struggling to her feet, her foot throbbed as it took her weight, taking off through the trees limping for real this time, Lexia cursed herself for being so stupid.

Lincoln watched Lexia as she marched off into the trees. She was limping, and heading in the wrong direction. He'd been so close to kissing her; what was he doing? He'd set out to find her weakness, and now he was falling for her. He should have let her hit the ground, but his instincts had taken over; he wasn't the type of man to let a women fall. What he couldn't quite understand was why she was so clumsy. The fence shouldn't have been a problem for someone like her, but the more he watched her the more she just seemed…ordinary. *Well, maybe not ordinary, god damn sexy and confusing!*

He couldn't see her anymore but could hear her noisy path through the forest. "Lexia. You're going the wrong way," Lincoln shouted.

He laughed when her angry face appeared through the trees.

"Why are you limping, beautiful?" he asked, walking towards her.

"I… well, I was attacked by a panther last night, and I hurt my foot again in the fence."

"A panther, really? I could carry you? Hold you real close." He winked at her, knowing he was being a dick, but it was the only way to create some more distance between them.

"Lincoln, I am fine to walk, thank you.

They walked in silence. Lexia stumbled along, cursing every rut and tree root that tripped her. There were no trails here, but Lincoln seemed at home; the dense undergrowth and tightly packed trees didn't slow him down at all. She watched him, fascinated, as his body relaxed; she couldn't stand the silence any longer. "So what have you done today?"

He paused allowing her to catch up before saying, "Just a few business calls, and organized some travel arrangements."

"Oh... Are you leaving?" *Why did I have to sound so disappointed?*

Lexia glanced at him noticing a slight smile on his lips. "Just for a few days, I'll be back Friday morning sometime; I have a friend in, Rapid City, I'm going to meet."

"Oh ok... So what business do you do then?"

"We run an investment company."

"We?"

"It's a family thing. I don't really have much to do with it, never been one for business."

"Just spend the money then?" she laughed.

"Not really a big spender either, my parents left me a lot of money when they passed, and my grandfather, and the company board deal with most things. I used to be more involved but living in the city, and being cooped up in an office all day drove me mad."

"Hmm, can't really imagine you in a suit." she laughed, trying to lighten the suddenly somber mood.

"I'll have you know I look sexy as hell in a suit," he said in a mock serious tone.

They both burst out laughing and Lexia wiped the tears from her eyes. She was so caught up in the moment, she never noticed the root that snaked in her way, tripping, Lexia twisted her foot as she fell. Her eyes widened as she was pitched forward but then she felt Lincoln's strong hands stopping her, putting her back on her feet. She looked up into his face, feeling blood rush to her cheeks. "Thanks."

"Best stop laughing at me, and pay attention," he said.

Lexia glared at him but it never reached her eyes; he made such simple things fun. The more time she spent with him, the more her reasons for not seeing him seemed silly.

She walked the rest of the way chatting to him about the places he'd visited, how she longed to leave Deadwood, and travel. She stumbled a few times but Lincoln was always there to steady her, his warm touch doing funny things to her tummy. When she reached her driveway, she didn't want to leave him, she had a night of studying and avoiding her dad ahead of her; her final exam was tomorrow.

"I'll see you in a few days then?"

"Maybe," he said with a mischievous smile. Running his knuckles across her cheek, he walked away without another word.

Frozen for a minute, she watched him walk away, her cheek tingling from his touch. How did he do this to her? She shook her head clearing the fog and walked down the drive. *Yes, he's so wrong for me but I don't think I care anymore.*

When the house came into view, Lexia breathed a sigh of relief, he's not home yet. As she opened the door the phone began to ring; hurrying, Lexia ran into the house and picked it up. "Hello?"

"Hello, may I speak to Professor Burton, please?"

"Sorry, wrong number." She went to put the phone down but the lady screeched into the phone.

"Wait! I must speak to him; it's a matter of great urgency!"

"I'm sorry, no professor lives here."

"He must, this is the number he gave me for emergencies, a Professor Jonathan Burton."

"Nope, no Jonathans, sorry." The door opened, Lexia looked up as her dad walked through the door, the woman on the phone was still shouting.

"I said wrong number." Lexia put the phone down.

"Who was that?" asked her dad.

"Someone asking for a Professor Burton, I told her no Professors lived here, but she wouldn't shut up, kept going on about a dire emergency...Crazy woman."

For a second Lexia was taken aback as her dad turned white as a sheet and a look of panic crossed his face.

Confused she asked, "Are you alright?"

"Erm, yes, fine. Did she say what the emergency was?"

"No. Anyway I'm off to go hide in bed, leg's killing me."

He looked down at her leg seeming to just remember she'd been injured. "Do you need it checking?"

"No, I... The nurse at school did, said I was very lucky."

"Hmm, yes," he mumbled, walking off.

God he's so up and down lately, I never know where I stand with him!

"Can you bring me supper, please?" No answer.

"Dad?"

"Oh what? Yes, supper."

"He's lost it," she mumbled, pretend limping up the stairs.

Chapter 11

The next morning she woke to find twenty missed calls from Alice. She groaned, "I'm going to be in shit when she finds me."

Her dad was distracted when he drove them to school, he had no meeting that morning, which meant Lexia arrived only thirty minutes before the start of school. Leaving her dad, Lexia walked in the front doors, coming face to face, with a very pissed off Alice.

"Hi," she said weakly. Alice glared.

"Explain now!" she growled; Alice could be scary as hell when angry.

"I... well my dad wanted to drive me home, and wasn't pleased when I said I planned to walk, and you know how he's been lately, Alice, so I kind of just ran, well not ran, limped fast and well, then I felt like crap when I got home so I went straight to sleep. I just wasn't up for speaking to anyone, I'm sorry." She took a huge breath and smiled at her. "Please forgive me?" Alice seemed even more pissed off. Lexia hugged her, hoping to shock the anger from her.

As Alice's mouth neared her ear she whispered, "Lex. I saw your dad here, so he never took you home, which means one thing: you are hiding something, or someone."

Gulping, Lexia walked.

"How's the foot?" Alice asked sweetly.

Shit limp! "Erm, better thanks."

She walked into school towards the gym, where their exam was being held; she pretend limped at a slow pace wondering how she was going to get herself out of this one.

By third period Lexia had, had enough, she needed to escape; all the whispering and staring was driving her mad, why did she run out of the school gates? Everyone was whispering about Lincoln. They either talked about how she must be dating an older guy or that she'd faked the whole panther attack for attention.

If she had to spend a moment longer trapped in school she was going to explode; her anger had been slowly building throughout the day. The fact that Alice hadn't spoken a word to her since this morning, wasn't helping her mood either.

Slowly standing, Lexia limped towards the teacher at her desk. She looked up, confused as to why she was being disturbed. "Miss Emerson, may I go find my, dad? I'm in a lot of pain."

"Oh yes, of course Miss Granger, I hope you are feeling better soon."

All eyes watched her as she left, her phone vibrated against her leg as she exited the room. *Alice is still my friend after all then.*

Wat U doin?

I need 2 get outa here cum over later if ur still speaking 2 me?

No reply.

Once she was alone, Lexia stopped limping, and hurried through the school to her dad's classroom, but when she arrived, he wasn't there and neither were his things.

Strange, I thought he was taking me home?

"Can I help you, Miss Granger?"

Lexia turned around to face the principal. "I was looking for my Father, sir."

"He went home to deal with an emergency."

"Oh, is he okay?"

"I wouldn't know, but I suggest you head back to class, Miss Granger."

"Yes, sir."

Sighing, Lexia limped away. When she was nearly to her classroom, she glanced behind her, finding herself alone. Racing towards the exit, Lexia burst through the doors into the bright sunshine and smiled; she was free.

When Lexia made it home there was a strange car in the driveway parked next to her dads. She stopped, *who's with my dad?*

Moving forward again, her every step silent, not even the gravel under her feet crunched; she'd turned into someone else. Like the panther that had stalked her, Lexia became the predator, her every move calculated, controlled.

A small voice in her head asked her why she was doing this. Why did she feel the need to stalk her own father?

Lexia had no answers, she didn't understand herself. This part of herself came from deep within, some lost piece of herself that she'd never known was there; it acted on instinct alone, and those instincts said something was wrong. Her dad was keeping secrets and she was going to discover them.

The front door opened silently, Lexia slipped into the house like a ghost; she knew every creaky board and joint. Pausing, she blended into her surroundings, waited, listened.

"You should have never come here!" her dad said, angrily.

"This is important. You can't hide from the truth any longer, no matter your feelings," replied a woman's voice, Lexia didn't recognize.

"You could have led them to us; I don't care what you've learned. You must leave now, before we are found."

"Is she all you care about? Do we mean nothing to you anymore?" snapped the woman.

"She's my daughter, she will always come first," her dad replied, harshly.

Lexia snapped back to herself, gasping at her dad's words; what did he mean? She felt sick, confused a tight not in her stomach. Questions ran around in her head, dizzying in their numbers.

Her foot shifted, causing the floorboard to squeak.

"Silence!" her dad ordered.

For a second the house was deadly silent, before Lexia called, "Dad?"

"Leave now," her dad whispered, angrily.

"You must tell her, she needs to know"—someone got up from their chair, the legs scraped across the floor, muffling the rest of the conversation.

"Dad?"—Lexia pushed through into the kitchen. Her dad was closing the back door—"Whose car is in the drive?"

Lexia's father remained silent, is hands on the door, head slightly bowed.

"Dad, are you alright?"

"Yes"— he sighed, turning around—"It was someone I met a long time ago, before I knew your mother. She...I...well, it's complicated but she's not a nice person. Don't worry, though, she will not be returning."

"What was her name?"

"It's not important. I actually need to go out, and I may be home late, will you be okay alone? Can you order in dinner?"

"Oh yeah, sure, I'll have, Alice, over." He looked at her, his eyes a minefield of emotion that she couldn't work out, then he left, leaving Lexia confused and alone.

Alice was walking into Lexia's drive when Mike flew past her, in his car; she jumped back to avoid the gravel flying up from his tires. The sharp sting of stone had her hissing out a breath. "Fucking hell!"

Rushing up to the house, Alice found the door open. "Lex?"—Walking into the hall Alice called her again—"Lexia? Are you here? Is everything okay? I saw your dad driving out of here, he nearly knocked me over, the idiot."

Lexia looked up as Alice walked into the kitchen. The tears pooled in her eyes, spilled over as Alice's face filled with pity. Alice was holding her seconds later, Lexia held onto her best friend, letting her emotions wash away with each tear.

"Better?" Alice asked when Lexia's tears finally ran dry.

"I'm sorry for breaking down on you."

"Don't be silly, that's what I'm here for. What happened?"

"I'm not sure. I came home and there was a car in the driveway, and I just had this feeling... I snuck into the house and listened to them."

"Who was it?"

"Well, that's the thing, I don't know. It was some woman and they were arguing about somebody... I think me. It was me, Alice, they were arguing about me!"

"What were they saying about you?"

"It made no sense, she was telling him that I had to know something but he was talking about leading someone to us. I just I don't understand anything that's going on anymore. Everything's messed up, Alice. How did my life fall apart so fast?"

"Listen to me, Lex, your life is not falling apart, okay! I'm not sure what's going on with Mike, but that's not your concern, okay? He probably has some crazy, ex-stalker girlfriend or something. So this is what you're going to do, Lex. First thing, don't see Lincoln ag…"

"Al…"

"No, Lex, listen! He's bad news and you are only going to get your heart broken. Second, if you're not going to give Dan a chance then stay single, and thirdly, just let Mike sort out his own mess. Stop sneaking about and thinking the worst, got it?"

"I just…" Lexia looked at Alice's stern face. "Okay I'll leave Dad alone, and I'm not interested in Dan. Maybe you're right, Lincoln has left town anyway, he should be back tomorrow but he might not come back." It was hard to not sound hurt as she spoke the last words.

“At last you’re listening to me. You do realize I’m the wise one out of us, don’t you?”

Lexia burst out laughing.

“Shut it! When’s Mike back?”

“Don’t know. He rushed out and said to order in.”

“Cool. Pizza and girls night it is then.”

CHAPTER 12

Looking at her wardrobe, the next morning, Lexia couldn't decide what to wear. Clothes were scattered all over the room. *Since when do I stress over clothes because of a guy?* She wasn't sure if Lincoln would meet her after school, they hadn't made plans and he hadn't given a definite 'yes, I will see you again' but still she stressed. Sighing she flopped onto the bed. "I've officially lost it. I told Alice I'd leave Lincoln alone, and here I am dressing up for him."

"Lexia, you're going to be late!"

Getting up, Lexia straightened her clothes, and took one last look in the mirror. *Ok I need to cover up more skin and show more cleavage.* Lexia pulled her leather boots over the thin bandage she had on her ankle, and swapped the tank she was wearing for a grey low-cut jumper.

Her dad's eyes widened as Lexia came down the stairs. But before he could protest, she was out the door and heading down the drive.

Normally she wore jeans or a long skirt to school. Troubled and excited all at the same time, her excitement to see Lincoln bubbled through her blood.

Reaching school, it took only a few seconds for Lexia to regret her choice of clothing. *What the hell was I thinking? What is Lincoln doing to me?* Every boy she passed, stared like they were seeing her for the first time.

Alice practically choked on her drink when Lexia joined her for lunch. "Spill now, Lex. This outfit best not be for Lincoln. And your ankle - how did you get those boots on?"

"I needed a pick me up, and what better way than to look good? The boots went on with a bit of tugging, but my ankle feels a lot better today."

"You really think I'm going to fall for that?" Alice scowled.

"Look it's just a skirt; what's the big deal?" *Why did I wear this?*

"The sexy leather boots, and the boobs you have on display for every, male, here."

"You wear clothes like this daily, just leave it, okay? Please."

"For now, Lex," she smiled sweetly. Lexia knew Alice would be following her every move until she found out what Lexia was hiding.

Lexia couldn't quite come to grips with her actions lately. Lincoln was wrong for her in so many ways, and yet she found herself doing irrational things because of him.

At the end of her school day, Lexia gathered her things,

with butterflies in her belly. Hurrying to escape class, her heart began to race as she neared the exit. Reaching the steps, Lexia looked towards the gate to find... nothing. No one was waiting. Her heart sank as he scanned the street looking for him.

Nothing.

The sudden, overwhelming urge to cry, hit her full force. Tears welled in her eyes, swiping at them, angry with herself, Lexia headed down the steps. *Get a grip, Lexia, he's just a man.* But he wasn't *just* a man; Lincoln was exciting, and a little wild, he was gorgeous and a *badass.* He could be kind and sweet, make her heart race, yet make her feel so angry she wanted to scream, all at the same time. He was like no one she'd ever known, it didn't matter how many times she told herself there was something off about him, because with one single touch he made her feel alive.

Walking home, her arms wrapped around herself in an attempt to keep all she felt inside, Lexia ran up the stairs the second she entered her house. Flinging herself on the bed, her head hit the pillow as her tears fell. Lexia cried until her tears ran dry, every conflicting emotion washed away.

At nine o'clock that night, Lexia heard a soft knock at the door, followed by her dad's footsteps as he answered. Listening, Lexia jumped to her feet when she heard the familiar voice - *Lincoln.*

"Lexia!" her Dad's voice growled up the stairs.

"Shit," Lexia muttered. Leaping off the bed, she ran downstairs completely forgetting the state she was in from crying.

Lexia reached the front door, her dad was red-faced, and fuming with anger, while Lincoln looked as stunning as ever. He was leaning against the porch, carefree and completely oblivious to the tension in the air.

She smiled at Lincoln then turned to her dad. "Yes?"

"Yes, yes! Lexia, explain to me, why a fully-grown man is calling for you," he said through gritted teeth.

God, seriously, could you be any more embarrassing?

"Well..." *What am I going to say?*

"If I may, Mr. Granger, I have been out of town, and returned later than expected. I only sought to let, Lexia, know I was back."

Lexia was speechless; Lincoln was pulling off sweet, and harmless. Her dad seemed just as stunned; he stared at Lincoln, motionless, before asking, "And why would, my daughter, need to know you were back in town?"

"Jesus, Dad! I'm nearly twenty, and Lincoln, is a friend." She glared at him suddenly feeling angry. She wasn't a child and she'd done nothing wrong. What did her dad think - she'd stay single forever?

Lincoln glanced at her, a flash of emotion crossing his face, before returning his attention back to her dad. "I can see it's a bad time. Nice to meet you, Mr. Granger. Lexia." His eyes locked with hers for a second, and with that one intense look, Lexia was hooked; she'd missed him, and seeing him made her want him more.

Her father slammed the door, Lexia turned and stomped up the stairs, ignoring her dad.

"Lexia, come back down here and explain yourself!"

Thundering up the stairs after her, Lexia's father stood in the doorway, the light from the hall casting him in a silhouette; she couldn't see his face, but she knew he was angry.

"Look, he's just a friend, I had no idea he was coming over. Just like he said, I expected him back earlier."

"Lexia, he's a grown man, and they only think of one thing," he said, his voice rough with anger.

"God, are you serious? Do you really not trust me? I'm not stupid, Dad, and I'm not a child anymore, but none of that is relevant because he's just a friend, nothing has happened between us. Now leave me alone, it's been a long day."

He stood for a second longer, before leaving without a word.

Lexia jumped to her feet switching on the light. She glanced at herself in the mirror. "God did I really go downstairs like this?" she muttered.

Her eyes were bloodshot, and her skin, red and puffy. Rubbing some cream on her face, Lexia then applied foundation in hopes of covering the blotchy patches. Straightening her clothes, before slipping into a long coat, Lexia pulled up her window and climbed out. The moment her feet hit the ground she ran for the cover trees.

Lexia couldn't see Lincoln in the dark but he couldn't have gone far. Jogging towards the road, avoiding the gravel—the last thing she needed was her dad seeing her sneak—she'd not gone far when heard something rustle. Lexia peered into the darkness but couldn't see anything. Her senses stirred; a prickle running across her skin. Reaching for her knife, only then realizing she'd forgotten it in her hurry, her heart pounded, her stomach flipped, and Lexia gulped as two gold eyes appeared in the darkness.

Lexia met his gaze, forcing herself to stay calm, to show this cat no fear. "Where have you been?" she asked, casually. The panther hadn't been around for a few days.

He growled low in return, taking a step forward.

"You have terrible timing. Can we maybe do this tomorrow? After I've chased down this, hot guy?" Lexia laughed nervously. *Why the hell am I talking to you?*

The panther cocked his head, and Lexia held her breath. *Did he really understand me?* As if he could read her mind, the panther growled again, then blended into the darkness. Lexia heard the faintest of rustles, then the forest was silent.

Running the last of the drive; afraid he may come back, Lexia reached the street, only to find it empty. "Goddam, panther!" she growled, spinning around, and slamming straight into a hard-muscled chest.

Lexia gave a startled yelp. "Shush, it's just me," Lincoln whispered, running his hands down her arms.

"Shit, how do you always manage to sneak up on me?" Lexia replied, looking up into his face.

He laughed, his hands lingering on her skin. "Who were you goddamming?"

"Oh, err, no one," she mumbled, finding it hard to concentrate when with his skin against hers.

"So how did you convince your dad to let you out?" he asked.

"I didn't, I climbed out the window," she smiled, as her heart kicked up a beat.

"I'm seeing an all new side of you," he said with a mischievous smile.

Lexia was finding it hard to breath, with him so close, looking at her with that dangerous glint she was drawn too, he was hypnotizing. Forcing air into her lungs she tore her eyes away, putting distance. "So…want to go for a walk?"

"Sure." Lincoln turned, heading into the trees. Taking her hand, he tugged her along.

"Lincoln?" Lexia whispered, planting her feet.

"You scared?" He smirked, pulling her closer.

"You realize there're wild animals in the forest?" Lexia told him, as her eyes search the gloom of the trees.

"Nothing that's going to eat you, come on, it's only a little way up here."

"What's a little way up here?" she asked, curious.

"You'll see." He smiled, making her tummy flutter. *How does he affect me with just one smile?*

Lexia walked in silence as Lincoln lead her further into the forest. It grew darker, to the point, she could hardly see.

She cursed herself for letting him lead her into here; somewhere in this forest was a panther. She looked around for danger, imagining the panther, slowly stalking them, his lean graceful body not making a sound as he crept nearer and nearer. *What will I do if he attacks? I've no weapon.*

Something rustled to her right, Lexia picked up her pace and stumbled. Tightening her grip on Lincoln's hand to keep from falling, Lexia looked wildly around; searching for two gold eyes.

"Lexia, you're okay; nothing's going to get you."

"I've seen things in the forests; this was a bad idea, let's go back. I was attacked remember?" Lexia replied, frightened.

"We're nearly there now. Come on, I'll protect you."

She moved closer to him, taking some deep breaths. "Okay."

Relaxing her grip on Lincoln's hand, Lexia took another deep breath, attempting to calm her mind; she was no good to anyone with her imagination running wild. As she did she felt a rush of adrenaline course through her, suddenly calm, her senses sharpened, and it became easier to make her way through the forest.

Lincoln thought it strange that Lexia was so frightened. She was his enemy, yet right now she was just a frightened girl. *Maybe this is all just a trick?*

Yet the more time he spent with her, the more harmless she seemed. *Well, maybe not harmless.* She squeezed his hand tighter as a rabbit dashed off. *Maybe she's looking for the panther? You're holding the panther's hand.* He smiled into the darkness.

He felt the second she calmed down; loosening the grip on his hand, a wave of energy rush through her. His skin prickled, the panther inside of him tensing to fight, yet Lexia didn't attack. His beast rose to the surface, on edge; it didn't trust her, this woman full of trickery and power. *How is she making me fall for her, why can't I kill her?*

With effort, Lincoln forced the panther back, and led Lexia into the little clearing he'd found. The moment they passed through the trees she gasped, her head tilting to the sky. Delight crossed her face as she wandered around the moonlit clearing; the sky was clear tonight and lit by a thousand stars.

Entranced by her beauty, Lincoln approached silently. Running his knuckles over her face, Lexia gasped, stepping back she smiled hesitantly.

"Who made you cry?" Lincoln asked her, closing the distance she'd put between them.

Confusion crossed her face for a second, then she turned, walking slowly, as she answered, "No one."

"Someone did. When you came to the door, you'd been crying."

"It doesn't matter, Lincoln," Lexia answered, glancing at him briefly.

"I don't like it when you're sad." Lincoln was startled by his comment, yet it had slipped out. The moment he'd seen her, he wanted to push past her father and make sure she was okay.

Turning back to him with a smile, Lexia said, "I'm not sad anymore. I love the forest, and being here now when it's so peaceful... It makes me feel free... alive."

Unable to resist the pull he felt towards her, Lincoln froze fixated on her every action. Lexia sat on a rock, leaning back on her elbows, she tipped her head and gazed at the stars. Moonlight lit her face as her hair cascaded over the rock, Lincoln's heart kicked up a beat, his breath caught in his throat as the overwhelming urge to claim her as his, took over. He strode silently towards her, scanning over her body; she'd bent leg up, exposing her toned thigh.

Unable to resist his need to touch, Lincoln ran a finger across her skin, trailing from her collarbone, and over the top of her breasts. He bit back a moan as she gasped, looking at him with desire.

When Lexia made no protest, Lincoln continued. Spreading his hand on her exposed skin, he slowly ran it up and around the back of her neck, pulling her upright. Pressing his body against hers, she sucked in a breath, eyes widening as her breathing quickened. Lincoln lowered his head, not taking his eyes from hers, and softly brushed his lips across hers.

Fire burned through him as she moaned, opening her mouth for him. He pressed his lips firmly to hers and deepened the kiss, when a howl shattered the quiet. Lincoln shot upright, his panther rising to the surface.

Lexia stumbled backwards as Lincoln abruptly let her go. Dizzy from his kiss and shocked that he'd just stopped, she watched in silence as he paced the clearing.

A second howl echoed into the night.

"We need to go now," Lincoln said, striding to her. He took her hand, dragging her into the trees.

"Lincoln, calm down, the wolf is probably miles away."

"Wolves can be nasty, and they never travel alone."

She heard the howl again and this time, felt afraid; she'd killed a wolf and he'd been alone. "Okay, will you walk me to my door?"

He paused for a second, the tension drained away from his face, kindness in its place. "Of course." He ran his knuckles over her cheek.

When they reached her house, Lexia led him below her window and turned, looking up at him expectantly. Lincoln realized she was waiting for a goodnight kiss. Wondering what he'd done; kissing her, and taking her into the clearing, all pointed to the start of a relationship. He'd made a terrible mistake, yet his eyes moved to her lips without his control; he needed to kiss her, he needed to feel the rush from her touch. *Just once more,* he told himself.

With a final caress, Lincoln let her go. She turned and climbed, jumping quietly into her room. "Goodbye, Lincoln," she whispered from above.

Lincoln returned Lexia's smile, but for a second she thought she'd seen sadness fill his eyes. He'd left before she had chance to question him, leaving Lexia looking into the dark night wondering why she felt filled with dread all of a sudden. Wanting to climb back out the window, and chase him down, Lexia shook her head, feeling silly.

CHAPTER 13

Lexia spent Saturday morning in bed. The past few weeks had finally caught up to her and her father was away for the weekend so when the light shone through the crack in her curtains, she rolled over and stuck a pillow over her head.

A while later some part of her brain registered the sound of vibrating but she never fully woke, until loud knocking sounded at the door, rolling over Lexia pulled her covers over her head and tried to ignore it.

"Lex get your backside down here!" Alice yelled.

Moaning Lexia walked over to her window, poking her head out, "Keys under the pot."

She was back in bed, her head under the pillow when Alice flopped onto the bed.

"Get up will you! We have a party to shop for."

"Alice, I'm really not in the mood for a party."

"Lexia," she moaned.

"Aww, Alice, don't make me feel bad, I'm not in the mood

for people," Lexia answered.

"But, Lex, I can't go alone! Come on you're supposed to be my best friend!"

Lexia pulled the pillow off her head and glared at Alice. "I am your best friend and I still don't want to go!"

"Fine! But you're still coming shopping!" Alice hit her with the pillow. "I'll be in the car you have five minutes!"

Hours later Lexia walked the streets of Deadwood, bags in her hands, which mostly contained the many clothes Alice had bought, it always amazed Lexia how Alice managed to buy so many things from a town with not many choices.

"Can we go to your house now please?" Lexia begged Alice.

"Okay! Are you sure you don't want to buy a dress for tonight?"

"I've told you I'm not coming!"

"Fine," she huffed.

Walking in the direction of Alice's house, Alice stopped, looking into a shop window.

"Alice, no! You said we could leave."

"Oh come on, Lex! Look at that dress." The door chimed as she walked into the store.

"I'm going to kill you!" Lexia huffed, following her.

She sank into a chair, waiting as Alice chatted to the shop assistant. They wandered off towards the changing room together.

Lexia's eyes narrowed, her mouth a hard line. *Why am I always running around after her?*

Alice emerged from the changing room, the multicolored dress clinging to her skinny frame. Each time Alice smiled in delight to the shop assistants compliments, Lexia's fists squeezed tighter. *Were they really going to keep talking and ignore her?*

Lexia almost laughed at herself; why did she feel so mad? This is how it had always been between them.

"Oh sweetie, that looks lovely on you!" the shop assistant sang.

Standing abruptly, Lexia's chair fell to the floor making the two of them jump. Alice looked at Lexia like she was being hysterical, and the wave peaked; all the anger that had been building crashed.

Trembling, anger boiled in her blood. *What are you doing?* Asked a small voice.

Lexia felt enraged, out of control even.

Alice looked at her in confusion, Lexia glanced at the shop assistant; the bright, sparkly girl, had fear in her eyes.

Realizing she'd lost control, Lexia needed to leave before another wave hit.

"Lex, wait!" Alice called, as Lexia ran from the store.

She crashed through the door, straight into a group of people, two tumbled to the ground, but Lexia carried on. She needed to get away; she could feel it; the power in her blood taking over, controlling her rational thinking. *What's wrong with me?*

She barreled through another group of people, and stumbled into a lone man, but instead of him staggering out of the way, he felt like a brick wall. Lexia bent over, gasping, as her skin turned to ice. Looking up, the man had gone. An echo of a memory tumbled through her mind. Lexia was back in the club with Lincoln, they were dancing. She was lost in the feel of him, his hands on her body, the heat that seemed to seep into her bones but someone knocked into her...the spell had broken and the feeling she'd felt then; lingered in the air now. It was exactly the same.

She'd brushed it off before, putting it down to being drunk, only her instincts hadn't been wrong, because that man was here now; she'd felt him, could feel his energy, his darkness, lingering in the air.

Lexia searched the street for the man, feeling strangely calm as the power within her awakened. This time Lexia didn't feel out of control, but strong and powerful. She saw everything in a new light, felt everything differently; it was like both her sides were in harmony, working together.

Lexia ran past Alice, barely registering her look of bewilderment; she'd become another face in the crowd. Lexia had only one goal; to hunt down the man.

At the end of the street, Lexia stopped. She was sure he was around here somewhere; it was like she could feel the energy he gave off. Turning in a circle, her eyes took in every corner, doorway, and window, but he wasn't there.

"Lexia," someone shouted.

"Where are you? I know you're here somewhere," she mumbled, turning slowly again... Something moved in the corner of her eye... *There!*

His hand curled around the edge of a building, each calloused finger gripping into the wood, and slowly he peered out. Lexia took a step, her whole body humming with adrenaline, ready to give chase, when their eyes locked.

Lexia froze as she took in his appearance. Everything about him was ordinary from his messy brown hair to his sun-kissed skin, except his eyes. They shocked her, made her question what she was doing, what she was seeing, because they weren't ordinary eyes. They were gold, and not golden-brown like Lincoln's eyes, but bright, pure gold; it bled out almost covering all the white of his eyes. They held no emotion, there was no depth to them. They weren't the eyes of a human.

He smiled at her; it was cruel and twisted, and turned his ordinary face into a monster's. Hands clenching into fists, Lexia prepared to fight, when an arm linked through hers. Snapping back to herself, her body drained, Lexia looked back to the building, but the man was gone.

"Babe, you ok?" Alice asked.

She didn't answer her, she had no idea. *What just happened? What's happening to me?*

"Hey, Lex, did you see someone?" Alice asked tugging her arm.

Lexia forced her eyes to move from the building to Alice's face. Her instinct to hide what was happening kicked in, and the lies rolled easily off her tongue.

"Yeah, I thought I saw, Lincoln."

"I thought you were leaving him alone?"

"I am, come on."

CHAPTER 14

Watching Alice try on a hundred different outfits, Lexia had given up paying attention about half an hour ago. The gold-eyed man, taunted her mind.

"Lexia!" Alice all but screamed at her.

"What?" she sighed.

Alice flopped down on the bed, and took Lexia's hand. "What's up, babe?"

Lexia, didn't feel ready to explain the crazy things that had been happening to her, the attacks, the out of control emotions, but she could tell her about, Lincoln, even though, Lexia knew Alice wouldn't be pleased. "Okay, but no shouting at me." Alice glared, but Lexia continued. "Lincoln, went away as you know, and I thought he'd be back Friday morning, that's why I dressed up, I thought he'd meet me after school."

"I knew you were meeting him," she hissed.

"Listen! He never showed at school, he came straight to my house when he arrived back. My dad, answered the door."

"Oh shit."

"Yeah, but anyway I won't go into his lecture, I climbed out the window at first chance, and met Lincoln."

"You really must stop climbing out the window. And what about our deal?"

"Alice, the night was amazing and...he kissed me," she answered, dreamily, remembering the feel of his lips.

"What?" Alice gasped.

"Shush, it was incredible, Alice, but when he left he had this funny look in his eyes."

"What do you mean?"

"It's hard to explain."

"Well has he called or text?"

"He doesn't have my number."

"What? Lex, you need to give him it, and get his. Look, stop worrying, and get yourself into a mood to party! Best cure for the blues is a good party!"

"But I don't want to go," Lexia groaned.

"Tough!" Lexia didn't argue, there was no point; Alice had always had a special talent at getting what she wanted.

A few hours later Lexia found herself dressed in a short,

silver dress she'd borrowed from Alice, it only just covered her backside, and with a deep plunging neckline, not much was left for the imagination. Her hair was pulled up high with tumbling curls crowning her head, and her shoulders and neck were bare. Lexia knew she looked good, and plenty of men had noticed, but she couldn't get in the mood to dance; there was only one person she wanted to see and he wasn't there.

Lexia watched Alice dance with some boy she liked, from the sidelines. Alice had a ridiculous grin on her face, which Lexia couldn't help laughing at. She tried not to be bothered about being ignored. Alice always left her when men were about; she'd been that way from the moment they'd met; erratic, demanding, but loyal. At least Lexia could always depend on Alice being a constant in her life.

Downing her drink in one gulp, hoping the alcohol would numb her brain, Lexia pushed off the wall to find another.

"Hey Lexia, I brought you a drink," Josh smiled, holding out the plastic cup.

"Oh, thanks." Lexia took it, smiling, he was cute she thought.

"So why you so sad, Lexia?"

"It's been one of those weeks." Lexia gulped down the drink. Josh's grin widened.

"I'll get you another." He ran off before Lexia could say a word.

"Here finish this, and we can dance," he said, when he returned.

Lexia looked at the drink; she'd only had two, another one wouldn't hurt. Maybe Alice was right; she just needed to have fun tonight. The drink went down in one.

Josh pulled her onto the dance floor and snaked through the bodies until they reached Alice. Alice grinned, grabbing her hand to twirl her around. Lexia couldn't help but laugh and dance with her friend, her enthusiasm was infectious.

Her body soon relaxed, and slowly Lexia began to enjoy herself. She danced with Josh, twisting her hips to the beat. Josh put his hands on her hips, and Lexia couldn't help but think of Lincoln; how it felt when he'd held her hips, and danced with her.

After a while Lexia began to feel dizzy, she stumbled away from Josh in search of a glass of water.

"You feeling okay, Lexia?" Lexia turned, looking at Josh; everything was becoming blurry.

"Just a bit dizzy." *But I've not drank that much.*

"Do you want me to get, Alice?" Lexia looked across the room at Alice; she didn't want to spoil her fun.

"No, I'll be okay in a minute."

"Here, come with me." Josh took her hand and pulled her forward, the world tilted and Lexia stumbled.

"Wow, you've drank a bit," he laughed. *But I haven't.*

Josh leaned her in a corner and Lexia felt grateful for having something to lean on. He moved in front of her placing his hands back on her hips.

"I think I best go." Lexia was finding it hard to concentrate, her brain felt foggy, all the sounds around her were to blurring together.

"Stay with me," he said. Lexia numbly registered his hands were on her body. She wanted him to stop, but was finding it hard to stand.

"Josh?"

"Shush, baby."

Lexia couldn't take it, she wasn't his baby. His hands were on the hem of her dress; she shivered as his fingers trailed across her bare legs, he made her skin crawl. Lexia wanted him off her, she wanted to go home.

"Josh, stop…" she slurred but he didn't listen. His hands were now lifting her dress.

"Come on, Lexia, don't be frigid." His cruel words cleared her head for a second.

"I said stop!" Lexia shouted, pushing him in the chest. Except he didn't just stumble back like she'd expected him to, he flew across the room landing on some dancers and they all fell to the floor.

"Lexia?" Alice called.

Everyone looked at her, Lexia looked down at her hands. She didn't mean to, she just wanted him to stop. She staggered forward needing to get away.

"Lex, Lexia, wait!" Alice's voice seemed far away. Lexia's head spun, she fell into the wall, her shoulder throbbed as it collided.

Falling out the door, cool gentle hands helped her. Lexia turned, looking into Alice's face. "I didn't mean to, but he wouldn't let me go."

"Of course you didn't, babe. Josh is a creep. Come on, let's get you home."

"No stay, it's still early, and I want to be alone."

"Lex?"

"I just need a little air, I didn't drink that much."

"Lexia, you were falling over."

"I just want to be alone," Lexia snapped.

Alice stepped back, looking hurt.

"Sorry…I just…I'm just tired. Go inside have fun, I'm going to sit for a min, then walk home."

"If you're sure, Conner is cute!"

"Go have fun. I'll call you tomorrow." She smiled, hoping it was convincing.

"Lex, get some air, but if you are still feel shit come get me okay?"

"Yeah."

"Bye, babe." Alice turned and disappeared into the house.

Lexia walked down the street away from the people, lingering outside the house; she hoped the fresh air would clear her head.

She slid down a wall and put her head on her knees. *I've only had three drinks* she thought.

"Hey Lex, where'd you learn moves like that?"

Lexia looked up at the boy from her school, but she couldn't remember his name.

"Pretty sweet, you throwing him across the room," he continued.

Lexia dragged herself upright.

"Wanna come inside with me?"

"No, I'm going home."

"Lexia, come on, that was so awesome! You're stronger than you look." He reached out squeezing her arm. A wave of anger roll through her.

"Sorry, I've got to go," she ground out, walking away before she hurt someone else.

Staggering from side to side, she tried to stay upright. The further she stumbled the worse she felt, everything felt wrong and standing upright was becoming a problem. The world tilted, and Lexia fell off the curb twisting her ankle.

"Shit," she muttered, trying to get off the road. Stood up on wobbly legs, she looked around; she'd reached a T- junction. The forest was to her right, and left seemed to head further into town. Lexia stumbled across the road, hoping once into town she'd find her way home. The road seemed to sway beneath her, tripping, Lexia scraped her knees on the rough tarmac.

Tears spilled from her eyes as she crawled over to the side walk and leaned against a wall; her knees stung and her head felt so foggy. She wanted to fall asleep, her eyes began to close, but then she saw a wolf slinking out of the trees, the cold gleam in its eyes made her heart pick up speed.

Lexia sucked in a breath, eyes going wide, she staggered back to her feet, but she fell back to the ground. Scrambling backwards, her dress ripped on the rough ground. Lexia sobbed as the wolf prowled closer. It had the same ice blue eyes that the other one had, but this one was black as night. It snarled savagely, running at her.

Crying out as it sunk its teeth into her ankle, Lexia kicked frantically with no effect. It sunk its teeth into her muscled calf, dragging her, and Lexia's head hit the pavement.

Bracing for another bite, the wolf froze as another growl filled the dark night; the wolf turned, racing. Relief flooded her system for a second before tall shadow towered above her.

"Lex, it's okay."

"Lincoln?" Lexia looked up at him but she couldn't see straight.

"Lincoln, the wolf."

"It's gone, I scared it off. Come on, in case it comes back."

Lexia attempted to get to her feet, but with her dizzy head and the pain in her leg, she couldn't. "I can't."

Lincoln helped Lexia stand, but the second he let her go, she swayed. "Jesus, Lexia, how much have you drank? Christ, you're bleeding."

"It bit me," she sobbed. "And I think someone put something in my drink."

Lincoln leaned into her neck, sniffing at her skin. She felt a rumble come from his chest, like the beginning of a growl.

"Come on, I'll carry you home, then we can fix your leg."

Lincoln cradled her body against his, and Lexia nuzzled her face into his chest.

Lexia tried to respond but nothing would come out past the lump in her throat. Her eyes felt heavy, and the warmth coming from Lincoln's body seeped into her bones. She sighed into his chest as a feeling of peace settled in her mind. Being near him, breathing in his smell, feeling his strong solid arms holding her with such care, it felt so right, like she'd finally found what she'd been searching for.

"You comfy there, love?" Lincoln chuckled, his chest

rumbling under her.

"Mmm," was all she could muster.

"What were you doing out here on your own, Lex?" His voice was soft and gentle, coaxing the truth from her.

"I wanted to be alone... Guess I kind of threw some asshole across the room at a party, Alice, and I, were at."

"Well I'm sure he deserved it, but why did, Alice, let you wander off alone?"

She didn't answer right away, her eyes closing against the thick fog in her brain. "I told her I was just getting some air but then some guy came up to me... I guess I wasn't thinking."

He didn't ask her another question for a while and Lexia drifted off, snuggling closer against his chest.

"What else is going wrong, Lexia?"

Silence.

"Lexia? Hey, Lex?" He poked her lightly. Her sleepy eyes opened and focused on his face.

"Mmm?"

"What else is going wrong?" he asked. But her eyes closed again. "Lex?"

"Pretty panther," she whispered.

"What?" Lincoln lifted her away from his body and as the cold whispered over her skin, her eyes reopened.

"Pretty panther," she smiled, looking at him.

Lincoln leashed the beast within him, shocked that it had risen to the surface for that second, and he'd lost control. It paced within his mind, confused about the girl he held in his arms, the girl he kept protecting when she was the enemy, and he was supposed to kill her.

When they reached Lexia's house, Lincoln tried to rouse her without being too loud. Whispering, "How are we getting in?"

"He's not here. You can be as loud as you like, I was supposed to be sleeping at, Alice's. Key's under the pot

"Did you carry me all the way here?"

"Yes, can't you remember?"

"Not really, I remember that wolf, and you... But not getting here."

Lincoln breathed a sigh of relief; she'd not noticed the panther in his eyes. Putting Lexia on her feet, she immediately tipped sideways and threw up.

Lincoln left her to it, and unlocked the door.

"You finished?"

"Yes, I'm so sorry. I swear I only had like three drinks."

"It's okay." He picked her back up, walking upstairs to find her bedroom. Placing her on the bed, Lexia rolled over hugging the pillow.

"Where's the first aid?" he asked, heading for the bedroom door.

"It's under the bed, Linc."

He paused and cocked his head to the left, studying her face. "Strange place to keep it."

On his hands and knees, his head disappeared below the bed to retrieve the kit. When he surfaced, his head level with hers, she gulped, sucking in a breath.

"I'm accident prone," she whispered, as her eyes travelled to his sculpted mouth; her tongue slipped out wetting her bottom lip.

His head moved a fraction closer, his eyes following her tongue. Heart pounding in anticipation, Lincoln could almost remember the taste of her on his lips.

Enemy. She's the enemy, he reminded himself. "Best fix you up." He was at her feet in seconds.

An awkward silence developed between them.

"You're quiet," she said after a while.

He looked up into her hurt eyes, and felt a pang in his chest. "Does it hurt?" Looking back at the wounds he waited for her answer.

"A little, I have a high tolerance to pain."

"That's unusual for a girl." He smiled, the cheeky glint back in his eyes.

"Well, maybe I'm not just an ordinary girl."

His grin was wicked." Oh I know".

"I'm so tired," she yawned.

Lincoln finished strapping up her ankle and calf then he sat and studied the sleeping girl on the bed before him. She looked so normal, acted so innocent, and yet he knew she was different; he might not have seen her kill for the sake of killing, but just one look at her leg with his panther senses and he could see the speed at which she healed. How her ankle had no scars from the bite he'd given her.

I should kill her now while she's asleep and vulnerable, and yet he stood, pulling a blanket over her barely dressed body. When he'd nearly left the room, he heard a faint whisper that stopped him in his tracks.

"Don't leave me, I don't want to be alone any longer."

She'd not opened her eyes or moved, but he found himself walking to her bed, sitting on her soft mattress. "You're not alone."

Lincoln woke with a gasp, sitting upright in Lexia's bed. Her head in his lap and his hands tangled in her long hair, she was sound asleep; her body half over him, clinging to him like her life depended on it.

He had to leave before it was too late. He felt what had woken him; the beast within savagely pacing in his mind, claws pricking at his skin. The panther couldn't handle being close to the girl who made him feel things he shouldn't.

Careful so as not to wake her, Lincoln slipped off the bed. Closing her bedroom door, he moved with silent predatory purpose from her house, pausing for a second to lock her safely in her home, and then let the beast out with a roar.

The panther raced across the ground, taking pleasure from the simple things that grounded him; the crinkle of leaves under his pads, the cool night breeze ruffling his fur, the scent of damp pine and animal trails. The panther roared again, snapping and snarling at anything in his way; the lines had become blurred, he'd let them become blurred. He'd become close to her, and now the man within him cared too much, yet he was more than just a man.

The panther within him was as much a part of him as the man, if not more; he'd never denied his heritage as so many others of his kind had. Lincoln had never chained the beast and hidden away from his true nature in cities, and skyscrapers. No, he'd clung to the fight his parents had fought their whole lives, what they'd died for; to protect his race from those who destroyed it.

But he'd messed up, he'd let his human feelings get in the way, and now his two halves where at war. The panther turned sharp when it reached a mile away from Lexia's house and began to run a circle around her home. A perimeter. He snapped and snarled, confused, but never once strayed further than a mile away.

Maybe the lines aren't so blurred after all; maybe my halves aren't at war. Maybe I've already crossed the line.

A wild, fierce roar sang out into the night, and silenced the forest, warning everyone a predator was near.

CHAPTER 15

The sun was high in the sky when Lexia woke the next day. Her head pounded as she sat up. "Ouch," Lexia groaned, as she moved, her whole body felt sore.

Pulling off the blanket over her Lexia found a thick bandage wrapped around the bottom of her leg, down to her foot. Brows creasing in confusion, Lexia laid back, trying to unearth memories of the night before. Rolling onto her side, Lexia hugged her pillow, pressing her face into it. Breathing deep, she moaned. "Lincoln."

A few brief memories came to her, but not of him in her bed. *Typical, he's in my bed and I have no memory.*

Her phone beeped.

Lincoln - Lex, you probably won't remember last night, someone drugged you. Your leg was injured by a wolf, rest it and it will be fine. I'll come over later today to check on you, Lincoln.

Smiling, Lexia brought the pillow back to her face, indulging in the wild musky smell of him. He'd rescued her again.

Lexia - How do u always mange to find me when I'm in trouble? She text him back.

A text came through seconds later.

Lincoln - Did you not notice my shiny armor?

Lexia laughed out loud; it felt good to laugh, to smile ridiculously over something silly.

Lexia - How'd you get my number?

She typed into the phone, and hit send, holding her breath until his reply came back.

Lincoln - Kind of went through your phone.

Lexia -Naughty!

Lincoln - You have no idea!

Concentrating, Lexia tried to recall more from the night before. She could remember dancing with Josh, and feeling a bit ill, but then the rest was blank. Her stomach retched, painfully, curling onto her side, pulling the blanket over her head, she breathed through the nausea. *I was drugged? Fucking Josh!*

She remembered, the look on his face as she took the drink from him, his eyes had lit up in delight when she'd downed it in one gulp, and then he'd tried to take advantage of her. *It's a good thing I'm stronger than I look,* she smiled.

But no matter how hard she tried, the memory of Lincoln in her bed wouldn't come back to her.

Hours later Lexia woke to a fading sky; her head had stopped pounding, and her stomach rumbled in hunger. Gently she got of the bed testing her leg, but it didn't hurt anymore.

Down in the kitchen Lexia made herself some food, and text Alice back; she'd left her like a hundred messages. As she placed the plates in the sink Lexia heard a howl in the distance, her whole body went on alert. An image of a black, blue-eyed wolf flashed in her mind. *It's come for me.*

She raced up the stairs, limping slightly, and grabbed a jumper and her knife. Pulling on boots, Lexia ran out of the house and followed the sad, lonely cries of the wolf.

As she ran deeper into the forest the animals grew quiet, the black wolf appeared, slowly stalking towards her, its jaws snapping and snarling.

"I don't want to hurt you."

The wolf exploded into silver lights just like the last one had. Stood before her was a wild-looking woman, her hair was matted, and her skin smudged with mud and blood.

She laughed at Lexia, a twisted smile forming on her lips. "But I want to hurt you. You killed my mate, little hunter, and now you will pay."

Hunter? Lexia had no time contemplate her comment; the woman leapt forward, turning into a wolf mid-jump. The wolf landed on Lexia, slamming her to the ground.

Pushing the wolf off, Lexia jumped to her feet, holding her knife tight and circled the wolf.

Lincoln walked up to Lexia's front door, but he couldn't smell her inside. He followed her trail into the trees, and as he traveled further he heard the snarls of a wolf.

"Lexia!" Lincoln full hilt toward the sound of fighting. Lexia was injured, she didn't stand a chance against the wolf, but as he stalked towards them he paused, shocked at what he saw.

Lexia and the wolf circled each other, they ran, clashing in a fury of knife and claws. Lexia kicked the wolf away, slicing her knife into its side.

Lincoln couldn't move, this wasn't Lexia; she wasn't afraid like she'd been with the vampires. She had a smile on her face, every move was thought through, and calculated.

How have I been so blind? As he watched her attack, moving with grace, she twisted out of the wolf's grip and sank her knife into its chest. The wolf gave a strangled yelp, before it fell to the ground.

Lincoln stumbled backwards and turned away, racing through the trees. He had to get away from Lexia, he needed some space between them to think. When he was deep into the forest he stopped, sinking to his knees, Lincoln grasped his head, trying to calm the beast within him.

He'd fallen for her. She'd seemed so innocent, so confused with her life, and he'd thought she was good. He thought she killed when there was no choice, but today... what he'd seen… he shook his head. She was a good fighter, with training she'd be near impossible to stop, but when he'd watched her, he was certain she'd enjoyed it.

But maybe she'd had no choice; the wolf had attacked her last night. His panther snarled, frustrated with the man. *Kill her*, it said, she is a killer. He wanted to agree with his cat, but what if he was wrong? No, he couldn't kill her yet; he needed more evidence before he'd make a move.

Lincoln let the panther take over. It ripped through his skin, and took off across the ground, running for hours deeper into the Black Hill ranges. The cold mountain air ruffled his coat in a way that would normally bring him pleasure, but not tonight. Tonight his human half was troubled, furious, about his feelings for a girl that killed his kind. He let the mix of anger and pain drive him on, until he'd ran so far, he'd left behind familiar territory. Blocking his human mind, he let the predator within rise to the surface, spending the night hunting until exhaustion took him over.

CHAPTER 16

Lexia woke Monday morning with the same feeling of dread that had troubled her all night. Lincoln hadn't come to her like he'd said, and hadn't answered any of her texts. The death of the wolf was also playing heavily on her mind. She hadn't had a choice, it was either her or the wolf, but Lexia hated to take a life; it felt wrong, she felt as if she'd lost a piece of her soul.

As the week wore there was still not sign of Lincoln. Lexia worried she'd said something wrong on Saturday night.

To make things worse, her dad had been very distant all week; working late most nights, and when he had come home he'd stayed clear of her. Even Alice had given up trying to cheer her up.

Heading out Wednesday evening for a run, not caring anymore about her safety, Lexia zoned out, escaping her mind.

The panther silently followed her, but Lexia was too far away to notice. She never heard the silent ping in her brain as he closed the gap between them. He leapt, landing on her, digging his sharp claws into her skin. Unprepared she fell forward, hitting her head on the ground. Rolling to the side, pushing passed the pain in her skull, Lexia quickly jumped to her feet. It took a second for her eyes to sharpen, and spot the black velvet panther. He attacked, she twisted out of the way, hitting him in the side with a kick. Sliding across the ground, the panther's his claws leaving grooves in the soil.

Bending to retrieve her knife, Lexia paused. She couldn't kill him; she didn't want the blood of this beautiful panther on her hands, already too much blood stained her skin, her soul. He leapt at her again, slicing into her flesh; Lexia kicked him away, wincing in pain, and fled.

Pushing her tired muscles to move faster, the panther snapped at her heels. He roared, making her heart lurch in fright. The forest fell silent around her, alerted to a predator's presence.

Lexia tried to outrun him, but he was faster, and she was far up the trail, too far away from home to call for help. As he snapped at her heels, Lexia turned sharply, heading off the track. He followed. Spinning around to meet him head on, Lexia watched his lean, graceful body sail through the air, the gleam of sharp teeth as they neared her neck, she heard the boom-boom of her racing heart. Dropping to the ground Lexia pushed up into the panther's chest sending him over the top of her. She rolled and jumped to her feet, bracing for his next move.

He circled her, watching her with his intelligent gold eyes. "Please," she whispered.

Lexia just couldn't take it; if this is what she was to become, a killer, then she would rather die. She knew in her heart, this panther was different. She couldn't kill him, even if he could kill her.

Lexia sank to the ground, tears spilling down her cheeks. "I can't hurt you," she said, looking into his eyes.

The panther cocked his head, slowly creeping towards her. Closing her eyes, wrapping her arms around her knees, she with fear; she didn't want to die, but she couldn't kill the panther.

Lincoln reined in his cat; stalking towards her, he looked at Lexia through panther eyes. She had a knife strapped to her leg, yet hadn't used it. He scented the air as he circled her shaking form. Fear. Fear filled the air. *Why didn't she fight back? Why couldn't' she hurt him like she'd hurt the wolf?* Lincoln took one last look at her, then disappeared into the trees.

Lexia knew the instant he'd left. The forest creatures around her began to move, and the birds began to sing. Standing on wobbly legs, Lexia looked around; *was this just all a game to him? When the panther finally makes his move, will I be ready?*

She walked home confused and frightened. The night had grown dark, when she returned home, her dad was waiting on the porch, his face full of concern. She tried to block out his voice as he lectured her on the dangers of the forest at night, and pushed past him into the house hoping he wouldn't notice the new cuts and bruises marking her skin. But he said something that made her freeze, made her skin go ice cold, and her heart lurch and stomach twist.

"Give me the paper," she said, snatching it from his hands. There it was on the front page; 'Man stabbed to death'.

"You must not go into the forest again until the killer is caught," he ordered.

Lexia gulped, and forced her tears not to fall. "Yes, Dad."

She climbed the stairs, getting into bed without any food and in her mud- stained clothes. As her weary head hit the pillow, she began to sob. *Why didn't I ever think about someone finding the bodies? Will they find out it was me?*

Lexia stayed home from school the next day. She hid in bed trying to block out the world. Her dad brought her breakfast before going to work, kissing her goodbye, Lexia had to fight back tears.

What's wrong with me? Why do I feel this way? She'd killed them in self-defense, and yet seeing it in the headlines made her feel like a...a murderer.

All day she tossed and turned, griping her stomach as it twisted and churned with dread. Eventually she got up, making her way downstairs Lexia fixed herself supper and sat in the front room, zoning out in front of the TV. Her dad called to say he would be home late, so Lexia settled deeper into the sofa, intent on a night alone.

Making her way to bed later, dragging her heavy feet up the stairs, Lexia couldn't seem to lift the gloom that hovered around her, making her feel sluggish and depressed. When she walked into her room, a cold chill swept over her body, warning her of the panther's presence.

Walking to the window and opening it, Lexia peered into the darkness; the tops of the dark trees rustled in the breeze, the night was clear, and a half-moon cast an eerie glow over the landscape. She could feel him watching her, the chill whispered over her skin making her shiver. It called to her, telling her to go to the panther.

She found herself stepping forward as if to follow. *No, I will not be fooled again.* She couldn't walk to her death, she had to fight.

A soft breeze played with her curled hair as she stepped back. The forest had grown quiet, too quiet; all the animals were aware of the presence of a predator. Lexia centered her mind, focusing only on the cool dark night, and the slight whispers of the trees. She let her mind wander till everything became white noise, and that's when she felt it. The rush of power as she connected to her new side; it heightened her senses, cleared her mind, until she thought of nothing but finding the panther, and finishing his game.

Jumping from the window, and landing in a crouch, Lexia absorbed the shock easily in the new, stronger body she processed.

Frozen, one hand on the ground, the other brushed the hair from her face, as she searched for his golden eyes in the darkness.

There you are!

Running with inhuman speed, Lexia chased him down. She followed him deep into the forest, her heart pounding with both excitement, and fear.

Coming to an abrupt stop, Lexia searched, *where are you, kitty?* She'd lost his trail; it ended where she stood. Reaching out with her senses, she focused on the slight hum of power lingering in the air. Finding him too late, the panther dropped down from above, knocking her to the ground.

The impact knocked the air from her in a rush, her head slammed into the unforgiving surface, causing Lexia's vision to blur. The blow would have killed an ordinary human, but as Lexia was beginning to realize; she was far from ordinary.

"There you are, kitty cat," she taunted, surprised by lack of fear she felt.

A low, deadly growl slid from his throat, as he snapped at her neck. His sharp claws pierced her skin, where he held her down, and warm drops of blood rolled from the wounds, dripping onto the leaf-covered ground. *Ok, time to get him off me. Come on, Lex, think!*

Lexia struggled against him in an attempt to knock him off balance. His claws dug deeper as she struggled, tearing through muscle. Grinding her teeth, not allowing the sound of her pain to escape, Lexia forced it away, and kicked with all she had, yet couldn't dislodge the panther. Then he made his mistake; his hind leg lifted from the ground, and in that split second, Lexia twisted her body, knocking him off balance.

Lexia flipped over, reaching down into her boot, she pulled her silver knife free. Within seconds, Lexia was on top, the knife to his throat.

"Now play nice, kitty," she whispered in his ear.

He let out a deep, deadly growl that vibrated down his body. Struggling beneath her, Lexia sliced the knife across his throat, just deep enough to warn the cat she meant business. Freezing the panther, exploding into pure golden light, her fingers no longer held fur, but what felt like water slipping through her hands. With a gasp, she leapt back into a crouch, knife in her hand braced to fight.

The light faded, and what was left behind was the most exquisite man she had ever seen, naked. Golden skin covered hard as steel muscles, with a light sprinkling of dark hair; he was tall, maybe 6'4", broad muscular shoulders and his face… Oh his face was heaven. His dark wavy hair framed golden-brown cat eyes, high cheekbones, a straight nose, his angular jaw covered in stubble. His mouth was so sensual, and beautifully sculptured. *Oh the things he could do with that mouth.*

Lexia froze. In that moment, as emotions crashed through her mind, Lexia thought her world had finally ended. Nothing was as it seemed. Her heart twisted in pain as she looked into the face of a man she'd come to trust, a man that had comforted her, protected her, and now, tried to kill her. The wolves had nothing on him, because the game, the panther was playing, was the cruelest of them all.

"Lincoln?" Lexia whispered, pouncing on him, as anger surged through her veins like fire.

He'd pay for messing with her head. *Did he think he'd kill me, now he's grown bored?* Lexia planned to show Lincoln what happened when you played sick games, but god was he quick; he kicked out, sending her over the top of him. She let the momentum carry her forward, tucking her body into a ball before springing back to her feet. They circled each other, claws out, knife held ready, waiting for the other to make a move. Lincoln rushed her, Lexia quickly turned to the left, swinging her knife around and into his back. He grunted, faltering slightly, but kept moving, turning with feline grace, he hit her with his elbow.

The force of the blow sent her head forward, causing Lexia to stumble. Stars burst in her eyes and she wasn't able to regain her balance before he'd pinned her to the ground. Forcing her hands above her, Lincoln slammed them into the ground, until Lexia could no longer keep hold of her knife. Struggling under his heavy weight, Lexia felt the first signs of fear take root in her gut; she couldn't budge him.

"Now that's better, Wildcat," he said, the smile on his face, cruel, and so unlike the man she'd known.

"Go on, kill me," Lexia screamed, feeling suffocated by fear.

"Kill you? But I've not finished playing yet, Lex," he taunted.

He hit her in the head; Lexia fought to stay conscious but she couldn't hold onto the scene before her, and her mind faded to darkness.

Looking down at her unconscious body, slumped on the ground, Lincoln's stomach twisted uneasily; he had no idea what he was doing, already regret and guilt gnawed at his mind. Panther snarling as it paced with, it wanted to hunt, and kill, yet at the same time, mark and claim.

She was the enemy, that much both man and cat was sure of. Those beautiful eyes had turned pure gold when she'd seen him shift, yet for just a second, hurt, and pain had flashed across their surface as she realized who he was. He'd protected her, he'd cared for her, and now he'd attacked her; no wonder she'd looked at him like that.

That one look had caused him to pause, made him wish they could go back. His heart twisted in pain; they couldn't go back. Those gold eyes marked her as a hunter, and he was a shifter; she was born to hunt him, and him to hunt her. But still that voice in his head whispered to both cat and man; *does she even know what she was born to do? Oh god what have I done?*

Confusion his constant partner, his panther scratched its claws on the inside of his skin; it wanted out, couldn't handle all these feelings. The cat hated to feel lost, but Lincoln couldn't let the cat take over, because the man might regret what it would do.

"Come now, Wildcat," he murmured, picking up her limp form. "Let's do something with you before you wake, and want to kill me."

Lincoln tied her up in an old aerie that had been abandoned—once, years ago, these forests had been full of life, a home for shifter kind, but then the hunters came...

It wasn't as far into the forest as his lair, but he was certain no one would hear her. Studying her now, chained up, his eyes devoured her. She was beautiful, with her long, chocolate brown hair that hung to her waist, it curled into loose ringlets at the ends. He wanted to run his fingers through them, feel them bounce at his touch. The panther growled in his mind, reminding him she was a hunter.

Yet she looked innocent; a few loose strands of hair had fallen forward framing her soft, feminine face. She had skin the color of cream, and deep down, his panther wanted to lick, taste, bite.

His gazed traveled down her body to her perfect plump breasts, small waist, and the curve of her sensually female hips. She was maybe 5' 9." *Just the right height for me.* He shook his head to clear his thoughts, as a rumble threatened to escape his throat. The panther wasn't happy, didn't know what to make of her; was she really the enemy or could he claim her as his?

As she stirred, Lincoln stepped back into the shadows to watch his prey.

Lexia's head and shoulders throbbed. Something was digging into her back and as she opened her eyes, it all came flooding back. Gasping, Lexia snapped her head up, her vision blurred for a second before focusing on the golden cat eyes, watching her from the shadows. Lexia pulled at the chains around her wrists feeling the bite of the metal against her skin; she pulled again, but they wouldn't budge. She slumped back in defeat.

"What do you want?" Lexia whispered.

Those cat eyes came out of the shadows, but it wasn't the panther who stepped forward, it was Lincoln. When he tilted his head to the side, studying her like she'd seen the panther do so many times, she wondered how she could have never seen them as being the same person.

Lincoln moved with a grace that could only be described as feline. His eyes turned back to human as he watched her, yet she could still see hints of gold through them; the same color as the panther's eyes. Everything about him screamed predator. *How did I not see? Maybe he held it back because I never felt this kind of power around him before, or maybe I didn't want to?*

He said nothing, just watched her, and the more he stared, the more she panicked. Her heart thundered in her chest. *What is he going to do with me?* She closed her eyes; she wouldn't let him see how scared she was. Slowly her breathing slowed and her heartbeat calmed. Taking another deep breath, Lexia opened her eyes. "I should have seen before, what you were. I was blinded by my feelings for you." She forced her voice to be strong.

Lincoln took another step forward saying nothing. Lexia let her gaze wander over him; he wore a pair of low-cut faded jeans, his chest was bare. The moon cast shadows across his hard, flat stomach. Dragging her eyes away from his body, she looked into his eyes. He took another step closer. Lexia looked away unable to bear the feelings he stirred being so close. Grasping her face, Lincoln turned her so she had to look straight into his eyes. Heat burned from his fingers, flooding to places he shouldn't have been able to reach.

"They glow when you fight," he said.

"What?" she whispered, confused.

"It's still there now, just below the surface; a gold ring marking you as, a hunter."

"Okay, Lincoln, stop talking crazy. Why did you do this to me? What was the point to it all?" She could feel the rage bubbling to the surface, slowly coursing through her blood, begging to take control of her. She dragged her gaze from his face.

"Look at me, Little Wildcat."

"My name's Lexia," she spat.

A low, cat-like chuckle left his throat. Dropping her face he walked away. "You look more like, a Wildcat, to me. So then, *Lexia*, let's get down to business, shall we?" All the humor had left his voice, Lexia shuddered. "So who's the hunter? You're Mom? Dad?

You must be half-human, I've never heard of a hunter being able to conceal their eyes before, but they give you away when you fight."

Staring at this deadly man, her mind struggled to understand what he was saying. Yes, her eyes had changed; they had that ring of gold through them and she'd seen them go completely gold when she lost control. Everything changed the night those vampires attacked, but a hunter, what was that?

"I don't know what you're talking about. I've never heard of, a Hunter."

"I'm guessing it was, your Mother. I've watched, your Father, and he's definitely human, but, your Mother - now she is nowhere in sight. What happened? Did someone finally get to her?"

Lexia's rage broke the surface. "Leave my, Dad, alone, and as for, my Mother, she walked out when I was a baby! I've told you this before, please, Lincoln, just let me go."

"That's it Little Wildcat, let it all out. Ahh, there they go glowing gold again; you must be real angry, huh?" he chuckled.

Breathing heavy Lexia noticed how a golden glow lit the darkness, with a gasp she shut her eyes. *Don't panic, Lexia, it's just your imagination, just breathe, breathe.*

Lincoln watched her, she stank of fear; it seeped out of her pores, clouding his judgment. Did she really have no clue at all what she was? *What am I to do with you?*

"You really have no clue, do you?" he asked, a softness filling his voice.

"No," she whispered, leaning forward, resting her head on her knees.

"The Hunters, were once just human, until the government experimented on soldiers, altering their DNA. The results of the experiment were stronger, faster soldiers, nearly impossible to kill. At first, the Hunters, kept the world safe, but over time they wanted to rule humans, instead of being their protectors. They went rogue, killing anything in their path. In the end the government issued an order for all, Hunters, to be terminated. I've not seen one until you. It's your eyes, Lexia; all hunters had bright gold eyes. I'm guessing yours only go gold sometimes because you're, half-Hunter."

He waited for a reaction but she sat there, head in her knees not responding. Lincoln wanted to go to her and pull her into his lap, hold her until everything was okay; that feeling had the panther prowling his mind again. She was the enemy whether, she knew it or not, she couldn't be trusted... But he had to do something, the guilt twisted at his insides.

"You're, a Hunter, Lexia," he said softly.

"It's not doing me much good now, is it?" she said in a low whisper.

Lincoln laughed. "Come on now, Wildcat, where has all your fury gone?"

Taking calm breaths Lexia answered, trying to keep a level voice; she would not let him provoke her. "So how am I supposed to be a, Hunter, if they're all dead? If they're as bad as you say, then why have you never seen one? What makes you so certain I'm one of them; that I want to rule; that I like to kill?"

He smiled at her, sending chills down her spine. "Because I've seen you kill, Lex, you'd almost fooled me; I almost let myself feel for you, but seeing you smile as you took that wolf's life squashed any feelings I'd had."

A single tear slipped down her face as she remembered the wolf. "Is that what you think, Lincoln? That I want this? That I enjoyed killing her? Do you think she would have enjoyed killing me? Because with every punch that she gave me, I felt her joy; I saw how much she wanted to kill me. I asked her to leave me alone, I told her I didn't want to hurt her but she wouldn't listen, Lincoln, she wouldn't. I had no choice but to let my other side take control, I couldn't just die."

"You didn't have a problem with dying when, my panther, attacked."

"My pretty panther," she whispered, smiling, eyes cast down. "I never saw, what I saw in the wolf's eyes when the panther attacked…when you attacked. I always saw good in you. Or maybe I wanted to, because right now I can't see it. Why did I ever want you?"

"You're confusing, Lexia. I want to believe you, but how can I, when you might stab me in the back? One minute you're just an innocent girl, the next you're killing my kind. I saw what you did to the wolf; saw the smile on your face as you attacked. You may feel guilty now, but that doesn't mean half of you isn't dark. Isn't a killer…I think I'll keep you up here for a while, then we'll see if your, hunter Mother, comes to rescue you."

"How easy it would be if everyone was simply good or evil. Are you telling me, your panther, is all good, and that you have no darkness beneath the surface? I don't understand what happened to me, or what I am, but I know part of me is good, and that part, fights to stay that way; isn't that what matters, Lincoln? That I don't simply give up and let the darkness consume me?"

Lexia thought over her words, it was almost too easy to imagine he was the Lincoln she knew, but he would never have done this to her. She hated him for what he'd done to. Even now, chained up, a small part of her still believed he liked her, still wanted her. He'd messed with her mind somehow.

"I know what I saw," he whispered, frowning to himself.

"Are you for real? You're confused! What about me? What the hell are you? First you stalk me as a panther, toying with me, chasing me, attacking me! Then it was almost like you were telling me to touch you, I could feel it, the pull between us making me never want to hurt you. But no, that's not enough for you, is it? You have to follow me as a man. You kissed me! I fell for you, God, I'm stupid. I should have seen you as the sick twisted freak you are!"

"I'm not a freak, Hunter, I'm a, Shifter. I'll see you when, your mom, arrives, Wildcat." He turned to leave.

"I told you, my mom, left when I was a baby - and my names, Lexia," she shouted at his retreating shadow.

His answer was a low cat-like chuckle as he shifted to panther, leaving her alone with thoughts racing through her head.

Lexia screamed Lincoln's name over, and over, but he never returned. Eventually she fell asleep, with a hoarse throat and tears dried on her cheeks. Nightmares followed Lexia into her dreams, she woke with a start; remembering the man with gold eyes, and wondered whether he was a hunter, and if he was, was she really half of that? Did she really possess such darkness?

Bright rays of early morning light shone through the gaps in the wooden panels, bleaching the old, gray timber, orange. Lexia glanced around; it looked like she was in an old wooden shed, but when she looked through the cracks, all she could see were the green tops of trees. *He tied me up in a tree house, what is he, twelve?* She smiled to herself.

"What's so funny?" Lincoln asked, standing in the one and only door, the sun shone behind him casting him in a silhouette.

She didn't answer his question, choosing instead to turn her head in the other direction.

"Like that, is it? Well, I had brought you some food, bet

you're starving?"

"Not hungry," she snapped. Her tummy rumbled. *God, shut up stomach!* Glancing at him, she asked, "Did you put poison in it?"

He bent so he was level with her face. "Far more exciting ways to kill you." His warm breath against her ear, sent a shudder through her. Nipping her neck, he then licked her skin; wet heat flared between her legs. "Get off, Lincoln!" she snapped angrily, her anger directed more at herself then him.

"Temper, temper. Do you think you can behave, if I untie your hands? Or shall I feed you?"

"I'll behave," she said, looking away from his hypnotizing face.

Lincoln went behind her, and untied her bound wrists. The panther crawled at his skin breathing in the scent of her arousal. She tasted just as he imagined, sweet and spicy.

Chucking the sandwich at her feet, he watched her eat. He and the panther both, found her fascinating, the more he watched, the more he wanted to claim her, as his, but could he forget she was the enemy? She looked harmless enough, until you had her cornered, and then she turned into a savagely beautiful, killing machine.

He threw the bottle of water at her, mesmerized, as she

caught it inches from her face without looking up. Her eyes widened as she realized what she had done. Yes, she was a killing machine, a stunningly, beautiful, killing machine, which his panther yearned for.

"So there are a few things I don't understand: why, when you had your teeth in my neck, did you not finish me off? Why the games, the chasing? I'd have been dead in seconds; no more threat?"

He studied her for a while he thought how to answer her question. She greedily drank the water, keeping her eyes on him.

He'd paced the forest, listening to her screaming his name, each call a fist in his gut; he'd battled most of the night with the beast within. "I attacked out of possessive rage," he said, in answer to her question.

"What's that supposed to mean?"

"It means…I don't share," he replied, vaguely.

"That still makes no sense," Lexia muttered, glaring at him. "Do you realize I'm missing my last-ever day of school? My dad will be going bat-shit crazy!" Lexia continued.

Ignoring her question asked one of his own. "Lexia, how long have you had your strength?"

She looked at him with those big eyes, he was sure if he looked long enough, he'd see into her soul.

Tilting her head slightly she answered, "I've always felt different, but those things began hunting me a few weeks ago.

Three vampires chased me, I was trapped, certain I was going to die when…" Lexia's eyes glaze over, as if she was back in the alley. "I don't know, it was a blur, I felt out of control, and then…red, red everywhere." Shaking her head she looked at him. "All those things I killed, they were real? I'm not losing my mind?"

Closing the distance between them, Lincoln lifted her head, staring into her blue-gold eyes. "You're not mad, Lexia, you have great power. Learn to use it. Those monsters will keep coming, they sense you now."

His words frightened her; Lexia wasn't sure she had the mental strength to keep on fighting as she had. Unlocking the chains at her back, they clattered to the floor, as he moved back. Pausing in the doorway, a black figure in the bright sun, Lexia gazed at him, fighting the urge to tell him not to go.

"Why?" she whispered.

"Because I can't listen to you scream anymore." He dropped from view. "It kills me," his last words lingered in the air.

CHAPTER 17

Frozen, it took Lexia a while before she was able to lift her trembling hands to pull the chains off. Climbing to her feet she slowly crept towards the door, and out onto the rickety veranda, which ran around the little wooden shack. Looking for some way down, Lexia walked the veranda before realization dawned on her; he'd climbed up in his cat form. She'd have to jump. "Damn it!" she muttered. "Can I make that?" she pondered, peering over the edge. "What the hell, it's better than waiting for him to return."

Climbing up onto the railing, Lexia took a deep breath, and jumped. Cold air rushed passed her face as she dropped to the ground. Landing in a crouch, she pitched forward, curling into a ball and rolling before coming to a stop.

Adrenaline pumped through her veins, bringing her back to life. Standing, she winced from the twinge of pain shooting up her leg as it took weight. Gritting past the pain, Lexia set off for home.

Lincoln observed from the shadows awaiting Lexia's next move. Still shocked he'd let her go, his panther continued to snarl at the surface, wanting to rip from his skin. It didn't like feeling confused; Lexia had been right, the panther had wanted her to touch him, to pet him. She made him feel things no one else had. He wanted her to be his, and that frightened him

When he'd heard her talking, and laughing with Dan; the cat had taken over. His panther, driven by possessive instincts, had bitten into her neck; leaving his mark. He had to let her go before he did something he would regret, he'd be lucky if she ever spoke to him again.

It had taken her a few hours to emerge through the door. On the railing about to jump, the look on her face, one of indecision, Lincoln silently cheered her on. It was a long way down, though no problem for his cat.

She twisted her leg upon landing, but felt a swell of pride fill his chest, as she pushed passed the pain, and ran away. The panther growled at his mind, wanting to hunt its prey down, but he remained in control. *She wouldn't be gone for long,* he smiled.

Panting, she bent over, bracing her hands on her knees as she surveyed her surroundings. Flexing her ankle in an attempt to lessen the throbbing, Lexia straightened up, pressing her hands into her back as she stretched. Regaining her bearings, she carried on.

No longer able to feel Lincoln watching her, Lexia slowed her pace to a walk. She was certain he was playing some game with her, yet for now it didn't matter; she had to get home before her dad organized a search party.

Finally home. She smiled, thinking of a hot shower. Stopping abruptly, her skin prickled, as her stomach filled with dread.

Slowly Lexia walked toward the house, careful not to make a sound. The forest around her was eerily quiet, not even the rustle of leaves could be heard. She reached the kitchen window, but found nothing unusual, so carried on around the side of the house. Glancing down the drive, Lexia felt nothing with her new senses, yet couldn't shake the feeling something was very wrong.

Dad's home. His car was parked in front of the house.

Then Lexia saw the front door half open. Her heart sped up as she stepped onto the front porch, fear formed in her gut like a heavy weight, threatening to drag her down. Lexia didn't want to walk in the house; if she stayed outside then everything would be okay. She'd never see what horrors waited within.

With trembling fingers, Lexia pushed the door fully open. An invisible force slammed into her, nearly buckling her knees.

Darkness lingered in the air; the darkness of death, and she knew. She knew her life would never be the same.

Her mind refused to translate what she saw. Feeling numb

she enter the house, her legs like lead, and followed the grisly red trail down the hall. Coming to an abrupt stop, she stared, a wordless cry on her lips. Sprawled on the floor at the end of the hall was a body; pools of thick, dark, blood around him, and his was leg stuck out at an odd angle.

A rasping cough penetrated through her paralyzed mind, releasing her from her frozen state. Running forward she tripped on the overturned hall table. Glass cut into her hands and knees as she crawled toward her dad, yet she didn't feel it. She only felt numb; like this was all a nightmare and she would soon wake up. *Oh please let me wake up!*

"Dad? Dad... Can you hear me?"

"Lex?" he replied, in a strangled whisper.

"Yes, Dad," she answered, turning him onto his back, looking into his blue eyes.

"Lexia, listen to me...you must listen. Your mother... didn't leave." Blood filled his lungs making him cough.

"What do you mean, where is she?" Silent tears fell from her eyes as she struggled to breathe.

"I ran with you Lexia. She'd turned into a monster...it's in you, too." His breathing slowed. "Don't let it out...Lexia...promise me," he croaked.

"I don't understand?" she cried. She couldn't believe this was happening to her. Trembling, her heart felt as if it was slowly cracking, the pain so intense, she wanted to die.

She watched his face harden as he forced his next words out in a rush. "Upstairs in my closet there's a box under the boards, it will explain everything. Now promise me you will never become a monster like her," he whispered, closing his eyes.

"Dad! Dad, I promise. Don't leave me. Please don't leave me, I can't do this alone." She shook him, desperate to do something, anything. He couldn't die. Opening his eyes and focusing on her one last time he whispered, "She's coming for you, Lex. Run."

"Who Dad? Who?" she sobbed, grief cutting off her airway.

"Hunters," he whispered with his last breath.

A feral cry ripped from her throat as she collapsed. Great sobs shook her body as Lexia hunched over her father's body, his blood soaking into her clothes.

Her heart hammered in her chest, as a dead, empty feeling filled her; it ravished her insides, until her whole body hurt, her every breath felt like breathing fire.

Sometime later, Lexia heard the sound of tires crunching over gravel, lifting her head she squinted into the darkness. Footsteps thudded on the porch, but Lexia made no attempt to move. *What does it matter anymore? I might as well be dead.*

"Mr. Granger? FBI." A cool voice rang out, as he rapped on the door. The hall light switched on, flooding the room with light.

Two figures ran towards her. "Are you hurt, Miss? Are you

hurt?"

She looked up, blinking rapidly in an attempt to lessen the sting of the light. Confused, she thought, *am I hurt? No...Yes... I hurt everywhere, my hearts been ripped out.*

Instead she replied, "He's dead." As fresh tears fell down her face.

Dazed Lexia watched her home fill with people, they whispered, and glanced but none of what they said sank in. Instead Lexia fixated on the spot where her father had once been. She'd screamed to leave him alone, when they'd attempted to take the body. Stood on her shaking legs with her father's blood covering her body, she'd threatened to kill anyone who came near him. They'd looked at her with a mixture of pity, and revulsion. An FBI agent had taken a step forward, not heeding her warning, Lexia had knocked him to the side like he was a mere fly. That's when she'd realized what she was doing. Remembered her dad's final words; she did have a monster in her, and she couldn't let it out. The people around her were just trying to help, and she'd wanted to kill them, of course they'd never believed her when she'd screamed it. But Lexia knew she could, and that's what had made her stop, what had made her take a step back and slide down the wall; she could *kill* them all.

Two legs appeared in her line of vision. "Miss Granger, you need to come with me."

She looked up, taking in his muscled build. He had a broad face, and his mouth was set in a grim line, his dark hair in a buzz cut. Lexia's breath caught in her throat, as she gazed into his eyes. Lincoln's honey-smooth voice whispered in her mind, *their gold eyes mark them as Hunters.*

"Come with me, please." He held his hand out to pull her up. Confused, she allowed him pull her up. His hand touched hers, and a sharp shock zapped through her as he made contact. Cold radiated from his touch, chilling her to the bone. She forced down a gasp, trying to hide her reaction as she followed him outside.

This man was a hunter, and FBI? Her dad had said they were coming for her, but nothing he'd said had made much sense. *Why didn't I get that box?* Lexia didn't understand what was going on, and she had no idea what her next move was. Her dad was dead; all she wanted to do was curl up and cry. But her body was screaming at her to run and the last time she'd ignored her body... *I will never ignore my instincts again.*

He met another man in the drive and they walked together towards their car, it was parked near the edge of the forest. Her dad's voice whispered in her head. *She's coming Lexia. RUN... Hunters.* As his voice drifted away the haze cleared, her mind sharpened.

Taking a deep breath, Lexia closed her eyes and focused on the power deep within. It felt like energy rushing through her body. Everything became clearer; she could think through her suffocating grief. The gaps in the trees weren't just gaps but an escape; she saw every rut, every patch of ground, which would slow her down. Calculating the best place, Lexia made her decision.

As they approached the car, Lexia dashed into the forest.

Trees blurred past her as she ran at impossible speeds, heading away from the two men close on her heels.

Buzz Cut was nearly on her, she urged herself faster but it wasn't enough; he was going to reach her.

Out of the corner of her eye she caught the glint of black velvet fur. Whirling around, the panther leapt on Buzz Cut, ripping out his throat. The other FBI agent aimed his gun at the panther. *No!* Lexia launched herself him, her legs wrapped around his body and she grasped his head. Twisting with all her strength, Lexia heard a sickening snap. They fell backwards as the FBI agent slumped to the ground; his empty gold eyes stared at her. *What have I done?* Scrambling to her feet, Lexia backed away until she hit a tree. Her knees gave way, sliding to the ground in shock, Lexia stared at the eyes that seemed to taunt her.

It was all too much, she couldn't cope. This wasn't an animal, he was human, and she'd killed him. Trembling, she clutched at her head, desperately, rocking back and forth, wanting to pain to stop. Someone was talking but she was unable to look away from the dead man.

I killed him, I'm a killer. It's too much. It's all too much. Lexia wanted to cry but the tears wouldn't come. Her dad was dead, she was a killer, but the tears wouldn't come. She was cracking, slowly coming apart, piece by piece.

Lincoln shifted back into human form looking at Lexia sat at the base of the tree, shaking like a frightened kitten, staring at the hunter she'd killed. *How could I ever think she was a threat?*

Kneeling at her feet he put his hand on her. "Lex, move, we have to go." Grasping her shoulders he shook her slightly. "Lexia, look at me". Her frightened eyes met his. "More will come, get up, Lex."

Her eyes focused on him, her distraught face changed suddenly, filling with rage. He felt the power ripple through her, and as his beast strained to take control she launched him across the forest, slamming him into a tree.

Lexia got to her feet and stalked towards him, every one of her muscles vibrated with anger, her fists were clenched into tight balls, and her eyes shone the brightest he'd ever seen.

"You!" she said through clenched teeth. "He's dead because of you!"

Lincoln clambered up, stepped away from her, his palms up. "Lexia, he was going to attack you, just calm down."

"Calm down? My dad is dead because of you!" Lincoln looked at her, confused.

"Lex?" he whispered.

"No! You don't have the right to be sorry… It's your fault!" she screamed.

Lincoln said nothing as he slowly retreated. His panther

clawed, and snarled to be let out, but Lexia needed comfort not aggression.

"It's all your fault," she whispered as a tear leaked from her eye. "If I'd been there...If...If...I could have saved him." She dropped to her knees.

Lincoln ran to her, taking her into his arms. She thumped at his chest, sobbing, and shouting.

"It's your fault, you had me, and I wasn't there...I wasn't there...I could have saved him!"

"No, Lex, they would have killed you. You couldn't have saved him; they would have killed you, too."

Lincoln held her as she sobbed, well aware they needed to move. He had to ask her to be strong, because if too many hunters came, he feared not even his panther could save her.

"Lex, we need to go. Please, Lexia, I need you to be strong"

Lexia looked into Lincoln's golden eyes, they still seemed cat-like. She took a breath and nodded, climbing to her feet. Lincoln shifted into his panther again. He was incredibly fast; he glided across the forest having no problems with the dips and ruts, which slowed her down. She pushed herself, determined to keep pace with the beautiful creature that had fascinated her for so long.

CHAPTER 18

They arrived a short time later on the outskirts of town. Slowing, Lincoln shifted. She watched the gold lights glow and sparkle like fireworks before they grew tall and faded away. He walked to the edge of the tree line, and retrieved some clothes, he'd stashed there. "We'll cross through the center of town then head out into the forest on the other side," he said as he pulled on the clothes. "They will expect you to come back into town so keep your head down, and don't look at anybody in the eyes." Straightening up he turned to face her. "Lexia do you think you can get them under control?"

"Get what under control?"

"Your eyes. They're glowing bright as the sun."

"Oh God, are they?" She buried her head in her hands.

Strong hands squeezed her shoulders, lightly brushing up and down her skin. "Hey, just breathe. Calm down and they'll go back to normal. That's it, deep breaths, center your mind."

His smooth voice wrapped around her like silk, caressing her mind. Opening her eyes she looked into his face. *God he's stunning.*

"There you go, blue again. Ready?"

"As I'll ever be."

Lexia walked next to Lincoln. She could feel the heat coming from his body; like an electric current between them. Struggling to keep up with his long strides, Lexia dropped behind to let a couple pass. As she jogged to catch up he turned sharply, and backed her up. His hands came up on either side of her head, pushing her backwards until she met the wall. He leaned in, whispering, "Hunter up ahead, walking this way."

Lexia's heartbeat quickened. His body was so close, a wall of lean muscle pinning her. Looking up into his eyes her breath caught, and warmth travelled up her spine. She couldn't even think of the hunter, her every thought instead on Lincoln.

"Lexia, your eyes are lighting up again." His back stiffened, suddenly. "He's nearly on us. Your eyes, Lexia."

"I can't control them!" she hissed. Cursing her body for reacting. *Come on, Lexia, calm thoughts. Don't think about his lean, hard muscles, or how close he's pressing... God, get a grip.*

"Close your eyes," he growled.

Her eyes slid shut. She concentrated on the rhythm of her breaths. With effect Lexia felt herself relax, when his lips touched hers. She gasped as his hands slid up, cupping her face. Opening for him, Lexia gave in to his hard demands. She melted against him, surrendering completely to the man that made her feel such intense things.

He broke away abruptly. The loss of him on her lips, shocked a pained gasp from Lexia, she stared, stunned. Grabbing her hand, Lincoln pulled her along, striding down the street, her stumbling after him.

Turning between two buildings that led to the forest. She let him drag her along in a daze, her mind reeling. Only Lincoln could make her feel like that by a simple kiss. Utterly consumed; when he kissed her it was as if the world stopped.

He dropped her hand as they entered the trees. Lexia tripped, landing painfully on her knees. "What the hell was that?" she shouted, feeling stupid for her reaction, and guilty she was kissing Lincoln only hours after her father had died.

"That? It was a kiss."

"Lincoln," Lexia sighed sadly, climbing to her feet.

"Look, your eyes were lighting up like the fourth of July. I had to do something to hide your face, didn't I?" He smiled sheepishly. "Come on let's go."

"Argh." Lexia followed, determined not to be left behind.

Lincoln pushed his human form to travel through the forest at impossible speeds. *Who am I kidding? That was more than just a kiss.* Her scent still lingered in his nostrils; she smelt like a sunny day; a cool breeze, with just a hint of autumn spice. Her scent was a drug to him.

He brought his hand up to touch his lips; they still tingled. As soon as he'd kissed her, a shockwave had passed through him all the way to his now rock hard cock. *What is she doing to me?*

He sensed her behind him. She'd become quicker; finding it easier to tap into her hunter strength. He kicked up his speed, notch just to see if she could push herself more. When she did, he smiled to himself, *that's my girl.*

Lexia was surprised how easily she kept up with him. He'd picked up speed, every time she'd close the distance between them. Frustrated she pushed herself, pleased for the distraction.

He kept to the edge of the forest and ran passed the town limits. Lexia focused all her energy into sprinting. Her eyes on Lincoln's tall, muscled frame. If she could keep herself together, and not let her mind wander to the horrible images, lurking below the surface, then she may possibly survive this.

He stopped. "We'll cross here."

Lexia followed him across the road and back into the forest. He threw her cheeky grin and then set off again. Lexia couldn't help but smile. He was being so childish and yet it was the only thing keeping her going.

Slowing down to a steady jog, Lincoln slipped through a gap in the thick vegetation before them. She would have never found it on her own, the small clearing was surrounded by trees and plant life; it created a barrier from the rest of the forest.

Lincoln came to a stop at a huge tree in the center.

"What's here?" she asked.

"Home," he said, looking up.

Lexia followed his gaze, surprised to find a huge house high up in the tree nestled among the branches. *An aerie.*

"Climb on."

"What?"

"Well unless you can jump very high, you will have to climb on." He looked at her, the look on his face, daring her to say no.

Lexia walked to his back, aware of the effect he had on her body, but jumped on anyway. Wrapping her legs around his waist, he smelt of the forest, of damp earth, and pine. His hands slid onto her thighs branding her with his heat.

Wrapping her arms around his neck, she tucked her chin over his shoulder. "Ready," Lexia whispered into his ear.

Lexia watched fascinated as his claws ripped through his fingertips. He leapt onto the tree sinking them into the bark, even as a man he climbed almost as good as a cat.

Her body rubbed against him as he climbed, and even though she'd promised herself not to allow him to see what she felt, her body flushed with heat anyway.

As he reached the top, Lexia immediately jumped off, ready to put as much distance as possible between them. Opening the door, Lincoln let her inside. "Bedroom's up the ladder, so is the bathroom. You'll probably want to get cleaned up? Go on up, I'll bring you a drink, and leave you some clothes on the bed."

"But I thought you said you were passing through?" she asked, confused as to why this place looked as if he lived here all the time.

Lincoln looked at her for a second and she wasn't sure he was going to answer. "I was. I never stay in one place very long. I have a lot of places to crash around the country."

Lexia didn't respond. Climbing the ladder, she found the bathroom. Turning on the water, Lexia took off her clothes and climbed into the shower in a daze.

For a few seconds Lexia stared at the tiled wall, to numb to have any coherent thought. Bringing her hands up to run through her hair, she saw the blood staining her skin. Her father's blood. *Dad.* That single word caused the box in her mind to burst open. Crippling pain, heart crushing sorrow, rushed through her, crashing against her mind. Huge sobs escaped her throat as she slid to the floor.

Lincoln walked into the bathroom. Picking her up out of the shower. He cradled Lexia against his chest while carrying her to the bed. Grabbing a big, fluffy towel he dried her skin and then her hair. She didn't care that she was naked; what did it matter when her whole world had crashed around her?

Pulling a t-shirt over her head Lincoln picked her back up and pulled back the duvet. Laying her down gently, as if she might break. Lexia felt his heavy weight dip the bed as he crawled beside her and held her close.

"Shush, baby, shush. I've got you." His voice was like a soft lullaby and it soothed the ragged edge of her pain.

A tiny voice in her head asked her if she could trust Lincoln; what had made him change his mind about her? Yet she squashed it down. He was all she had right now and she wasn't ready to face the world alone.

Chapter 19

The angel sang over her in a sweet soothing voice, "Goodbye, little Hunter," it cooed. "You will be mine again." The gold light turned to darkness as a familiar voice shouted, "She's coming for you, Lexia. Run!"

Blood, blood everywhere. She was drowning in blood. There was only blackness, it surrounded her, suffocated her.

Gold cat eyes shone in the darkness; searching, hunting.

"Run, Lexia," her Dad's voice called out. "A box in the wardrobe." His voice drifted away, but his face remained. He was dead, and the blood...the blood was everywhere!

Lexia woke screaming, drenched in sweat. Her heart trying to beat out her chest.

A fierce growl broke the darkness. Lexia gasped, jumping away.

"Lex? What's wrong? Lexia talk to me."

"Y...You growled at me."

"Not you. You were screaming, it...just slipped out. I thought someone was trying to kill you with all the racket you're making."

"Sorry...bad dreams."

"Get back in bed, you're shaking."

Lexia hesitated but climbed back under the duvet, now very aware, she only wore his t-shirt; it smelt of him. *God, he saw me naked! He dressed me. Good job, Lexia, the first time he sees you naked, and you're a blubbering mess.*

"What you thinking, Little Wildcat?" he said, his voice barely a whisper.

"Lots of things…Like why you are suddenly being nice to me…and what I'm supposed to do next? My dad…before he…" She took a deep breath. "Before he died, he told me to get a box in his closet."

"You do realize the hunters will be watching your house? They'll expect you to return."

"I have to get what he left for me. It's information on who I am. Please, Lincoln," she whispered.

"We'll figure it out later. Right now you need to sleep."

Her first instinct was to object, but his voice was hypnotic, she found her eyes closing.

His voice brushed her neck, "Shush, I'll keep you safe, sleep."

When Lexia woke the sun was high in the sky and beams of light shone through the wooden slats of the blinds, making a pattern across the floor. For those first few moments as her memory caught up, everything was alright. Lincoln's arm wrapped around her shoulder, and his hand was in hers, their fingers entwined. Their legs were tangled, and even though she was sweating from his heat, she didn't want to wake him. In that moment she felt safe. Everything felt right in the world. This could just be any other morning, and Lexia held onto that thought, held onto his hand, because the moment her memory reset, her world would come crashing down.

His eyes half opened, staring into hers. Her breath caught at the beauty of them, but the magic broke as he realized she held his hand as if her life depended on it.

"Good morning, Lexia. Can I have my hand back?"

She stared at him a minute more, noticing the faint laugh lines around his mouth. His eyes lit with laughter as he smiled at her; amused she still hadn't let go.

Blinking, Lexia let out her breath. Releasing his hand, she continued to stare at him as an empty, dead, feeling, settled in her stomach, twisting at her insides.

Lincoln gazed back, and instantly Lexia needed some distance. She could feel the darkness that circled her mind threatening to drag her down. Questions loomed the more he stared, and Lexia was both desperate, and afraid to hear the answers.

Rolling out from under him, Lexia retreated to the bathroom. The door clicked shut as she pressed her palms against it. Catching her breath, Lexia bent her head, leaning her forehead against the solid wooden door, when he asked, "Where's the fire, Wildcat?"

Her clothes from the night before were still in a small rumbled pile in the corner. Letting out a long deep breath Lexia put her underwear back on – gross – She hoped less nudity would help her deal with what laid ahead. Picking up her jeans, Lexia slid one leg into them before realizing they were stiff with her fathers dried blood. A tortured cry ripped from her chest as a single tear rolled down her cheek.

"Lex?" Lincoln knocked softly at the door.

Her legs crumbled beneath her, as images tumbled through her mind.

The door creaked. Lexia looked up at Lincoln, feeling utterly lost. "I have no clothes ...my father's... blood. I have nothing," she croaked.

Walking forward, Lincoln crouched before her and wiped the tear from her cheek. "I'll get you some clothes, what's important is you have your life, Lex. Your father would want you to live."

He's right, he would want me to live, he kept me safe from them so I could live and now he's dead... They will pay for what they've done...

Her mood shifted. Where once had been unbearable pain, now was a need for revenge. "They can't get away with killing him. I need to go home and get that box. I need answers. I need to understand all of this." Lexia pulled away from Lincoln, her clothes long forgotten.

"Okay, Lexia wait. You can't storm up to the house, the hunters will kill you."

"Let them try," she snapped, eyes glowing gold as she stormed from the bathroom.

Lincoln leapt on her, pinning her to the floor. She struggled under his hold, but couldn't shift him.

"Hush, Little Wildcat. You will have your time for revenge, but right now, is not it."

"Let me go, Lincoln."

"No, love. If you were truly ready, I wouldn't have been able to pin you down. You've so much potential, if you'd just learn to use your hunter side."

She stopped struggling beneath him; he was right, she was weak. *How am I ever going to kill all those highly-trained hunters?* Her stomach lurched again, pain twisting her insides.

"Let me up," she said, defeated.

"Lock your anger away, Lex. When the time comes, let it fill you up and that will be what gives you an advantage over them. They're pure hunters but they have no comprehension of what it means to love. They have nothing to fight for. That is their weakness."

"Okay." She nodded, not able to hold his gaze. She felt silly for her sudden outburst.

"I'll go into town and fetch you some clothes, then it's time to stop fighting the hunter within you." He smiled. "I hope you're ready to have your ass kicked."

"Ha ha, Linc! I nearly had you once, remember!" she said to him as he dropped to the first floor. She climbed down behind him.

"Nearly, being the important word. Now stay," he said, jumping down to the forest below. She ran to the edge, calling, "Hey Lincoln, you realize when you're back, I want to hear all about what you are, and what you know."

She couldn't see him for the trees, but his laughter sang out into the forest behind him.

His laughter faded, and she was left with a suffocating silence. Lincoln, with his larger-than-life presence, his jokes, and smiles had kept the pain away, but now he was gone, all that was left was emptiness. The shroud of darkness surrounded her and she dropped to the floor, whimpering. Images of her dad broken, and lifeless, bombarded her mind. Clutching her head, Lexia begged the images to stop. "Dad," she sobbed, curling into a ball unable to control her tears now they'd started. Lexia clutched at her chest as her sanity slowly crumbled away; her whole body began to shake as pain stabbed at her heart.

Eventually Lexia's tears ran dry and the violent tremors that struck her body stopped. A dull emptiness filled her, and she became unaware of the world around her. Her mind had shut down in order to cope, Lexia had gone within herself, where the outside world couldn't reach her. Lexia was an empty shell.

When Lincoln walked into his home hidden within the depths of the Black Hill ranges with bags of clothes in one hand and culinary treats in the other, he found Lexia curled into a tight ball on his living room floor. Her small frame trembled as soft, broken whimpers left her throat.

Bags forgotten, Lincoln ran to her side, dragging her stiff, numb body onto his lap. "Lex, baby, Lexia," he whispered, stroking her face and hair. She didn't respond, or even register his presence. *I should have never left you...*

He held her gently, rocking her. Unsure how to help, Lincoln went with his gut instincts and lifted Lexia into his arms. Carrying her up the ladder, and into his room, he placed her on the bed. Rolling over, Lexia gripped his pillow, hugging it against herself. Laying behind her, he wrapped himself around her. Shifters were a tactile race; when in pain they craved the comfort of a gentle touch. Lexia wasn't a shifter, but Lincoln knew of no other way to help her. Eventually he felt her limbs relax as she drifted to sleep, yet he still held her; arms a protective cage, they laid there for hours.

For days Lexia did nothing but wallow in bed, only leaving to use the bathroom. He fed her and never left her side for long, but she'd let the darkness claim her. Lexia was a broken, empty shell, and he didn't know how to get her back.

Time lost all meaning, days turned to nights, and still she laid lost in the endless darkness of her mind; she'd retreated so far into herself, he wondered if she would ever come back.

Lincoln had let her be for the first few days, he'd stayed with her so she wasn't alone as she mourned the loss of her father. He'd tried to reach her a few times but she seemed too lost in her sorrow to come back. But now five days had passed and as he stared at her beautiful, sad face, he wished he'd done something sooner, this couldn't go on any longer.

"Lex, Lexia... It's time to come back now." He shook her gently but still her eyes wouldn't focus on him. "Damn it, love, come back!" Still nothing.

Lincoln pulled Lexia into his lap, and cradled her, she snuggle into his warmth. He ran his fingers through her soft wavy hair, speaking softly into her ear, "That's it, baby, I'm here, it's time to wake up now."

She turned into his chest, sobbing. "It's okay, Lex, let it out, you can't keep all that pain in. I need you to fight, Lex, you need to fight this so we can find out why he was killed. Mike wouldn't want you to just give up would he? Come on, Lex, show them what you are, let's get your revenge."

Revenge. The word whispered through her mind breaking the darkness. She turned her head focusing on the face of the man who held her so gently. *Lincoln.* Slowly it all came back to her from the first time she had killed vampires to watching her father die. *Yes. Revenge!* She held onto Lincoln using his raw, living heat to anchor herself. She could deal with this pain. She was strong. She was a hunter.

"It hurts."

"I know, Lex, and it will never go away completely, but with each day that passes the pain will become less."

"Why are you helping me?"

"Because I care about you, Lex, and I've spent my entire life hunting those who take innocent lives. I've been waiting for the moment the hunters returned."

"I don't know where to start, I'm too weak."

"I'll show you how to be strong, and I'd start with a shower." He flashed a cheeky grin, and that' all it took for hope, light, to replace the darkness within.

She wiped at the tears running down her face, looking down at herself, still dressed in Lincoln's T-Shirt. *How long have I been in bed? God I stink!* Jumping from his arms she ran to the bathroom feeling self-conscious.

"That's the Wildcat I knew," he chuckled. "I'll be downstairs making food...will you be alright?"

Silence. Then a faint whisper, "Yes."

When she climbed down the ladder, cleaned and wearing new clothes, Lexia felt lighter. The darkness had lifted a little. The pain and the grief would always be there, but the moment her feet touched the first floor, and Lincoln looked up and smiled at her, she knew it wouldn't rule her life. With every smile and touch, Lincoln filled the gaping hole of pain in her heart. He had an aura around him that was filled with energy, with a love for life, and anyone that was in his presence felt it.

He was cooking so she took the opportunity to wander through his home, taking in the details that told her things about the panther that fascinated her so much.

Lexia was quite surprised how nice his home was, considering it was out in the middle of nowhere, she guessed it was powered by generators. The main floor consisted of a small kitchen, which seemed even smaller with Lincoln stood in it. He was bent over the stove, his lean muscles flexed over his shoulder blades as he stirred whatever he was making.

She dragged her eyes from his back, focusing on the kitchen doors. They were made from rustic wood; he seemed to like everything natural, a little wild. An island sat in the middle with tall chairs around the bench where he now placed plates for the food.

The living room had huge windows across both walls,

making the most of the view; vines and branches crawled around the outside, and the veranda, blending the house perfectly into the forest. The wooden floors were covered in several thick rugs; he liked soft things. Two large sofas sat in an L-shape, huge green throws hung over them bringing the forest colors inside. There was no TV, just a sound system and a collection of CDs stacked up.

Upstairs was the bedroom and bathroom, he'd kept the furniture simple, just the huge bed covered in silk sheets. A lazy boy sat in the corner looking out another huge window, this one had a wooden blind hung in it. The bathroom was simple and modern; the walls were all tiled in slate, a huge bath sat against one wall with a shower above it.

Lexia decided she loved it, he had blended the modern features perfectly with the forest and everywhere you looked there was something soft to curl up into. Smiling Lexia walked towards Lincoln, who was serving up their food.

"Eat," he said.

For a while they sat in silence but eventually Lexia couldn't keep her questions back. "What's, a Shifter?"

He looked up meeting her eyes, they appeared guarded, the panther flash in them for a second before he spoke. "A Shifter, is someone with the ability to shift into an animal."

"Any animal?"

"No, only the animal that is their other half."

"So you only change into a panther?"

"Yes, my panther is as much a part of me as my human side."

"So the wolves that attacked me were, Shifters, not, werewolves?"

"Wolves? You were tracked by more than one?"

"He was the first thing I killed after the vampires." Lexia shuddered, suppressing the memory of his blood covering her skin.

"Werewolves can only change on the full moon, and when they do they lose all thought from their human side. Like vampires, their souls, their conscience, are gone."

"Wow, it's still so hard to get my head around all this supernatural stuff."

Lincoln stayed silent, and dropped his eyes to his food. Lexia got the feeling he wanted her to stop prying but she needed answers, and he was the only one who could give them to her.

"What other animals do, Shifters, turn into?"

"Mostly wolves, and big cats. Sometimes I'll come across a lion, tiger, or a non–predatory Shifter, like dogs, or deer, but most of them were wiped out by hunters."

Lexia fell silent at his last comment. Her kind were killers, she had half of that blood running through her.

Lincoln looked up and studied her. Lexia dropped her eyes unable to hold his stare. "Lex, don't blame yourself for others' actions. Just because you're half hunter doesn't mean you're evil.

Just like shifters, we choose whether to follow the light, or the dark. Those wolves who attacked you, had chosen to embrace their animal sides completely, but not all wolves do."

"Yes, but from what you've told me, no hunters were good. We weren't born as hunters, but created. How do you know we weren't created for evil?"

"Come on, Lex, you were born, and do you honestly believe you're evil?"

"Maybe not all of me, Lincoln, but sometimes I feel so…so out of control, like something's taking over me."

"So you fight. Do you not think I fight to control the panther? And you've seen that I lose control."

"Mmm." Lexia absently rubbed her neck remembering the moment she felt sharp teeth piece her skin. "Do you think he wanted to kill me? Your panther I mean." She held his eyes and gasped when she looked back at a panther wearing a human face.

"Not kill, just mark." His smile made her heart flutter, heat pooled between her legs.

"What does that mean?" she whispered.

"You'll see," he murmured. Lexia couldn't pull her eyes away from him, she tracked his movements as he left the kitchen and shifted, leaving in a blur of gold lights, and black velvet.

Chapter 20

The next day Lincoln went into town for more supplies. Lexia watched him walk onto the veranda. He turned back, frowning. "Are you going to be alright?" he asked.

She smiled, "I'll still be here."

He turned, dropping from view. Though she said she would be fine, the second he dropped from view, her heart gave a lurch, her breaths coming in quick, and shallow.

His voice whispered through the forest, "I can hear you Lexia. Breathe."

Lexia suddenly felt angry with herself. She'd become reliant on him to keep her nightmares at bay. She had to pull herself together or Lincoln would get sick of babysitting her.

Lexia paced the room, thinking over why Lincoln was helping her. He'd spent the last few weeks stalking her, hunting her, and now what? What did he want from her? How was she ever going to avenge her Dad's death? And after that, what would she do? So many questions whirled through her mind, but she had no answers.

Realizing she'd walked outside, Lexia paused to take in the day. The air was clean and crisp, and a slight chill lingered causing goose bumps rise along her skin. Sitting on the swing, slowly rocking back and forth, thought over what troubled her most - Lincoln. She had feelings for him, feelings she had never had with another man. She'd had a few boyfriends, but had never felt as drawn to them as she was Lincoln. Her eyes wandered to him whenever he couldn't see her watching, and the slightest touch set her nerves on fire.

But what does he want for me? He'd been so caring towards her, held her when she had fallen apart, and he had saved her life when he had first set out to take it. *God he was confusing.* Getting up she walked the length of the veranda, hoping he'd be back soon.

Sensing someone out amongst the trees, Lexia walked quietly to the rails, and peered over, listening. Attempting to relax, Lexia pushed out her senses, but heard nothing. Her feet carried on their relentless steps, when she caught his scent from above. Moving just as he dropped from above, Lexia twisted to the side, and brought up her elbow slamming it in the back of his head.

He grunted, stumbling forward and then burst out laughing.

"I've warned you before, about sneaking up on a girl," she grinned. "What were you doing anyway? Thought you were helping me, not attacking me?"

"Just a test, my Little Wildcat." He jumped back onto the roof.

"Guess I passed then?" she called.

He jumped back down carrying bags. "Hungry? I bought some food." He rubbed his knuckles across her cheek and walked inside.

Stunned Lexia brushed her fingers over her cheek, the skin burned from his touch. *You are so confusing.*

Following him inside she realized Lincoln had been paying for everything she needed. "Thanks for this, I'll pay you back as soon as we get into my house."

"Hey not a problem…so you wanna eat?"

"Sure."

CHAPTER 21

Two hours later Lexia raced through the trees following Lincoln. This was his idea of increasing her stamina; he ran at speeds some cars couldn't sustain. She stumbled over logs, rocks, roots, and natural potholes until she was so exhausted she wanted to vomit. Stopping to lean against a tree, Lexia panted hard; the cat had obviously held back when he'd chased her before. *Would he carry me back if I passed out?*

He snaked through the trees; a low growl rumbled up his throat. Stalking towards her, the sun reflected off his black velvet fur, giving it a warm golden gleam. Lexia was memorized by the beautiful deadly, creature. She longed to run her fingers through his coat, to hear him purr. Stopping a few yards away, he growled again, a deep threatening sound, as his golden cat eyes searched her face.

"You've got four legs, I can't run anymore," she smiled at him, thinking she should maybe be afraid.

He crouched, ready to strike. His eyes lit up as if laughing at her. "Now, now, kitty, play nice," she said, holding up her palms.

He leapt with a snarl, claws and teeth glinting in the sun.

Lexia twisted around the tree, watching as he landed on the trunk, and jumped back to the ground. Momentarily hypnotized by the sight of him, Lexia didn't move fast enough, as he charged again. His claws sliced, shallowly into her thigh. "Mother fucker! Lincoln that hurt!"

Showing no signs of quitting, as he came again, Lexia twisted around, kicking him in the side. The cat fell to the ground but quickly recovered, prowling towards her.

Doubt filled her mind. *Was he just playing or had the beast taken over?*

"It's like that is it? Well, here kitty, kitty, kitty!"

Lexia cleared her mind, letting her power to the surface; it filled her muscles giving her a rush. She flashed a wicked smile pulling out the silver knife strapped to her ankle. Lunging, she swiped a shallow cut across his side as he jumped out the way. He growled at her, and she felt guilty for damaging his beautiful fur.

"Play nice then, kitty! I don't wanna hurt you."

He answered by attacking. Knocking her to the ground, Lexia recover quickly and jumped to her feet, facing him. This time as his teeth lunged for her, she hit the side of his head. He faltered, stumbling slightly on landing and she took her chance. It would take him seconds to recover, but she could be quick, and deadly, like the panther. Letting go of her fear, Lexia's instincts took over. Lexia spun around, her leg curling up and lashing out, catching him in his side. The cat slid across the ground with a stunned look in his eye. Lexia took her opportunity and sprinted towards his home. This time she had no problems with the roots, and branches that threatened to trip her before, and she no longer felt tired. She felt great, adrenaline coursed through her, she felt like a...a hunter.

Lincoln walked out of the trees into the clearing around his aerie. He had on just a pair of faded jeans, they hung loosely on his hips. Lexia dragged her eyes to his face as he looked up at her, an odd expression on his face. She sat on his veranda, legs swinging over the edge.

"How'd you get up there?"

"Erm, not sure really...I kind of jumped and climbed. A bit scary how I do these things when I let the hunter take over," she laughed nervously.

He climbed up, too, jumping over the railing, and stood in front of her. Lexia looked up at him, taking in his lean muscled body, the top button of his jeans were undone. His chest was dusted lightly in dark hair, the trail narrowed as it trailed down under his jeans. She blushed, looking away. *God what's wrong with me?*

"So you got that beast of yours under control now?" she asked to distract herself from the naughty thoughts in her mind.

"Have you, little hunter?" he laughed unlocking his door and walking inside.

Lexia flushed fever-hot. She was certain he knew the effect he had on her, and with his shifter hearing and senses he would quite easily pick up her racing heart.

"You want me to cook? You must be starving after all that

running."

"Sure," she whispered out into the darkening night. Closing her eyes she let her thoughts whirl. *How did my life get so messed up in such a short span of time?*

The next few weeks carried on the same - he'd run her through the forest morning and night, always in cat form. She kind of thought that was cheating but after a few weeks she could keep to his incredibly fast pace. They did hand-to-hand combat, which mostly consisted of Lincoln beating her until she was black and blue. A few times he knocked her out.

He also made her meditate. "Center your mind," he'd say. "Learn to tap into that hunter power." She mostly became mad, and frustrated by meditation, spending most of the time picturing images of kicking his ass, instead of empty of any thought.

Then there were the surprise attacks. He'd never managed to catch her unawares; she had a knack for sensing danger, and she couldn't help feeling a little smug by this. Most of the time Lexia felt safe with Lincoln, yet every now and then, she'd glimpse the wild animal beneath his skin, and wonder whether she was being a fool.

Yet no matter how confused, or frustrated she felt; Lincoln's methods worked. Her muscles grew tighter, and more defined, and she felt more in control of the power she had within.

Three weeks into her training they were fighting on the veranda. He had given her a good few punches in her side, and her every breath hurt.

"You need to let go, Lex. You're over thinking every move."

She let his honey-smooth voice calm her. Dispelling the images of beating him senseless from her mind. Taking deep breaths, letting her instincts take over, she blocked his two blows, and struck with an uppercut. He grunted; the sound urged her on.

He blocked her twice, and on the third let down his guard. Without hesitation Lexia saw her opening, and drove her fist into the side of his head. He stumbled. Spinning Lexia, kicked him in the gut. Lincoln tumbled to the floor with a smile on his face.

"Now that's my Wildcat," he cheered.

"Ha! At last I have you at my feet," she laughed, feeling exhilarated.

Lincoln's smile turned wicked, before for she could react, he hooked his foot behind her knee, and pulled. Lexia's knees buckled, and fell on top of him, he flipped her over, pinning her body to the floor with his arms framing her face. She stared at him shocked, and a little breathless.

"That's better," he drawled.

"L-Lincoln," she stuttered, her heart thudding erratically.

He smiled sweetly, caressing the sensitive skin at the nape of her neck. Taking her earlobe between his teeth, he bit down gently. The slight jerk of her body was unmistakable. Lexia turned her head away, cursing her body for reacting.

Letting go of her nape Lincoln cupped her cheek and turned her face towards his. Their eyes locked, gold on gold, looking at each other with raw heat. Lexia's heart raced and her thighs clenched restlessly.

Is he playing, or does he want me, like I want him?

Chapter 22

Lincoln ran his thumb over the softness of her lower lip, the urge to tease her had turned into a craving for more. Giving in, he bent his head, running his lips across hers; warm, soft and delicious they made his body come to life. He kept the kiss soft, sucking slightly on her lower lip. A soft female moan escaped her lips as he deepened the kiss, caressing her lips with his tongue. He could feel the rise and fall of her beasts against his chest. The sound of her pounding heartbeat, and jagged breath, only made him want her more. He'd never wanted someone as much as he wanted Lexia. Yet he held back, not wanting to pressure her into something she wasn't ready for.

Lexia had never before felt this much pleasure. Her body tingled, every nerve on fire. He kissed her with such greed, as if she were the most exquisite thing he'd ever tasted. Moaning into his kiss, Lexia wrapped her arms around him, lacing her fingers into his soft hair. She'd given up deciding whether this was a game, he was the most dangerous of temptations, and she didn't care.

Too soon he pulled away, a soft whimper escaped her. Lexia locked her hands around his head pulling him back for more. He stared at her with those cat-gold eyes before compiling.

He kissed her with hunger, his tongue invading her mouth and tangling with hers. One hand caressed her nape; branding her. The other lazily roamed her body, cupping her breast, he squeezed. Lexia moaned into his mouth, digging her nails into his back, making him purr.

Rocking against her, his rough jeans created delicious friction. With every slow rub, Lexia's pleasure increased. Her back arched as she gasped softly, her eyes sliding shut, she dragged her nails down his arms, leaving a mark of her own.

He pulled away, giving her a soft sensual kiss, before nipping at her lower lip with his sharp, predatory teeth.

Lexia watched him stand above her, feeling flushed with desire, and confused as to why he'd stopped. Her eyes travelled his body, a lazy smile forming on her lips as she saw his hard flesh straining to escape from his jeans. *So I'm not the only one who feels this.*

He caught her looking. Glancing away she flushed fever red.

"Time for a run, Lexia."

Lexia glanced at him just as he turned, dropping his jeans. She got a glimpse of his hard round ass before he vanished into sparkling lights and jumped from the veranda as a panther.

God. Lexia rolled over, burying her head in her hands. She had no intention of following him. Groaning, she fidgeted; her body felt tight and needy. *What have I gotten myself into?*

A few nights later Lexia was dreaming; it began like all the other dreams she'd had lately. She and Lincoln were back on the living room floor, wildly kissing. Only in her dreams he didn't pull away and leave her wanting more. Pulling off his T-Shirt, he hover above her, the gleam in his eyes promising naughty things. As he stripped her of her clothes, she reached behind him, a silver knife glinting in the moonlight. His eyes widened in surprise as the blade plunged into his back. She smiled as the light left Lincoln's eyes, and her father's voice filled her head, "You have that monster in you."

Lincoln woke to Lexia's screams. She thrashed wildly on the bed, the covers twisted around her, and sweat beaded across her skin, "No! Nooo!"

Leaping onto the bed, Lincoln held her down. "Lexia, shush...shush, I've got you." Her eyes opened, clouded with fear. "It's just a dream, baby, shush."

Eyes locking with his, she said in a haunted whisper, "It's not a dream. My dad's right, Lincoln, he's right."

"About what?"

"A part of me is evil." She looked away.

"Baby no, no. Not a single part of you is evil. Are you listening to me? Lexia look at me. You're not evil, okay?"

Lexia nodded, tears spilling from her eyes. He pulled her to him, holding her close.

"I'm so scared, Lincoln. If I give into the power, will it take over? My dad told me as he died that I should never let it out."

"Your dad didn't understand. Having power doesn't make you evil. It's what you use your power for that defines you."

"Don't sleep on the floor tonight; I don't want to be alone," Lexia said, not quite meeting his eyes. Pulling her down, Lincoln wrapped her into his warm embrace. "Sleep, baby," he murmured against her ear.

Lincoln held Lexia as she slept. He looked at her innocent face, she was so beautiful, with her perfect creamy skin; a soft, rosy pink lightly dusted her high cheekbones. Playing with a curl hung across her face, his mind wandered. An image appeared in his head; she stood before him naked, her hair hanging over her breasts. He didn't know how long he could hold his feelings back. Once his panther had a full taste of her, they'd be no escaping, and she was still so young. *Can she handle that? Can she handle me?*

Running through the forest with Lincoln the next day, Lexia felt lighter, freer.

Not a single part of you is evil...

She smiled, picking up her speed, and raced past him. "Catch me, pretty panther," she called, her laughter singing out into the forest.

She raced through the trees exhilarated by their new game when her skin prickled. Slowing her pace, Lexia concentrated on any life forces in the forest. She couldn't hear anything, not even Lincoln's quiet footfalls. The forest had grown deadly quiet.

Catching movement between the trees Lexia stopped. About twenty feet ahead two hunters walked quietly. Dashing behind a trunk to conceal herself, Lexia shucked in a breath. *Shit can I take on two? Lincoln where are you?*

In an attempt to clear her mind, she closed her eyes, yet it had no effect. Fear choked her, its fingers squeezed around her heart, causing it to lurch violently. She considered running to the house, she'd become quicker recently. Casting a quick glance she saw they'd closed the gap between her while she'd been warring with her body. Taking another deep breath, Lexia exhaled slowly. This was why Lincoln had been training her, for exactly this purpose. Now was the time for revenge.

She recalled him telling her to use her rage as a weapon. Imagining of her father, the rage within Lexia ignited. She had one goal - to kill.

Standing quietly, her back pressed to the tree, Lexia listened for their approach. Sensing Lincoln up above, a feeling of calm settled over her. His musky, earthy smell wrapped around her, the energy he gave off, uniquely Lincoln, and with a smile on her face, Lexia stepped out from behind the tree. Striking the hunter square in the chest, he doubled over. She curved her fist, forcing it up into his face.

Black velvet caught the corner of her eye as the panther dropped from the tree. He landed on the other hunter, his claws digging into flesh. She heard his growls fill the air as she blocked a punch from her attacker.

Clipping her in the face, she stumbled back, her vision blurring for a second. An evil smile spread across the hunter's lips as he realized he'd hurt her. Lexia used his moment of distraction to pull her knife free. His smile faded from his face. Moving with lightning speed, Lexia slammed her foot into his stomach and then, swinging her knife upwards, she sank it into his heart. He stilled, eyes widening before falling backwards.

Tensing as she prepared to fight the last hunter, but Lincoln had already finished him off. The hunter laid discarded, his throat ripped out. Stood in human form, Lexia caught Lincoln watching her. She forced her eyes to stay on his face and not run down his naked body.

Wiping the blood from her knife, she slid it back into its sheath and looked up glaring at Lincoln, still watching her. "What?" she demanded.

"You're amazing to watch."

"Sorry?"

"Nothing...Are you okay?"

"Yeah. What are we going to do with the bodies? Someone might find them."

"I'll come back later, and sort it out, let's get you back to the house in case there's more."

Lexia followed the cat back through the trees feeling confused by his comment '*you're amazing to watch.*' She'd caught him looking a few times at her with that intense look since they'd kissed. He never brought it up, which made her think that she had maybe imagined the bulge against his jeans. Maybe she should just try and kiss him again? But what if he pushed her away? She didn't think she could handle the rejection.

They slipped through the vegetation into the clearing, and he shifted back to human form. Lexia walked past him as he broke out into golden sparks. In front at least she'd not have to torture herself with his naked body.

Lexia made it only a few paces, before his strong arm pulled her back. Lincoln crushed her against him. She blushed scarlet trying not to think about his naked body pressed against hers.

"Lincoln?"

He responded by claiming a savage kiss that left her breathless. Releasing her he turned, walking towards the tree trunk.

She swayed on her feet before he pulled forward by the hand. Following dazed, heat flaring through her body.

"Climb on," he commanded as they reached the trunk, she obeyed too stunned by his actions to object.

Fire flared through her body as she clung to him. Her mouth brushed over his smooth skin and she had an overwhelming desire to sink her teeth into his exposed fleshed. Letting go of her legs as he landed, Lincoln strode into the house leaving Lexia outside.

"Lincoln...what was that?"

He turned, stalking towards her, a panther in human form. She froze as his head dipped down to run sharp teeth along her neck. "A kiss," he smiled.

"Lincoln, stop. You can't keep playing with me." Looking away from his heated gaze she whispered, "I can't stand any more pain."

"I like to play." Cupping his hands around her face she looked into his beautiful eyes. "Let me take away the pain." He bent his head touching his lips to hers in a soft, sensual kiss. Lexia melted as pleasure rippled through her body.

Pinned to the floor seconds later, the soft rug tickling her bare arms. Lexia had no time to think as she was surrounded by his rich, earthy smell; intoxicating to her senses. His sharp claws grazed her skin, leaving her clothes in shreds, naked, exposed to him.

His hand ran up her body, cupping her breast, pinching her

nipple, pools of sensation flooded to her damp core. All thoughts of embarrassment were replaced with exquisite sensation.

Lincoln closed his mouth around her neglected nipple while still tweaking the other; she arched her back, a sharp moan escaping her lips. His big male hand ran down her body and cupped her boldly, making her gasp. She looked up into his eyes seeing an explosion of gold lights reflected from her own.

"So beautiful," he murmured.

Rotating his palm slowly against her; each rub more delicious than the last. A rush of sensation flooded her as his finger delved into her flesh. Screaming, arching her back at the jolt of pure pleasure; her muscles clenched tight as he pushed her closer to orgasm. *More, more! Yes, more.*

A harsh noise of protest escaped her mouth as he removed his finger, kissing, and nipping, Lincoln sucked his way down her body.

He'd passed her navel when Lexia's mind kicked in. "Lincoln," she cried, tugging at his hair.

Chuckling his golden eyes locked with hers as he dipped his head. Placing one long, slow, lick onto her soft pink flesh; Lexia's mind went blank as a wave of pure heat washed through her nerves. He spread her thighs wider, parting her delicate skin with his fingers all the while exploring her with his knowing tongue.

He carried on lapping at her like a cat; she could barely breathe through the sensations. He pushed at her legs wanting them wider and she let him spread her, tasting deeper.

Her face was burning, every muscle trembled as muscles clenched tighter, waiting for the moment she'd snap. Mouth ravaging her with raw need, his fingers thrust inside of her, her back arched and a scream tore from her throat as Lexia shattered into a million pieces.

"Better?" he asked, when her breathing returned to normal.

She smiled, incapable of words.

He skimmed back up her body, claiming her mouth.

"I need you, Lex," he whispered against her ear.

Surprised at her hunger for this wild panther she clawed at his back, drawing blood and wrapped her legs around him, pulling him closer. "I won't let you go if we do this," he said, pulling back, looking into her eyes.

"I need you, too," she whispered.

He let out a growl as the end of him brushed against her damp entrance. "Mine," he murmured, pushing into her wet core.

He felt so big stretching her to the limit. "More," she moaned. He thrust deep into her, filling her up. She clawed at him, needing him closer. *More. God yes, more!*

Lincoln pulled out excruciatingly slowly making her whimper. Sinking her teeth into his neck, she felt out of control. He growled, picking up speed. His teeth closed over the soft curve of her neck; the sting of his teeth only made her more aroused.

No longer able keep pace with him, Lexia melted against him, accepting his hunger. The pressure built deeper this time; the sensation painfully sweet. She screamed, scratching at his chest as her body shuddered underneath him.

He pulled out, twisting her onto his lap. Staring into his eyes, seeing only panther, he slid her slowly down over his throbbing cock. She gasped; he was so deep inside of her. Being like this with him felt more intimate; she felt his every emotion along with him. She'd never felt this way about anyone, and never had she given herself over so completely to a man. She bared her soul to him, and relished in their wonderful, intimate dance.

Lexia felt possessed, overtaken with need she pushed him, pinning him to the floor with a wicked smile. Riding him hard, digging her nails into his flesh she dragged them across his chest, he growled, eyes flashing savagely wild. She twisted her hips riding him faster, tipping her head back and feeling the rush of sensual pleasure streaming through her veins.

Lincoln tried to pull her back but Lexia resisted. She felt the rush of power flow through her veins and smiled wickedly at him, her eyes turning to gold. Lexia watched the panther appear in his eyes, felt his claws break through his skin. A growl rumbled up in his chest, and she arched her back further, and clenched around him as she climaxed.

Collapsing forward, Lincoln flipped her over, claiming her mouth. Their eyes locked, Lincoln's shining brightly as he cried out. Lexia clung to him as he sank his now-sharp panther teeth into the curve of her neck, marking her, claiming her as *his.*

CHAPTER 23

When Lexia woke later with Lincoln wrapped around her – she didn't remember making it to bed. She felt relaxed and happy. Her body throbbed in a good way; reminding her of the moment he'd lost control and marked her. *Goddam possessive cat.*

Yet she still wasn't sure what it all meant. He'd said he wouldn't let her go, but Lexia struggled to let go of past events. A fresh churning of anxiety blossomed in in the pit of her stomach.

He looked young and innocent while asleep, his soft dark hair had fallen across his forehead. She itched to brush it aside and tangled her fingers in it. *Oh god what are you doing with this man, Lexia! He's 23. Why would he ever want you?*

"Stop thinking, Lex," he murmured, eyes still closed.

Lexia sighed; wishing she could turn off her brain. If she wasn't having nightmares about her dad, she was daydreaming about Lincoln, and not to mention feeling overwhelmed with being a hunter.

Needing to move as her head become clouded with thoughts, Lexia tried to slip from his hold.

"Where do ya think you're going?" he chuckled, locking his arms around her.

"Lincoln... I need space to think." He opened his eyes and looked into hers.

Lexia looked away.

"Lex, look at me." When she didn't, he growled low until she obeyed.

"What's on your mind? You can talk to me."

She looked into his golden-brown eyes, into the human eyes of a man who had come for her when there was no one left. He'd shown her how to hunt, how to kill, but he'd also brought her laughter and joy. He made her forget the death and the people hunting her, made her relish in the fact, she was alive and well. If she was honest, she was terrified, one day he wouldn't be there to keep the darkness away, but no matter how happy she felt, she couldn't forget he'd originally set out to kill her.

"A lot of things have happened lately, Linc. Some things I don't ever think I'll get over. I sometimes wish they'd just killed me, too, so I wouldn't have to deal with the pain of losing him. The darkness, Lincoln...it...it follows me. I'm scared it will consume me, but when I'm with you, the pain, the darkness, it's bearable. Yet there is this voice in my head reminding me of what you are, that you're my enemy and that you set out to kill me," her words trailed off into a haunted whisper. She felt like the world had stopped, staring into his unreadable eyes, waiting for his answer.

"Lex, I will never forgive myself for doing that to you and I will always be here to keep the darkness away. You've lost so much, but you've come back stronger. Have faith in yourself, have faith you *can* contain the hunter inside."

Lexia let out the breath she hadn't realize she'd been holding, but the little voice in her head still nagged with questions.

"But why? You set out to kill me, and now this... What's changed? What makes me so different?"

"Lex, you're over thinking things. Okay, yes, I set out to kill you. The first time I saw you, you were ripping vampires apart with your bare hands."

"You were there that night?"

"My panther was drawn to something that night, and before I'd even realized I was in town, I heard your cries but then I saw your eyes and...You've got to remember, hunters are the enemy. When I was a kid we had to hide who we were. We were told to fear the hunters, how they killed our kind without a second thought, but for me it's personal."

"What do you mean?"

"When I was six my parents left me with my grandparents. They were going out into the mountains to run, be panthers, but they never returned. They were killed by a group of hunters and when I saw your eyes turn gold, all I saw was the race, which had killed my mom and dad. Which had taken away my childhood."

Lexia sucked in a breath as she looked into Lincoln's sad,

haunted eyes. Her kind had killed his parents; how could he ever love her?

"Lexia, I never told you this because I knew you'd do this."

"What? What am I doing?"

"You're blaming yourself for something you had no control over, just because you share some of their DNA. Yes, the hunters killed them, and I had set out to kill you. I've spent my life wanting revenge for their deaths. But I never could, I had so many opportunities to do it, but I couldn't. I told myself I was just getting to know your weaknesses but I just wanted to know you, everything about you fascinates me."

"But you attacked me, kidnapped me?"

"Okay, I kidnapped you, yes; can't you just forget about that? It's hard to explain...I was so conflicted…and I suppose…I thought if I took you, you'd show me your true side."

"So you hoped I'd turn into a monster and make things easy for you?"

"Maybe," Lincoln admitted.

"Don't think that smile's going to let you off the hook."

"Lexia, I never could have killed you. You're not just a hunter…you're human, you feel. You were mine from the moment I watched you first kill...so beautiful."

"I'm yours?"

"Mine."

"Possessive, aren't you," Lexia smiled.

"Very," he drawled, pulling her down. He pinned her under him. "That's better," he laughed.

"Lincoln!" But she couldn't keep the smile from her face.

Fire flared throughout her body as she felt the hardness of him brush against her. He kissed her hungrily until she gasped for air. Exploring her body lazily this time, loving her with slow torturous strokes. She felt every inch of his thick hard cock as it rubbed against her swollen flesh. The pressure built slowly, somehow deeper, and when he finally pushed her over the edge, deep waves of pleasure rolled over Lexia until she was incapable of thought.

She fell to sleep, feeling sated; every muscle heavy and weak, with Lincoln wrapped around her, protecting her.

Lexia woke later knowing she was alone, rolling over she saw a note on Lincoln's pillow.

Lexia, I've gone to take care of our friends, I hope you don't wake. I'll be home soon, sleep my Wildcat, sleep, L x

Lexia smiled at the note; the heavy weight on her heart lifted. She rolled over breathing in his smell, remembering their wild lovemaking. She had never been with anyone who made her feel so much; his every touch drove her to madness, and the orgasms were the best she'd ever had. His body was—Lexia snapped upright as all her senses went on high alert; something was wrong.

Jumping out of bed, Lexia pulled on random clothes before climbing down the ladder. She heard no sound in the house but still she moved with caution. Picking up her knife, and a longer one of Lincoln's as she passed by, Lexia crept out into the dark night.

Standing on the veranda she calmed her mind letting power wash over herself. A brisk breeze played with her hair whipping it into her face, and she briefly thought she should have tied it up.

The sky was clear tonight, a full moon hung high above her, surrounded by twinkling stars. On any other night Lexia would have stopped to appreciate the beauty, but right now she could sense danger in the forest.

Climbing higher up the tree, Lexia looked out over the forest. Seeing four hunters walking quietly through the trees, her hand hovered over her knife on instinct as she thought over her next move. They hadn't reached the wall of vegetation, which hid the house yet – maybe they would walk by and never realize it was here – Yet she couldn't take the risk of Lincoln losing his home.

Decision made, Lexia climbed along a thick branch and dropped onto another tree. She slipped upon landing, the rough bark grazing her skin, reaching blindly her arms clung tightly to the branch and she managed to pull herself up. *This would be far easier if I were a cat.*

Her plan was to slip out of the clearing at the opposite end to the hunters so that they wouldn't see the entrance to Lincoln's home. Climbing from tree to tree, Lexia dropped down without being seen. "Shit," she mumbled as a branch sliced into her arm, the feeling of warm blood spreading over her skin.

The cut would heal as quickly as it was opened though. Lexia moved silently away from the hunters, looping behind them. Taking a deep breath, she made a silent prayer, hoping she could fight four hunters alone. "Oh, Hunters," Lexia called.

All four turned together, their gold eyes eerily bright in the darkness. They raced towards her at impossible speeds. Lexia's heart jumped in her chest as she sprinted away, in the direction she hoped Lincoln would be. She wove through the trees, adrenaline pumping in her veins, and jumped high, catching a low branch. Lifting her legs, she swung up into the tree.

They were close behind, but Lexia was hidden from view when the hunters came crashing past her hiding spot.

The hunters slowly retraced their steps, she gripped the long knife in her hand, pointing it downward, and prepared to drop on top of the hunter as he walked beneath.

He crashed to the ground with a thump as Lexia brought the blade down through his back, piercing his heart. The others circled around her, wary, as she sprang to her feet, retrieving her smaller knife with her left hand. No one blinked as they waited for the other to make a move.

The hunter directly in front of her lunged first. Lexia didn't take the bait, having already sensed another closing the gap behind her. Throwing the knife in her left hand at the hunter to her front, she whirled to avoid the blow from behind. As she spun, Lexia brought up her blade and with a single swipe that reverberated up her arm, she passed it through the hunter's neck, bringing it out the other side. His eyes held hers in surprise before his head rolled, and fell to the ground.

The two remaining Hunters rushed at her, furious. The one with her knife lodged in his chest, reached her first. Blood slowly dripping down his body, and he moved slightly hunched over. Dodging his blow, Lexia slammed her elbow into his face. Yet didn't move quick enough to miss the uninjured hunter.

Lexia saw the glint of his blade at the last second; moving just enough to miss her vital organs, the knife sliced through her flesh. She screamed at the excruciating pain exploding through her body. The hunter didn't stop, light exploded in her eyes as he hit her head and she fell to her knees.

Fighting nausea as she crumpled to the ground, Lexia rolled away, then jumped to her feet. Gripping her blade in her sweaty palm, Lexia slouched slightly on her injured left side, each step painful as they circled each other.

Not waiting for their next move; Lexia kicked at the injured hunter to her left, whilst pulling the knife out of her side, throwing it at the hunter on her right, she stumbled forwards as pain exploded from the wound. Gritting her teeth, Lexia recovered quickly, blocking a punch, and returning one of her own. The jolt of pain as the blow reverberated up her arm made her falter, and Lexia was unable to miss the next attack.

Fighting past the pain, she swiped out with her blade aiming for his neck, but she'd moved too slowly. The blade sliced across his chest instead, leaving behind a slash of crimson. He grunted and stumbled giving her time to bring the knife back and thrust it upwards through his heart.

The last Hunter was already aiming his fist as her blade sank in. As she pulled the blade out trying to protect herself, his fist travelled towards her face. She felt the blade slice into his skin as the fist connected. Pain burst inside her skull, and she saw stars before her vision went hazy. Hearing his strangled cry of pain as the blade carried on through flesh, Lexia hit the ground, smiling before the world went black.

Lincoln was jogging back to his home, his mind on getting back to the beautiful woman he'd left naked in his bed. He hadn't wanted to leave her, but the bodies of the two hunters they'd killed earlier needed to be hidden. He had carried them both far up into Black Hill ranges and buried them were they would never be found. *It won't do us any good if they find more bodies in these woods.*

He was distracted by the erotic images playing through his mind that he nearly missed Lexia's scent. Backtracking, he picked up her trail, heading away from the house. "What are you up to?"

Running at a steady pace he followed her trail letting his animal come to the surface. This was the panther's territory; it knew every rut, stone, and branch. He scented the air, anger boiled in his blood as he picked up the scent of three....no four hunters.

Pace quickening, Lincoln pushed the fear for her safety out of his mind, before it took hold. She would be fine, she was half-hunter, and he'd prepared her for this.

Picking up the scent of her blood, Lincoln saw red; a violent rage rushed through his beast, and it split through his skin, going wild with bloodlust.

The panther covered the ground with incredible speed, his pads not making a sound as they skimmed the forest. Lexia was up ahead fighting with two hunters; she taken out two, their bodies lay slumped around her, but the remaining two were on top of her. She couldn't hold them back.

He roared, the need to protect her so strong he struggled to hold on to his humanity. The panther within him took complete control as its need to shed blood became overwhelmingly strong. Lexia drove her blade through one of their chests but the other hunter had already aimed his fist. She noticed, turning and bringing up her knife. Lincoln watched in horror, desperately forcing his muscles to work harder, as the fist connected with her skull. Lexia's eyes widened, then she crumpled to the ground.

The panther landed on the hunter in a fury of teeth and claws, savagely ripping him apart. The hunter had no time to scream, no time to fight back; the panther killed him in seconds. Yet it wasn't enough for the cat; he'd failed to protect her, he wanted the blood of any man that dared to touch her. Cold rage spread through his veins as he ripped apart the bodies of the hunters around him. The impulsive need to protect was so strong that it didn't matter that they were dead, the animal needed to feel the flow of their blood. He needed them to pay.

Up until this moment Lincoln hadn't realized how much he truly loved Lexia, how his heart beat only for her. He no longer lived for revenge, but for her happiness, her smile. He'd protect her, he'd die for her. She was the heart and soul of both man and panther.

Only when the panther laid eyes on Lexia did his humanity surface. On her side, dirt and blood covering her body, her hair was splayed out around her, twisted and matted; she looked broken. Shifting, Lincoln kneeled as he brushed a leaf from her hair.

"Lex, baby?" His voice gentle, soft.

Lexia gave no reaction to his voice and her breaths were too shallow. The panther thrashed at his mind desperately needing her to be okay.

"Hold on, Lexia," he said firmly. An order; he could not lose her.

Standing, Lincoln lifted Lexia into his arms, his hold far gentler then anyone would've believed. Running through the forest he cradled her to him, wrapping her in his strength while being careful not to jar her body. Slipping through the vegetation that hid his home, her eyes fluttered open for a second but she made no sound. He stopped, swearing to himself; how was he going to get her up the tree gently?

Blood seeped through her top onto his chest. He needed to stop the bleeding before she lost too much blood. Putting her over his shoulder as gently as possible, Lincoln climbed. Letting his claws slice through his fingers he sunk them into the bark, her every whimper like a knife to his heart. He laid her gently on the floor of the kitchen and grabbed the first aid kit. Ripping open her top open, Lincoln set to work on her injuries.

Lexia felt like she was floating in a cloud of perfume, it smelled of the earth, the trees; rich and wild. It smelled of Lincoln. She felt his arms strong around her, cradling her against a solid wall of heat and muscle. Opening her eyes seemed an impossible task; they felt so heavy. Yet she needed to wake up, she forced them open, everything was blurry. Focusing on Lincoln, she saw they were under a tree, and up in the tree was a house. *Home.*

Lexia struggled to keep hold of consciousness, her head felt thick and heavy. Sharp pain exploded in her side, she heard the strangled, tortured, cry before realizing the sound was from her. Biting her lip to cut off the noise, Lexia welcomed unconsciousness this time.

CHAPTER 24

Opening her eyes, Lexia looked out of the windows on the main floor. Gold and pink beams filled the sky, and she could hear the early morning chatter of birds.

Turning her head she looked at Lincoln's face inches from hers. He was sprawled out across the floor, a streak of blood staining his jaw, his face a mask of worry, even in sleep. He wore no clothes and, dirt stained his feet and legs. Sitting up she bit back a gasp from the pain in her side; a thick bandage had been wrapped around her waist.

Sitting for a minute until her head stopped spinning, Lexia then stood. Looking at Lincoln; blood spattered his body but she couldn't see any cuts, so she presumed it wasn't his. Picking up the blanket she'd been wrapped her in, Lexia gently placed it over him. Smiling, Lexia crept towards the ladder.

Lincoln rolled over, tucking the blanket around his shoulders. He reached out in sleep for Lexia but felt nothing but rug. Pinging to his feet, the blanket pooled around his ankles as he eyes scanned the room. A lethal growl grew in his chest and rumbled up his throat.

A feminine chuckle. "I'm up here, Linc."

He was up the ladder and by her side with panther speed. "Lexia, what are you doing? Go lay down." Every word was said with the lethal edge of a predatory panther.

Turning she looked into his eyes, cupping his face with her hands. "Less of the dominance. I'm fine, just a little sore, hunter blood heals quickly." She brushed a soft kiss over his lips before returning to the sink to clean her face.

He reached out pulling a leaf from her hair. "You were stabbed Lexia, let me check your wound."

"Fine. But don't think you can boss me around all the time, and I didn't see you all concerned when you did a number on my ankle. In fact I remember you pretending you had no idea why I was limping. Funny, hey!" She strode out of the bathroom with remarkable ease. The panther was pleased with her strength, but the man needed to double check before he could breathe a sigh of relief.

"I'm sorry about that but things are different now; please let me take care of you, make up for my mistakes."

Lincoln carefully peeled back the dressing and sucked in a breath as the stab wound came into view.

"What? It hardly hurts, it can't be that bad?" Lexia looked down trying to get a view of what had made Lincoln so speechless.

"It's nearly healed... Give it a few days and you'll never have known it was there."

"That's great...so what's your problem?"

"You heal as fast as me, if not faster." His voice held a tone of surprise, he hadn't expected this; she was a half-blood, that should have made her weaker.

"Lincoln, isn't that good?"

"Yeah...just...well, you're a half-blood. Why are you healing at this rate; you never healed this fast when I bit your ankle?"

"I did, I just had to fake being injured. I have no idea why I heal this fast, but I'm not complaining. Sooo can I go get cleaned up now?"

He wrapped the wound back up and sat full of thought. She laughed brushing past him. He looked up when she smiled sweetly over her shoulder, "Want to join me in the shower?"

Lexia walked into the bathroom, carefully peeling off her clothes. She left the bandage on; she'd replace it after the shower.

Turning on the water, Lexia stepped under the hot stream, sighing as it melted her sore muscles. She heard him come into the bathroom a few seconds later; she had her back to the door and one hand in her hair trying to rub in shampoo. He pulled back the screen and stepped into the tub behind her. Her heart kicked up a gear, her tummy fluttering with anticipation. "Let me do that before you hurt yourself."

"Thanks." She let go of her hair, it slapped gently against her back. Lexia felt strangely shy, they might have had sex, but this felt more intimate. His fingers massaged through her hair, and she relaxed, a groan escaped her lips.

"That nice?" his voice brushed against her neck.

"Mmm, very." Leaning into him, Lexia melted under his touch. When he'd finished her hair, he worked his way down her body, rubbing her shoulders and neck, then gently over her breasts.

Gasping, heat pooling in her belly as he rubbed harder, pinching her nipples. She leant her head back feeling dizzy. Her body tingled with sensation; the hot water trickling over her skin adding to the pleasure. His hand trailed down her right side and back up over her breasts. Each time his hand slid over her skin, he brushed lower towards the hot need between her thighs, the anticipation had her quivering. His finger brushed lightly over her clitoris. "Lincoln," she groaned. He continued torturing her with his gentle quick strokes until her whole body trembled. The clawing, aching need for release had her digging her nails into his thighs; moaning and panting she begged for release.

"Harder," a rough command escaped her lips.

She was clawing at his sides, biting her lip as the pressure built. He slipped his finger through her soft lips and rubbed, pressing hard over her sensitive nub. Lexia screamed as fire burnt through her veins jerking her body until it peaked and washed away leaving her muscles like jelly. Her legs crumpled but Lincoln held her tight.

When she came back down to earth, he'd turned her around, her still sensitive breasts pressed against his chest. Feeling his hot hard tip rubbing between her thighs, Lexia looked up through her lashes into his lust- filled eyes. Smiling sweetly, Lexia shimmied down his body until she was face to face with his large throbbing shaft.

Holding his gaze she slowly took his cock into her mouth. He growled, taking hold of her hair as she sucked harder. Licking her lips, savoring his sweet, salty, taste, Lexia wrapped a hand around his shaft, squeezing tight while her tongue teased. Releasing him, Lexia began to run her hands up and down his length, licking off the moisture that collected at the end. His scent filled the air as she stroked him to the edge, licking and sucking as he moaned and gasped. Taking as much of him as possible into her mouth, she looked into his eyes seeing only panther.

"Lexia," he growled.

Teasing with her mouth, she squeezed a hand around his base.

"Jesus, baby stop!" he tugged at her hair.

"I want to taste you," she whispered.

"Fuck!"

Lexia lowered her mouth back over him, sucking and pulling. She dug her nails into the back of his legs dragging them up over his butt, holding him against her, forcing him further into her mouth. She could feel his body shaking, his breaths broken pants as she sucked him closer.

He jerked, swearing as he went over the edge. She held onto him, digging her nails into his hard muscular legs, tasting every last drop. As she let him go, he slid to the floor and she crawled into his lap soaking up the feel of him. His warmth, and the smell of their arousal.

She loved that she could bring this strong, overprotective man to his knees, but what she loved most was that he let her. With her he was more than a panther, he was a man with a heart, and soul so beautiful, she couldn't understand what she'd done to deserve him. He understood her in a way no one else had.

She smiled at him, brushing his wet hair from his face. "Come on, baby. We're wasting all the water."

He chuckled, standing up and placing Lexia on her feet. "My Wildcat," he whispered, kissing her softly before turning the water off and carrying her out.

"Lincoln!" she giggled, "put me down."

"Nope, you're going to rest. No more seducing me."

"Ha, didn't take much doing."

He laughed putting her down on the bed and wrapping a towel around her. "Stay. You'll need a dry bandage, and if you behave then I might bring you breakfast in bed."

"Well, when you put it like that," she smiled ever so sweetly. "Whatever you say, Sir!"

Chapter 25

Lexia couldn't think of a better way to spend a day, they dwindled away the hours talking and lounging around the aerie. Curled around his body, Lexia had her head on Lincoln's chest listening to the steady rhythm of his heart. With Lincoln she didn't have to hide, he didn't care that she was half-hunter. Looking at his face she smiled; whenever she looked at him a warm heavy feeling spread from her heart.

Oh god I love him, I can't lose him! Sucking in a breath, Lexia attempted to control the fear. Losing her dad, and never having a mom had taken its toll; made her irrational when it came to those she loved. A single tear rolled down her face, she looked away from him, the pain too much.

"Hey baby, what's wrong?"

"I love you, Lincoln, but I am so scared of losing you," she whispered.

He lifted his hand to her face, gently wiping away the tear. Lexia leaned into his touch, closing her eyes she breathed in his rich, wild smell. His lips brushed lightly over hers making her shiver.

"I love you, Lex, please believe me. I know I've done wrong, but I will spend the rest of my life making it up to you. You. Are. Mine."

Wrapping his arms around her, Lexia nuzzled her head into his neck falling into a dreamless sleep.

She woke the next morning feeling the happiest she'd been in a long while. Slipping from the bed, Lexia crept across the bedroom towards the bathroom. She'd made two steps before cat eyes appeared before her.

Lexia jumped in surprise. "God Lincoln, can't I even go to the toilet?"

"Of course, but then you're back in bed to rest until you're fully healed."

"You are so overprotective, I'm fine. Doesn't even hurt... See?" Lexia poked a finger in her side.

"Lexia! You could have done more damage!" Forcing her back to the bed Lincoln unwrapped the bandage, and sucked in a surprised breath.

"What's wrong? Honestly I feel fine."

"It's healed."

"That's great! Why have you got that look on your face? Oh god, is there a huge scar?" Standing, she quickly crossed the room to the mirror and looked at her left side, but saw nothing. Where thirty six hours before there had been a deep stab wound, now the skin was perfect, not a single scar line in sight. Smiling she turned back to Lincoln sat on the bed with a dumbstruck look on his face. "Earth to Lincoln! I'm fine."

"You heal quicker than me. How is that possible when you're only half- hunter?"

"I have no idea, and I don't really see the problem. Now I'm off to shower then we can go to my house." She shut the bathroom door, bolting it before he could lecture her on the dangers of going back.

Showered and dressed, Lexia jumped down from the ladder expecting an argument from Lincoln, but found breakfast awaiting her instead. Surprised she sat next to him and they ate breakfast in silence. He'd made her pancakes, all soft and fluffy with just the right amount of maple syrup on top.

"Okay, enough silence, give it to me."

He Laughed. "I'm not going to stop you, but how about one day with no drama?"

"No drama?"

"Just you, me, and fun?"

"O-kay, what's fun?"

"Follow me and find out." He left leaping from the veranda in human form.

She ran after him, jumping from the veranda like he had. Landing lightly in a crouch she looked up and smiled into his scowling face.

“Lexia, you were half-dead only a few days ago,” he scolded.

“I thought you said fun?” She ran past him, slipping through the cutting shouting, “Catch me if you can!”

Lincoln followed the sound of her laughter as it filled the forest; he loved to hear her laugh, and see the mischievous smile on her face. He’d do everything in his power to never see her hurt again, and today he’d make her laugh.

Sprinting faster, Lincoln followed her sweet, sexy scent. Realizing she was playing games, and had circled back around onto her track, he froze, using his panther’s keen senses as he scanned the trees. He heard the ‘whoosh’ of air as she dropped from above but didn’t manage to move in time. She landed on him, knocking him to the ground, and pinning him before he could respond.

“Got ya!” she giggled, kissing him breathless.

Jumping up she disappeared again.

Lincoln growled, “I’ll get you this time, my Wildcat!”

“We’ll see, Kitty Cat,” she teased.

Lexia ran through the trees, adrenaline and excitement

pumping through her veins. The feel of the wind whipping across her face, and the sound of her rapidly beating heart only added to the exhilaration.

Lexia knew she wasn't as fast as Lincoln…yet, but she'd had a head start, so he wasn't on top of her yet. Doing everything he'd taught her to mess up her scent trail, Lexia splashed through a few little streams, soaking her clothes, but she didn't care; it was so much fun. She then doubled back and retraced her steps before heading downwind. Cheeks flushed with color, heart drumming in her chest, Lexia looked around. The forest was too silent; he was close. Too close.

Smiling, Lexia messed up the trail a little more then crossed a larger body of water before hiding behind dense bush. Looking over the top she searched for a sign of him. Nothing. *Where are you?* He was far better at this then her. She ducked back down, keeping silent, not daring to breathe. Using her hunter senses Lexia attempted to pin point his location.

A rabbit shot out of the undergrowth a yard away, and his musky, earthy smell filled her nose. Lexia jumped up and leapt over the bush just as Lincoln sprang into the spot she'd been hidden in a second ago. "Found you," he said, a cheeky, cocky grin on his face.

Lexia smiled and leaned slightly forward over the bush inviting him for a kiss; she saw the hungry glint in his eyes as he bent to claim her mouth. Her hands clasped his shoulders, as she locked eyes with him. Their lips brushed to kiss when... Lexia tightened her grip and pushed down. Lincoln's eyes widened in surprise as he fell into the bush. Lexia raced off, laughing hard as she heard him swearing under his breath.

Lincoln hadn't had this much fun in...ever. Lexia's laughter filled the forest as he went head first into the bush. He couldn't believe she'd gotten the better of him. Chuckling softly he shook his head, and set after her again. She'd had a few minutes head start this time; he could feel the soft vibrations on the ground as she ran flat out. He would have her this time; his panther came to the surface of his mind, picking up her seductive sent. Yes, he would have her.

Lincoln ran as a man but his panther was in control, the only evidence in his eyes. His thought processes were no longer those of the cocky, playful man, they were those of the panther; the predator who lived in his soul. The trees whipped past in a blur of rich green. The forest became denser, making it harder for Lexia to pass without leaving a trail, but she hadn't done a bad job. If he didn't know every inch of this forest he may have missed her. Scent becoming stronger, his body tingled with anticipation, and he picked up his pace; he couldn't wait to catch his prey.

Lincoln stopped, glanced around, but saw nothing. Lexia's trail ended here in this densely packed crop of trees. How had she gotten through without leaving a trail? He looked up, his answer on the branch above him. Jumping into the tree tops, he picked up the single long brown hair that was caught on a branch, inhaling. God she smelled good, he was going to make her scream when he caught her, and soon he would.

"Your first mistake Wildcat, never try to beat me in my own territory."

He may know every inch of the forest, that was his home, but the tree tops were where the panther thrived; they lived in the trees. He leapt silently through the tree tops, climbing nearly as well as he did when he was a cat. She wasn't far now, her scent had rubbed against each tree she'd passed. As he reached the end of her trail he spotted her pile of clothes on the ground. Dropping out of the tree he bent and sniffed her clothes, the smell making him more aroused. *What are you up to?*

Lincoln listened to the forest around him. The animals had gone silent at his presence, and he could hear running water to his right.

A sudden wave of anger hit him, she would be scratched to hell running about this far up; very few trails crossed this part of the forest. It had been left to go wild, the forest creatures all that past. He made the decision to head for the water, she'd been very careful not to leave a trace of her presence but he could see a stray hair glinting in the sun a little further up.

Lincoln found the source of the running water, a small waterfall filled a pool with crystal clear water, and there in the middle was the most beautiful woman he'd ever seen. Lexia was facing away from him; the sun glinted off the gentle curve of her back. Her hair was pulled over to one side, leaving her nape, naked, vulnerable. Turning slightly, he caught sight of the curve of her breast. He couldn't contain himself anymore.

Stripping out of his clothes he dived into the pool. The shock of being surrounded in icy water did nothing to calm his raging arousal. He reached her splashing water up her back as he stopped. Gasping, Lexia arched her back. He groaned at the sight, wrapping his arms around her, and boldly cupping her breasts.

"Caught you," he murmured against her exposed neck. Sinking his teeth into her soft flesh, not to hurt, but mark. Lincoln turned her around.

"Want to swim?" she asked.

"Sure," he lied.

Lincoln watcher her turn, and dive into the cold water. Coming back up, her long hair was plastered against her skin.

"Cold?" Lincoln laughed.

"Just a little," she replied, splashing him, and swimming away.

He was beside her seconds later, his well-muscled body easily cutting through the water. "Did you enjoy your cat games?" she asked.

"Mmm very. You make a very good cat, but the best game is yet to come." Flashing her a cocky grin he swam through the water, kicking his legs to splash her. Lexia squealed and raced after him.

Lexia shivered as she excited the water, but soon forgot as a big, hot, male body wrapped around her. Whispering, "Time for the best game."

Finding herself suddenly flipped around, Lincoln lowered himself to the ground, pulling her along. She sat with a sexy male between her thighs and giggled, the cold forgotten as heat surged through her.

"Mmm, definitely the best game." She sank her teeth into his neck.

Lincoln growled, thrusting his hard cock into her already damp core. Lexia rode him, it was raw and primal. Nothing was held back as she slammed against him, driven by her sexual hunger. Shockwaves of pleasure rippled through her body as she pinned him to the earth. His fingers clung onto her hips, the edge of his claws scraping against her skin as they pierced through his own skin. She'd never made love to a man with such wild abandon in her life. She loved it. Loved him.

His hands hungrily trailed up her body squeezing her breasts, pinching her nipples. The pressure built, hotter, tighter as she moved harder, and faster. His hands caressed her body, his skin so hot she felt branded by his touch. She was pure sensation, her body felt agonizingly tight. Screaming as she reached boiling point, Lexia exploded around him, and collapsed forwards as he thrust once, twice, then lost control. He jerked and shuddered under her. "Lexia," he said in a hoarse whisper,

She roused later sprawled against his warm body, her hair splayed across his chest. The sun had travelled lower across the sky, and Lexia shivered as a light breeze blew over her naked skin.

"Cold, baby?"

"Mmm, best go find my clothes."

"Put this on, I'll go get your clothes." He handed her his t-shirt, then gold light shimmered around him revealing his beautiful, black panther. He rubbed up against her before disappearing into the undergrowth.

Lexia pulled on his t-shirt wrapping his intoxicating scent around herself. She'd never felt like this before, the way she'd made love to him with no embarrassment, holding nothing back until every wall she'd ever built around herself had fallen. She'd bared her soul to the wild panther that was now her life.

He prowled out of the trees, growling low, carrying a bundle of clothes in his mouth. "Stop with the scary cat routine, you're a sweet boy really," she smiled.

His response was to growl again, opening his mouth slightly to reveal the sharp gleam of his predatory teeth. "Sorry, you're a big, bad pussy cat," Lexia teased.

He jumped on her softly, knocking her to the ground. He discarded her clothes and his sharp teeth bit lightly down over her neck in warning, but she wasn't afraid, he was her panther, and she trusted him with her life. "You are my magnificent panther, and all I want to do is pet you until you purr."

He let go of her and settled over her body; his head rested on her breasts. His gold cat eyes stared into her own. Lexia ran her hand through his velvety soft fur; she loved the feel of it sliding between her fingers, so soft, so warm. She felt him purr, rather than heard it, the soft vibrations tickled across her skin.

"Mmm, I could lay here forever stroking you, but I am starving and it's getting late. Time to go, my beautiful panther," she whispered, looking into his sleepy eyes, stroking her fingers between them.

A rumble vibrated on her chest, before he jumped off, and she got dressed. Lincoln stayed in panther form, so Lexia picked up his clothes and followed. The path he chose through the trees was big enough to accommodate her easily. Even as a cat he took care of her; she realized both man and panther loved her with all their hearts.

When they reached familiar territory Lexia stopped and crouched in front of him. "Shift for me, baby." Gold lights sparkled around her and she shut her eyes, the blinding lights too much.

When his warm fingers gently pushed hair from her face, Lexia opened her eyes to gaze into the gold-brown eyes of the man she loved. "Hey."

"Hi, you had a good day?" he asked standing.

Lexia stood and hooked her arms around his neck. As his

hands glided down her body and rested on her thighs, she jumped, wrapping her legs around his waist. Looking down into his eyes, Lexia brushed dark hair from his face.

"I had the best day, thank you." She bent her head, kissing him softly. He groaned into her mouth as she deepened the kiss, tangling her tongue with his.

Jumping to the ground she said, "Get dressed, baby." And took off, laughing.

CHAPTER 26

Ten minutes later Lincoln walked hand in hand with Lexia, listening as she spoke of how she found it easier up in the tree tops. Mesmerized by her beautiful smile, and the twinkle in her eye, he never scented the intruders lurking by their home.

Lexia's eyes widened as she was dragged her to the ground by her throat. Two more hunters moved toward him, guns glinting in their hands. Lincoln leapt, shifting mid-air and landing on the nearest man, he sank his teeth into his throat; blood filling his mouth.

Casting a glance in Lexia's direction, Lincoln wanted desperately to help her. The hunter had his arms clamped around her throat, trying to knock her unconscious. Bloodlust raged through him but he couldn't help her. The sound of gunfire reverberated through the forest. The bullet grazed his side as he twisted sharply around. The hunter had no time to fire again, his teeth ripped into his flesh, ending the hunter's life.

Lincoln turned to find Lexia free. Circling the last hunter, she waited for her moment to strike. He let out a savage roar and raced across the clearing. The hunter turned his head, eyes widening in fear at the sight of him. Lexia spun, kicking the man square in the gut. He fell backwards as Lincoln leapt, sinking his claws into his chest as he landed. The Hunter was dead before he hit the ground.

Lincoln shifted rushing to Lexia, panic twisting in his gut as he looked her over for injuries. "I'm fine, Lincoln, just bruises," she croaked, rubbing at her throat. "Lincoln you're bleeding!" she gasped.

"I'll be fine, just a graze from a bullet."

"A bullet! Those bastards tried to shoot you?"

"Lex, don't fret, we need to leave. More might come."

"Lincoln, I'm so sorry, you've lost your home because of me."

"Hey." He rubbed his knuckles against her cheek. "It wouldn't be home without you and we'll be back, when we've killed every damn person who ever thought to hurt you." The sentence ended in a growl.

They went into the aerie and packed some clothes. Lincoln gave into Lexia's protests and allowed her to patch up his wound. Once done, Lincoln watched her dash into the bathroom quick, to collect a few things. She paused in front of the mirror, absently rubbing her hands against the few bruises forming. The hunter had nearly choked the life out of her; just the thought had him enraged again.

"Are you alright?" he asked her, forcing his voice to be

gently.

"Yeah, fine," she answered, looking away and picking up the things she'd originally gone in there for.

Lincoln knew she'd never tell him but he could tell this attack had really shaken her. She never sensed the danger, just as he hadn't. They'd been too caught up in each other and it had put them at risk.

"We need to go now," Lincoln said, descending the ladder. He watched her sadly take one last glimpse at the bedroom before following.

"Where are we going to go?" she asked.

"I'm not sure. We may have to check into a motel…but… they will be watching those. Might be best to leave town and work out our next move."

'What? No Lincoln, I need to get that box my dad left me. I need answers."

"I know," he whispered, feeling torn.

He locked the house behind them, and together they jumped to the ground. Walking in silence towards town, both were on high alert, yet Lincoln could almost see Lexia's brain churning for an answer to keep her in this town.

"Alice!" she gasped suddenly.

"What?" he answered, not looking at her. He wouldn't be letting down his guard until they were safe.

"We can stop at my friend's house, at least until we get into my house then I'll leave town."

"Ok, baby. Lead the way."

Lexia and Lincoln made it across town to Alice's house without any problems. The second Alice opened the door, Lexia rushed inside; she had a feeling when Alice got over the shock of seeing her, she'd start shouting – it's what Alice did.

"OH MY GOD! Lexia? What the fuck!" Alice screamed at the top of her voice.

"Shush!" Lexia hissed, noticing Lincoln wincing from her volume. His Shifter hearing couldn't be turned off like hers.

"Shush! Have you any idea what the police are saying about you? That you killed your dad - killed your dad. I mean, what a fucking joke, you wouldn't harm a fly. And…I have spent the last week being questioned by police about your whereabouts…and I keep saying I have no idea where you are, but do you know what? I should know where you are because you're like my best friend… and if you had a problem you'd come to me, right? But no…I have no idea! You've been missing all this time and your best friend had no clue if you were alive, or dead. Do you realize what I've been through, Lexia?" Alice took a huge breath, her hands resting on her hips.

"W–" Alice cut her off; she hadn't noticed Lincoln yet.

"Don't give me excuses, Lexia; you're lucky I even let you in! I mean where you have bee—" Alice focused on Lincoln, then back to Lexia, focusing on the bruises forming on her neck.

"Oh no...no," Alice said, shaking her head. "What the hell is that asshole doing here? Look at you Lexia. Your neck, what the hell has he done to you?"

"Alice, wait. Calm down, and I'll explain. Lincoln hasn't done anything to me."

"Are you stupid? You think those bruises are nothing? Where did your spine go? You—"

Lincoln interrupted with a deadly growl that vibrated over Lexia's shoulder. Alice's eyes widened in fear. "That's enough insults for one day I think," Lincoln added, his voice calm, level. "I need to shower. Where's the bathroom, Alice?"

Alice said nothing, pointing a shaking arm behind her, and returned her gaze to Lexia.

"Will you be alright, baby?" he asked softly against Lexia's neck. He nuzzled at her skin sending shivers down her spine. Lexia closed her eyes and breathed deep, wrapping his scent around her for strength.

"Yes, Alice was just shocked."

He kissed her neck lightly. "I'm so pleased I killed him for marking your skin."

"Linc, I'm fine, you're the one who was shot. Now go get

clean, I'll be there soon."

Lexia stared after Lincoln forgetting about Alice. When she was with Lincoln, it was like the whole world dropped away, nothing mattered but being close to him.

She was startled out of her daydreaming by Alice. "Ahem!" She glared at Lexia.

"Ok, I'll tell you everything but first you must promise not to freak out anymore."

"Me, freak out? Never!"

They both giggled and headed into the front room, like it was any other day with her best friend whom she could trust with anything.

"First of all, when are your mom and dad due home?"

"They're not here, remember their cruise? You were supposed to be staying here with me? Had to basically chuck them out the door with everything that's happened."

"Yeah, I remember now. God, I'm sorry, Alice," she whispered.

"Look, Lexia, just tell me what's going on, I promise to keep quiet until you've finished."

Lexia closed the curtains then turned to her friend; would she believe her? Well, there was only one way to find out. She sat down and began at the beginning, keeping it together when she reached her dad's death wasn't easy; a few silent tears ran down her cheeks but she waved Alice off until she'd finished the story to date.

Alice was silent, her eyes growing wider as the tale unfolded. Lincoln walked in near the end, dressed in a new change of clothes. Alice whiten in his presence but said nothing.

"Say something!" Lexia said, her heart thundering in her chest; she'd expected millions of questions, or a good old Alice rant, but silence… Alice was never silent and it frightened Lexia more than the idea of facing hunters.

"Super-human fighters, and men that turn into animals?"

"Well, yeah, kind of."

"Lexia...I...I...What is there to say?" She took a deep breath, then looked at Lincoln, and back to Lexia. Her eyes softened in pity before answering, "Lexia, sweetie, I think you need help."

"I AM NOT MAD, ALICE!"

Lexia heard Lincoln make a disgruntled noise behind her. Alice's eyes widen. Looking around, Lincoln was in the process of stripping. Lexia realized what he planned.

"Lincoln! No she'll—" but she never finished before bright gold lights shimmered around him.

Alice jumped up as he turned to light, a startled squeak left her throat as she fell backwards, scrambling away as a huge black panther stalked towards her.

"Alice, it's okay, he won't hurt you, look." Lexia walked over to her panther, and crouched at his side before running her hand through his fur. Lincoln purred as she petted him, his head rubbing softly against hers.

"See, he's still Lincoln."

"He's purring...like a cat." Alice didn't move but her body softened.

"Alice, please, you have to believe me."

"Can I stroke him?"

"Oh, erm... Lincoln?"

He growled softly in return, and she got the message; Alice could now, but skin privileges were not for everyone.

"Yes, this one time."

Alice crept forward slowly, her trembling hand outstretched towards Lincoln. As her fingers slid into his fur, she sighed. Lexia guessed how she felt, feeling his fur so soft and warm; she just wanted to curl up next to him and rub her whole body against him.

Alice was now at his other side slowly running her fingers down his back. "He's so soft," she murmured.

"Mmm, he is," Lexia rubbed her face against his side wrapping her arm over him. Lincoln purred softly then shifted back. Alice jumped, startled, but Lexia sat still and looked up into her man's face.

"Enough you two, I am not a pet," he said it in a serious tone, but Lexia could see laughter in his eyes. Her cocky man loved to be swooned over whether he was panther or man.

"But you're so soft and..." Alice's eyes trailed up, "hot!"

"Alice!" Lexia gasped at her friend's blatant remark.

"Now, now ladies, no fighting," Lincoln laughed, pulling on his clothes.

"Alice, eyes down. He's mine," Lexia hissed.

"Oh alright. God you always get all the hot guys, it's so not fair!"

"Lexia, you need to get clean. A good hot bath will help your bruised body. I'll help you." With that he dragged her out of the room.

Alice's voice trailed behind them, "So. Not. Fair!"

Lexia sunk into the bath, the hot water encasing her body. She sighed deeply, closing her eyes and laid back. Lincoln had filled the bathtub; the water covered all of her body and her hair floated on its surface like a black cloud around her head. She relaxed deeper as Lincoln's strong fingers stroked over her forehead and into her hair, massaging her scalp. Lexia moaned, slowly drifting off to sleep. The tension and stress from earlier washed away into the hot water with each tender touch.

She wasn't sure how long she'd laid in the bath half-asleep when Lincoln lifted her out. Shivering, goose bumps broke out across her skin as the air whispered over her wet body. She snuggled deeper into his warmth as he cradled her, carrying her from the bathroom to the spare room.

He laid her down on the bed, and began to towel off her skin; she moaned with pleasure as he worked down her body. Looking at him through sleepy eyes and smiling dreamily as he neared her thighs.

When she'd been thoroughly dried Lincoln explored her body with his hands; he loved the feel of her silky soft skin and loved the way she wiggled and moaned beneath him. Gently massaging down her body and she moaned deeply making his cock jump in his pants. "That nice, baby?" he whispered in her ear.

She shivered, looking at him with gold, desire-filled eyes. "Yes," she replied in a breathy whisper.

Lincoln thought she was the most beautiful creature he'd ever seen, especially when her eyes turned gold with raw hunger. He knew she didn't like her gold eyes, yet she didn't understand when her eyes turned gold showing her hunter genes, hers were completely different. Lexia's eyes weren't the matte, lifeless gold he'd seen in the few pictures that had been captured of the hunters, but bright and full of life. They seemed to sparkle and dance with joy, and whenever he saw them she reminded him of an angel sent down from heaven.

Her eyes held only goodness; a fire so bright it hurt to look sometimes. He'd seen the way the hunters looked as they flashed to gold in front of them. It wasn't shock from discovering that she was different, it was fear. Fear because when they looked into her eyes they saw goodness, life, and the power running through her veins, they'd never possess.

He worked his way down her body, kissing and sucking at her skin; she shuddered and gasped beneath him, exciting him further as he neared the apex of her legs. Gently rubbing his stubble-covered jaw across the sensitive flesh, she cried out softly, arching her back, wanting more. He trailed his fingers over her and she pushed against his hand wanting more friction, but he continued with his tender strokes, torturing her a little longer.

"Lincoln," Lexia moaned.

He parted her soft pink flesh and gently blew against her swollen clit. Moaning, Lexia tilted her hips toward him. "Please," she begged.

"Please what? Tell me what you want."

"Oh Linc, please, please touch me." He lowered his mouth to her awaiting core, slowly licking his tongue upwards.

"More," she cried.

He unleashed the panther that he'd been holding back, sucking and licking at her, lapping up her juices. He held her down, his claws slicing through his skin and drove her to the edge. He felt her tightening, bracing for the moment she snapped.

Lincoln pulled away from her, smiling at her little moan

of protest. He quickly removed his clothes, freeing his himself and thrust it into her desire-swollen heat. He pounded her hard and fast holding nothing back and relished in the wild cries and moans that left her mouth.

She opened her eyes and stared into his which were flashing from human to panther as he lost control. Tightening around his cock, he shuddered at the added sensation, crying her name as his warm juices flowed into her. Lincoln collapsed forwards, rolling to his side. Lexia snuggled into his body and almost instantly fell to sleep. He watched her for a while, stroking her soft skin before sleep claimed him as well.

CHAPTER 27

Lexia woke early feeling disoriented. She was in an unfamiliar room and bed; she missed waking to the sun peeking through the wooden slats of Lincoln's blinds. She missed seeing green tree tops and the peace of the forest; already cars were busy outside. As the days had gone by, she'd become more in tune with her hunter abilities. She rolled over and looked at Lincoln's peaceful face; his eyelashes casting shadows over his cheekbones. She wondered how he slept through all the noise around him, his hearing was even better than hers; no wonder he lived in the middle of the forest with only the scurry of animals and the chatter of birds to break the silence.

She slipped out of bed leaving Lincoln to sleep and crept into the kitchen to find Alice already there nursing a cup of coffee. She glanced at the clock, it was only 5:30 am.

"You're up early."

"Hmm, got a lot on my mind, and so are you?"

"Yeah, I have a lot on my mind, too." She smiled, pouring herself a coffee and joining her friend around the table.

"You look well-rested, though. Lincoln must have done

a good job wearing you out last night. Sure sounded like it," she smirked, trying not to laugh.

Lexia felt her cheeks flush with heat, "Oh god." She hid her face in her hands and burst out laughing. Alice joined in, and soon both girls were crying with laughter.

"What's so funny, girls?" Lincoln asked, walking in with just his jeans on.

"Put some clothes on," Lexia laughed, whilst Alice covered her mouth trying to stifle her laughs.

Lincoln seemed completely unfazed by their hysterics. "Nope. Shall I make breakfast?" They never answered too busy laughing, tears streaming down their faces.

Eating breakfast with Lincoln and Alice, Lexia felt better after her laughing fit. She should be mortified that Alice had heard her having sex with Lincoln, but somehow it just didn't matter. It was Alice, she knew every secret that she'd ever had. She smiled to herself looking at the two people that meant the world to her.

Alice spoke, her words ripping Lexia's soul back open, and the smiled dropped from her face; a feeling of dread settling in her stomach.

"I didn't mention it yesterday, but I attended your dad's funeral, Lex." Alice sat in silence, waiting for Lexia's response.

Lexia didn't respond, she stared at a crack in the table, yet really saw was the last time she had seen her dad. It didn't matter how many happy memories she had with him, that moment was imprinted on her mind, slowly eating away at her. She didn't want to talk about this; the grief was too much, a swirling vortex trying to pull her in. Just one slip up and Lexia would never get out; she had to forget, she had to move on.

"It was just a small funeral, my mom and dad went and his work colleagues, some of his students. I put a picture in his grave for you. It was that one I took three years ago on your birthday, do you remember? I said goodbye for you, Lex."

Lexia looked up, tears blurred her vision, and she felt Lincoln's warm hand slide onto her thigh. It eased the hurt a little but not even Lincoln could heal this wound. "I said goodbye, Alice... I said goodbye when he died in my arms."

Alice sucked in a breath. "Lex, Lexia I, I…" Lexia knew Alice didn't mean anything by her words but she was upset and angry. Angry at the hunters for murdering her dad, angry that she couldn't attend her own father's funeral. Angry that everybody thought she'd killed him. Lexia felt so angry that she wanted to scream; scream until her throat felt hoarse.

Lexia sighed, "I know you didn't, you're my best friend, Alice. Thank you for being there when I wasn't."

"I can take you there if you like?" she whispered.

Did she want to go see her dad's grave? Did she want to open a wound she barely kept closed? Did she want to feel the pain, fresh, and raw? Yes…No…Yet she might never get a chance again. She might die today…tomorrow...She owed her dad this much. He'd given her, her life, the least she could do is visit the place where he was laid to rest. She hoped it might help to let out some of her pain and sorrow; lately it had become harder to control. She could feel it eating away at her and, Lexia knew sooner or later she'd have to let some of it out, before it consumed her.

"I'd like that," she whispered.

Later she walked into Deadwood's graveyard with Lincoln at her side; she could feel the energy bouncing off him. He didn't like this, she was putting herself in danger, but as he kissed her and walked away to patrol the area, he said nothing, and she knew he'd walk into hell if she asked.

Alice led her to a freshly dug grave, the earth was still rich and moist. "I'll give you some space, babe." Alice left her in front of the clean crisp headstone her dad had picked himself, she collapsed to her knees and let her tears fall.

"God I miss you, Dad," Lexia whispered.

She missed his overprotective ways, and bickering with him over dinner. She'd always complained about her plain, ordinary life, yet now she'd give anything to have it back. Everything felt surreal, like she lived in a constant dream-state, because monsters weren't real, boyfriends didn't turn into animals, and mothers weren't monsters. These were the things of fairy tales, these were the things written in books. But it was all true, and her father was...*dead.*

Laying the flowers that she held in her hand on the earth, Lexia spoke to her father, "God things are so messed up, I wish you were here. I'm trying to do the right thing, I'm trying to be the daughter you raised me to be but I...I..." Lexia was sobbing so hard she could no longer speak. *I'm so sorry I couldn't save you, Dad, please forgive me.*

Crying looking at his headstone, marked, 'beloved father' she thought he was the best dad she could have ever asked for. He'd taken her away from her mother, and she wasn't sure she understood exactly why, but he'd said she was dangerous, to run from her, and Lexia trusted her dad. She couldn't bring him back and no matter how many hunters she killed it wouldn't make the pain go away, but she could make sure no one else had to feel this way because of the hunters.

Her tears slowed as a sense of calm wash over her; she was going to destroy all hunters, anger replaced her grief.

She felt Lincoln's approach before he spoke, "Lex, I'm sorry, baby, but we've got company. We need to move, now." Lincoln's voice was soft but she heard the undertone of urgency.

She looked at the gravestone again, tears spilled over her eyes; she couldn't even have this time at her dad's gravesite. Anger swirled around and around her. They were taking everything away from her. Lexia felt like she was trapped in a raging storm, it whipped and swirled around her, feeding her fury. "I won't let evil win, Dad. I love you."

"Baby, now."

"Goodbye, Dad," she whispered, and stood wiping the tears from her eyes. It was too much, she couldn't control the storm much longer; it raged, burning her soul.

Lexia heard Alice squeal and spun around to find six hunters blocking their path. Lexia squared her shoulders. The time to grieve would come, but right now she needed to fight; right now she needed to be a hunter.

"Alice, stay behind us," Lexia said through gritted teeth. Her body was trembling all over. She looked at Lincoln by her side and for a second the storm cleared as she gazed into his fierce face. *How I love you.*

The hunters all took a step forward, towards the people she loved, and the storm broke.

Walking forward, the rush of power poured over her body as the world dropped away. All that existed were the men threatening those Lexia loved. She'd never felt the kind of fury running in her veins; she'd lost control. Lexia let out a wild scream. Running forward and channeling all her pain and anger into her every kick and punch, she cut through them with blind rage. She had no thought to what she was doing. Spinning and kicking on pure instinct, she blocked hit after hit, the knife she pulled from her boot ran with blood as it sliced through flesh and muscle. She didn't stop, she didn't falter, not until every hunter lay dead at her feet.

Panting Lexia held her knife, ready to strike but as she looked around all she saw were Lincoln and Alice. The red haze cleared and the storm in her soul settled. She looked at all six men laid dead at her feet, their blood splattered her hands and arms. Lexia looked at Lincoln; who hadn't a mark on him. Confused she asked, "I killed them all?"

"Yes, love, you killed them all. Come on, we need to move before more come, or the police."

"But I..."

"Grief does strange things to us, Lex. Do not feel bad for protecting those you love."

But she did feel bad. She hadn't just protected those she loved; she'd lost control, let the anger consume her until her body acted, and killed on its own. She'd killed them and it had been easy; she'd taken a breath and in the next they were dead, their blood covering her body. How had she killed them without even knowing what she was doing?

Lincoln reassured her not to feel bad, yet she couldn't help it; every life she took chipped away a piece of her. She worried that one day no one would recognize her. She'd be a monster, and she would be looked on with fear. The power in her scared her; what would happen if she lost control again and she never came back? Would she kill those she loved and be powerless to stop it? She'd vowed to kill all hunters who posed a threat to the world but what if she was the biggest threat of them all?

CHAPTER 28

As she tried to sleep that night, Alice's face drifted through her mind; the way she'd looked at her in the graveyard. Alice hadn't seen the friend she'd known all her life, she'd seen a monster.

"Lexia!"

Lexia rolled over and looked into gold cat eyes.

"Mmm?"

"Stop it," His voice was stern, the voice of a predatory panther.

"I can't, Linc," she said in a haunted whisper.

"Baby," he sighed, "Do you enjoy killing? Does it make you feel powerful?"

"No…No, it kills me a little each time. I don't want this power, Lincoln. It's changing me... I'm becoming the monster my father feared."

"No, Lexia, you're not. Your life changed, not you; you've always had power. Always been you. Those hunters will not hesitate to kill you, or your friends; they live for the kill, for the rush of power. Your father didn't want this life for you but do you think he'd want you to die? Do you think he would have wanted you to let them kill Alice?"

Lexia laid in silence for a while thinking over Lincoln's words. He laid by her side, his limbs tangled with hers. The feel of him, his warmth, his steel-hard muscles that held her with such tender care, this is what she lived for now. To live everyday with Lincoln, to make him smile and laugh; to feel the rush of pleasure from his every kiss.

"I live for you, Linc, I don't live to kill." Lexia kissed him softly on the lips.

"No more torturing yourself over this, you need to accept what you are, Lex."

Accept what I am, can I do that? "I'll try to, Lincoln," Lexia reassured.

"Good," he said softly, with a smile.

"There's something else that's been bothering me."

"Go on."

"There must be loads of half-Hunters out there, so why me? What makes me so different? And why can I take out pure hunters when I'm only half?"

"I had been thinking the same thing. Hopefully you can find your answers tomorrow in that box."

"I hope so." Lexia snuggled further into the heat of his body. Resting her head on his chest she fell to sleep listening to the steady rhythm of his heart. Without him she may have lost control a long time ago; he anchored her, kept the darkness away.

The next morning Lexia and Lincoln moved quietly through the streets of Deadwood, both of them with a gold gleam in their eyes. They kept to the shadows, invisible predators ready and waiting to strike. Lincoln stalked behind Lexia, she could feel the energy rolling off him like static against her skin.

Lincoln clasped her hand as they entered the familiar forests that surrounded her home, and they walked hand in hand stopping at the edge of the tree line behind her dad's shed. Lincoln shifted and disappeared into the trees. She heard him move a few paces ahead then he became silent, became one with the forest, a panther on the hunt.

Lexia closed her eyes and concentrated on the sounds around her; she could hear two men talking in the front garden but they seemed relaxed so she guessed her panther hadn't been detected.

Time seemed to slow down as she waited for him to return, the longer Lexia waited the more bad memories resurfaced in her mind. In an attempt to get her mind onto something else, Lexia tried to focus on the conversation the two hunters were having not that far away. It didn't help; Lexia began to pace, her hands fisting and releasing in agitation. *Where the hell is he?* Panic and anxiety clutched at her, she turned and...The panther prowled out of the trees, turning into bright gold lights as he approached.

"Lexia, what's wrong?" Lincoln asked, concern in his still cat eyes.

She let out her breath and uncurled her hands. "It's just being back here…It's…" her words died in her throat. Lexia shook her head unable to continue.

"We'll be gone soon." He hugged her tightly. Soothing her jagged, raw, wounded soul. "Most of the men are on the ground floor and around the edge of the house. From what I could see there doesn't seem to be anyone in the bedrooms; maybe a dozen hunters in total."

"If I could get past the two out front, then I could climb up to my window."

Lexia watched the war in his eyes. His need to protect her clashing with the task she had to do. Reluctantly he said, "Okay, if I distract them and lead them away, then you can climb in. But Lexia, you get in and out, no fighting or going downstairs. Alright?"

"I will, I promise. Where shall I meet you?"

"Run straight for Alice's, make sure you're not followed. I'll find you, okay? No matter what happens, you go in and out then straight to Alice's. Don't wait for me."

"Okay," she whispered, feeling nervous all of a sudden.

Rubbing his knuckles against her cheek, Lincoln shifted and disappeared into the trees.

Minutes later Lexia heard a commotion in the back yard;

followed by gunshots, the hunter's shouts, and Lincoln's returning growl. Lexia fought the urge to run to him; her every instinct was to protect the man she loved. Yet she couldn't; she had to get the box, she had to find answers.

The two men that guarded the front door ran around the side of the house. Lexia dashed undetected across the grass. She stood for a second and looked up at her window, remembering all the times she'd climbed in and out of her room. Scaling the side of the house and opening her window, Lexia jumped through and took a step forward into the room. Something crunched under her foot; looking down Lexia lifted her foot, revealing a photo frame. Picking up the frame, Lexia looked at her father's smiling face, his warm eyes stared at her. The picture was from three years ago, Alice had taken it; the three of them had, had a dinner for Lexia's birthday. Her heart twisted in pain.

Looking around the room, Lexia felt oddly detached. Her bookcase had been tipped over, draws pulled open, their contents spilling onto the floor. All her memories lay shattered and broken around her. That's how she felt, broken and shattered. It took all her strength to not collapse to the floor. To not succumb to the tears burning behind her eyes, the sorrow ravaging at her soul.

How dare they destroy her memories like she didn't matter? Everything in the room had been a memory of her life, and the hunters had broken them without a second thought. Blinding anger raged through her veins, washing away the sorrow. They would pay. She did matter. Lexia marched for the door. Hands clenched into fists, adrenaline pumped through her veins as she clasped the door handle.

In and out… Lexia paused, taking a breath.

She couldn't go downstairs and put herself at risk. It didn't matter that her body hummed for vengeance. She'd promised Lincoln, he'd let her do this alone even though it went against every one of his instincts. He was a shifter, they protected what was theirs to the end; they didn't let them go on their own. But he had, for her, because she needed to do this one thing alone and he trusted and loved her enough to not be rash.

Lexia took a deep breath and let her anger go as she stepped back. *I'll need something to put the box in... my backpack.*

Lexia turned; looking around the room, she found the bag and emptied out her school things, replacing them with a few trinkets and the broken photo frame. Padding to the door, Lexia listened for movement in the hall; hearing nothing she cracked open the door.

Lexia slowly walked towards her dad's room, careful not to make a sound. When she stepped inside, she ignored the mess, going straight to his closet. Opening the door, Lexia pulled up the boards, and just as her dad had said, there amongst the cobwebs sat was the box. Picking it up, Lexia ran her hands over the smooth wood around to the brass clasp.

The floorboards creaked outside the bedroom door.

Lexia froze, listening as whomever was on the landing walked past, and opened her bedroom door. *Shit!* Realizing she'd left the window open, Lexia had a split second to decide her next move. She either jumped out the window behind her, hoping she could outrun the dozen hunters he would likely alert, or she faced him and took him out before he could utter a single word.

Running lightly across the landing and through her door. He had no chance to turn around; Lexia jumped on his back, clamping her hand over his mouth to muffle his shout, they fell forwards, towards the bed. Positioning her other hand, she twisted, hearing the sickening crack as they landed on the mattress.

Lexia leapt back from his body, and crossed to the window she'd left open. As she glanced out she saw the two guards had returned to the front. *How am I going to get out now?*

Quietly Lexia returned to her dad's room, putting the box in her bag, she took calming breath's, and thought through her options.

Peering out her father's window, she judged the height. If she jumped, the group of hunters in the yard would see her, and the aim had been to go in undetected. Or she could climb onto the tree that brushed up against the side of the house, but would it hold her weight?

"Well, only one way to find out," she muttered, pulling up the window.

The branch hovered above the window frame, it had scraped off the paint on the house from its movements over the years. With her back facing away from the house, Lexia tucked her fingers into the wooden planks, and pushed up, her feet resting on the window sill. Reaching one hand for the branch, her heart a jackhammer in her chest, Lexia clasped the thick tree branch and jumped, reaching out with her other hand. The branch bowed slightly from her weight but held. Slowly Lexia walked her hands towards the trunk, her legs dangling lifelessly.

Half-way across, a hunter headed her way, his head cast down looking at his phone.

Lexia held her breath as hung silently from the branch, releasing it in a rush when he turned the corner.

Hurrying along until she reached a part of the branch strong enough to pull up on, Lexia heaved herself and crawled with a speed, her panther would have been impressed with, to the trunk. Jumping to the ground, she froze, listening, then took off through the forest.

Trees blurred together and the air whipped past her face with such a force it brought tears to her eyes, yet she didn't slow down. She felt the first bit of hope blossom in her heart; she'd finally retrieved the box, and she finally had the information to answer the questions that burned in the back of her mind.

A flash of black caught her attention before her panther ran beside her. "I got it, Lincoln, I got it!"

No one followed them from the forest, and after finding Lincoln his clothes, they walked through the back streets of

Deadwood. As they rounded the corner to Alice's street, Lexia stopped in her tracks. Her body stiffened and her eyes bled to gold.

"Lexia?"

"Can't you feel it?"

"Feel..." but she'd already taken off, ripping her hand free from his.

Lincoln raced after her, his panther rising to the surface, but even then he struggled to catch up with her. As they neared the house he could smell it; hunters. His panther growled and paced in his mind.

They stopped in the front yard; the door had been kicked open. "Alice!" Lexia's strangled whisper hit him in the gut. She couldn't handle any more death, a fresh bloom of fear clutched hold of his chest as Lincoln realized he might not be able to bring her back this time.

"Lexia, wait. They could still be inside."

"Oh I hope they are!" Her eyes glowed impossibly brighter and she was gone, a blur of speed. As pushed the door aside and it shattered.

Her enraged scream met Lincoln as he rushed into the house, finding her in the kitchen near the back door, glass littered around her feet and a piece of paper clutched in her hand. Yet he didn't notice that first. First he noticed the blood slowly dripping to the floor from her hand and he became aware of the power humming through her. Shaking with rage as her eyes turned slowly towards him, they looked not of this world.

His panther snarled in his mind, its fur standing on end. His every instinct told him, she was unstable…a danger.

Lincoln walked slowly towards her. "Lex?" Her eyes focused on his own.

"They will pay," her voice was like a deadly blade, so cold, so empty.

Lincoln reached for her, as their hands touched, she lashed out sending him sliding across the room. He hit the wall with an "oomph." His panther growled and snarled, ready to attack, yet he forced it down because this was Lexia…he loved her.

Lexia gasped as she saw Lincoln fly across the room; she looked down at her hands like they belonged to someone else. *What did I do?*

Collapsing to the floor, great heaving sobs rocked her body. She'd lost control of all the power that flowed through her veins.

"Lincoln, I...I…I'm, I didn't mean to." She looked up, swiping at the tears that blurred her vision; she feared what she would see there. It would finally break her if Lincoln look at her like she was a stranger, a monster. Yet she saw only concern, love, and fear. Fear for her.

"What's happening to me?"

"Oh, baby." Lincoln rushed to her, holding her tight.

Clinging to him, Lexia buried her face into his chest, and breathed in his musky, earthy scent. He softly stroked her hair and slowly she relaxed. Lincoln was her anchor, as long as she had him, everything would be okay.

"They have her, Lincoln; they'll let her go if I turn myself in," she rasped.

"You know as soon as they have you, she's dead. As long as you're free she lives."

"She's my best friend, Linc, I have to do something. She's in this because of me."

"We will do something, but we can't going running in head first. Let me clean your hand and let's see what your father left you. Maybe he left answers that will help."

Twenty minutes later Lexia sat with her hand bandaged, though the wounds had nearly healed. Holding the backpack, she pulled out the box and held it in her hands. "It's funny; I've wanted this box for so long, but now that I have it, I'm frightened of what I'll find."

"My Wildcat, scared?"

She looked at him and smiled at the cheeky glint in his eyes, he was right. She opened the box. Inside she saw a letter; opening it she ran her fingers over the crisp white paper and read the scrawled handwriting…

My dearest Lex,

If you're reading this, then I have failed to keep you safe and for that I am truly sorry. Sorry your life has now been turned upside down, and I'm sorry I'm not there to help you. I can only say, I lied to keep you safe and I hope you can forgive me.

You must have so many questions. But to answer them I must start at the beginning:

I'm a scientist, Lexia. I used to work for a secret government agency. That's how I met your mom, Lucy Hunter. She was the head scientist on the project we worked on, to enhance soldiers so they'd become stronger, faster, and heal quicker than the average human.

In the year 2010, Lucy made the breakthrough that led to the creation of hunters. They were everything we had hoped for, built to fight and protect; the only difference in their appearance was that their eyes turned gold. Your mom volunteered to be changed, too. Before she was changed she had blue eyes just like you.

Lucy and I were very happy, and we married later that year. A year after we were married I started to notice some changes in her moods; she would lose her temper very quickly and often talked of the hunters feeling taken for granted. I didn't tell anyone. I loved her, Lexia, and I didn't want to admit my wife was slowly changing.

The government began to lose control of the hunters and your mom had changed so much that I no longer saw the beautiful, smart woman I fell in love with. But my plans to leave her changed in November 2011, because she told me she was pregnant.

When you were born, I thought I finally had my wife back. For the first five months we were the perfect, happy family. But the morning you turned five months old, I came into your room to find that the gold eyes you were born with, had turned blue. Lucy lost control; she screamed and smashed your nursery apart. I quickly took you away from her and when she calmed down, she demanded to take you into her labs and do tests. I thought at first she was merely worried about your health, but for some reason I couldn't let you go, something felt very wrong. So I convinced her to just take some blood and when she left for her labs, I went searching in her home office. What I found, Lexia, made my stomach turn, and I took all her work, and left with you.

Everything I found is in this box and you mustn't let anyone have the information, Lex. You see, you are not half-hunter like Lucy wanted me to believe. She's developed a new project to create better hunters, only she experimented on embryos this time. I don't believe the government knew about this, they had lost complete control over them by then. I have no idea how many of the babies survived, and at the end of 2013 the government terminated all hunters and closed the project down.

I hoped that with them all gone we could finally settle down but I never could be sure so I kept moving us about until you turned six, when I decided I had to try to give you a normal life. So we moved to Deadwood and you started school. After years of never being found, I finally stopped looking over my shoulder but always in the back of my mind I thought they would come for you. I never believed they had managed to kill them all.

I want you to know that to me, you were always my daughter. From the moment I first looked at your beautiful face, I was in love, and nothing, not even DNA, could change that. You've grown up into a beautiful young woman and I'm so proud of you, Lex.

You're not very different from any other girl, maybe a bit stronger, but nothing like a hunter. I suspect the power lays dormant inside of you, and a major emotional event will trigger the change.

My biggest fear is that the power will take over, and you will become the monster Lucy set out to create, but I have faith that you were born with this power, and can control it.

You must fight it, Lexia, and I'm sorry you have to do it alone. If your mother ever finds you, do not trust her, Lex. Please remember that. She may look and act like your mother but all her humanity died the day she became a hunter.

I will always love you, my baby girl. Stay strong and be safe,

Dad

Xxx

Lexia stared at the words on the paper, they blurred together as tears fell from her eyes; big drops fell smudging the ink. She wasn't even his real daughter, and yet he'd risked his life for her, died for her, when he knew all along a monster lay dormant.

Did Lucy even love her? Or was she just some experiment in an attempt for power? At least she knew why they wanted her so badly now, she'd been created to be stronger than them.

A sob escaped her throat, and Lincoln pulled her tighter against himself. He was sat wrapped behind her, his chin resting on her shoulder so he could read the letter with her. He hadn't said a word since she'd begun reading, and Lexia worried what he would think of her. As if he'd read her mind he whispered against her neck, "I will always love you, no matter what."

Turning into his embrace, she nestled her head into his chest, and finally let go of all the pain she'd been keeping locked inside.

She didn't know how long she'd been sobbing for; he didn't say anything, just held her tight and stroked her hair until her tears ran dry. Pulling back, Lexia wiped at her face, looking at Lincoln's t-shirt stained with black smudges of mascara.

"Sorry."

"It's just a T-Shirt."

"What am I going to do?"

"We are going to hunt." Lincoln smiled, his eyes flashing panther.

Lexia shuddered; sometimes her panther could be very scary. "It says I have until midnight."

"Well first, you'll arrive early, and you *will* be alone. Just not for long."

Lexia smiled and picked up the research her dad had taken from Lucy. She thumbed through it, the paper creased and stained with age. Most of it made no sense at all but she put it back into the box, promising to read it all when she had time; when Alice was safe.

"I can't see them killing me on the spot, Lincoln. Why create an elite army then kill them off?"

"I think you're right, they will want you to join them. My only fear, Lexia, is they won't let Alice go, but keep her as a motivator."

"They touch her, and I will show them what they created."

"You won't need to, Lexia. I will come for you."

"God everything is such a mess. We have hours until we need to go; I can't just sit here."

Lincoln looked at her hungrily, and she wondered why he never seemed to see the same image she had of herself. He looked at her like she was strong, when she felt anything but.

Leaning towards her he whispered, "Let me help you forget."

The moment Lincoln's lips touched Lexia's the world fell away. She clung to him, opening her mouth to let him deepen the kiss; his tongue swept into her mouth making her moan. Her legs wrapped around his body, pulling him closer, she needed him so badly, needed him closer. Lexia pulled at his clothes, needing to feel her naked skin against his. Her nails scratched along his back making Lincoln moan.

Lincoln pulled back pulling at Lexia's jeans; he dragged them off her legs and stood, stepping out of his own and pulled his torn t-shirt over his head. She locked eyes with Lincoln, then gazed down his body as he stood naked above her. Groaning, her eyes bled to gold at the sight of his hard flesh.

Lincoln crushed his body against hers. Thrusting into her; she cried out, arching her back to let him in deeper, welcoming him. He shuddered, taking a hard grip on her hip and then thrust again.

There was no managing the emotions she felt for Lincoln. Uncontrollable and infinite hunger, that's what she felt for him. His hand clenched and unclenched on her hips, a whisper of claws against her skin. She met his gaze and demanded more. He rode her with the uncontained power of his beast. Her body went tight around his velvet steel as she clawed his back, whimpering and moaning in need.

Lexia looked into Lincoln's eyes as they repeatedly flashed from man to panther. Hovering above her, his body a masterpiece for only her. Lincoln pulled her leg from his waist and pushed her wide, slamming into her, unrelenting.

Lexia's last thought, was the kiss of his claws against her soft skin, and the whisper calling her name. She had a fleeting thought, of how in that moment, her life was perfect.

CHAPTER 29

Just as the sun was setting that night Lexia walked out of the forest and up her driveway. The gravel crunched under her boots as she took slow steps towards the house, a feeling of foreboding in her gut. She looked to the sky as if praying to the cruel god that had messed up her life.

The sun was a rich, red ball dipping behind the dark green forest; bright streaks of pink, purple, and orange covered the horizon. Lexia sighed; it was beautiful. She'd never really appreciated how nice her home was, a little white, wooden house nestled on a green canvas; it was so peaceful. She realized now why her dad loved it here so much. It was such a stark contrast to the labs and cities he must have lived in before she was born.

Lexia stopped. Two men approached, breaking the peace she was just enjoying. *Time to work!* She held up her hands, palms out as they approached but the energy coming of them didn't feel at all non-threatening.

"I'm unarmed, just as you asked," she spoke in a low, level voice.

They smiled cruelly at her and it was obvious they planned

to fight. *Going to be like that then is it?*

Lexia centered her mind, breathing slow, steady breaths until she felt the rush of power run through her veins. They stopped a few paces ahead and her whole body itched to fight, but she held back, allowing one of the men to take hold of her hands, bringing them behind her back.

"I'm turning myself in, let my friend go." Lexia made no attempt to struggle against the hunter's hold even though it took all her resolve to restrain her instincts. She knew what was coming, she could see it in their eyes; the thirst to fight, to draw blood. Lexia hoped she was strong enough to get Alice out of this alive.

The hunter at her front smiled, evil intent etched on his face.

"Such a pretty face, but no brains." He swung his fist towards Lexia. She watched it move through the air, felt it whisper past as it brushed against her skin. At the last second Lexia forced her head back into the face of the hunter behind her, she broke free as he fell back from the impact. The unlatched handcuffs clattered to the ground.

Kicking the hunter square in his chest as he came at her, Lexia watched as he flew backwards. He cowered back as she closed the distance between them, and brought her boot down onto his skull. He grunted before collapsing unconscious.

"No brains, hey?"

She turned to find the last hunter sprawled on the floor;

his hand clutched his nose as blood poured through his fingers.

"You broke my nose!"

"Well I was told you wouldn't harm me if, I was unarmed, serves you right really." She turned, striding away from them.

Fear gripped at her as she approached the house. She had to succeed; Alice's life was on the line.

Failure is not an option.

Lexia knocked and took a step back. The hunter that answered the door froze as he saw her, confusion crossing his face. Stepping forward, Lexia punched him before he'd registered who she was. He slumped to the floor, and she jumped over him into the swarm of hunters filling the hall. Her fear had gone and her instincts took over, a small thrill ran through her blood as she began to fight.

They came at her from all sides, but she stood her ground fighting them off as best as she could in the tight space. Taking a blow to the back of the head that made her vision blur, she faltered slightly giving a hunter the chance to clamp his arms around her. Lexia bent forward, forcing all her muscles to lift the heavy weight off the ground and flipped him over her back. He landed with a grunt, knocking two other hunters down. Lexia spun around, kicking the man behind her in the gut. He doubled over in pain and Lexia brought her fist to his head, knocking him unconscious.

As she went to spin around, ready and willing to fight whoever came next she felt the cool metal of a gun being pressed to her head. She froze, fear clenching her heart.

"Oh I'm going to enjoy killing you. You'll wish you'd never touched me when I'm done." Each word was said with the cold edge of evil and Lexia wondered how she'd ever thought she was like them.

Slowly she turned, hands held up, to face the hunter that she had attacked in the drive. Dried blood stained his face and his bright gold eyes held no warmth, just pure hatred.

"Problem is I probably don't have enough time to torture you before Lucy arrives. I will just have to be satisfied with shooting you in the head, I guess." He smiled cruelly, making Lexia shudder.

"Hey!"

Lexia looked toward the voice to see a tall, well-muscled hunter walk in through the front door, his voice held the notes of authority. She looked back to the hunter holding the gun, to see his next move.

"She broke my nose!" he whined.

"I don't care what she broke, there's a no kill order on her."

"But, but look what she did," he gestured to the moaning men on the floor.

"I was told I wouldn't be attacked. All I did was defend myself."

"Shut up, bitch!" She saw the flick of his hand as he brought the gun towards her head. Lexia twisted to the side, the hilt of the gun grazed past her cheek. She turned her back to him and spun, bringing her elbow down on his head. He crumpled to the floor with a grunt.

"Don't move." Lexia held up her hands again, slowly facing the hunter in the doorway.

"Let my friend go, you have me now," she sighed.

"Do we? Something tells me you could leave any time you want. I think we'll keep your dear friend as leverage." He smiled sweetly but it never reached his eyes.

"I want to see that she's okay, or I'm gone." Lexia smiled sweetly back.

He laughed, "I like you, follow me...And no funny business." Lexia shivered; she didn't want to be liked by him, she was nothing like him.

As they walked past the groaning hunters on the floor he kicked them shouting, "Get up you worthless bunch."

Lexia followed him upstairs; he led her past her dad's room, and stopped in front of hers. "Here she is," he said, opening the door. "Only a few cuts and bruises, she put up quite a fight, you know," he chuckled.

She rushed past him, pushing him into the doorframe. Alice was sat leant against the wall in the corner of her room, her hands and feet were bound and there was a scarf tied over her eyes. She whimpered and cowered away as Lexia touched her.

"Shush, it's me."

"Lex?" Alice whispered.

Lexia pulled the scarf off her face; a dark purple bruise marked her cheek bone. She turned to glare at the hunter behind her, "I'm going to fucking kill you for touching her!"

He laughed again, fuelling Lexia's anger. "Now, now it wasn't me; in fact it was the guy whose nose you broke." He laughed again like his fellow soldier being hurt was rather funny. "Come on, then. I'm not letting you out of my sight."

"I'll come back for you," Lexia whispered to Alice. She nodded once, a tear sliding down her face. "I promise, Alice, you will get out of this."

Lexia stood and walked to the door. "Blindfold," he snapped.

"You put that back on her and I snap your neck," Lexia growled.

"Hmm, we'll see." But dropped the subject and moved from the doorway to let Lexia pass.

As she followed him down the stairs he said, "I'm Derrick, by the way." Lexia said nothing. Derrick would be dead soon enough; she didn't buy his 'I'm- a-nice-guy' routine.

Derrick put a pair of handcuffs on her and bound her legs. Sitting on a chair at her kitchen table, he picked up the book laid there, open on his page. "Titanium handcuffs by the way. Don't hurt yourself trying to break them," he muttered, preparing to read.

Lexia glared at him as he propped his legs on the table. She leaned back against the wall and smiled to herself; soon she'd hear her panther's calls.

Lexia couldn't get over how odd this situation was. Here she was, tied up in *her* kitchen, while a stranger sat at *her* table reading... *Is that my book?*

"Hey, that's my book you're reading!" Lexia cursed herself the second the accusation left her lips. This man was a hunter and she was tied up, defenseless. *What's wrong with me?*

Derrick looked up, his gold eyes staring at her. As she looked into them, she realized his eyes were different; yes, they were the same gold as every other hunter's she'd seen, but his eyes held a deep sadness. She wondered who this man had lost.

"Is it? Sorry about that, but it's really quite boring around here." Amusement twinkled in his eyes for a second before the sadness returned and he looked down to read the book again.

"Why are you here if it's so boring?" *Why am I talking to him?*

He looked back up, seeming to consider his answer before he said in a low voice, "Not everyone has a choice over what they do. I ... I have a family to protect."

"But ... I don't understand? If you have a family, then why are you here?"

His eyes hardened. “Because I’m dead to them, the government made sure of that. And…Lex is it? The hunters, they are far worse than the government.”

A cold chill slivered down her spine at his last words. Lexia didn’t ask any more questions, she could feel he was done talking.

She looked around the room and as her eyes settled on the spot just outside the kitchen door, she was sucked back in time. She could see his bleeding, broken body; she remembered the way her heart twisted in agony as he took his last breath. Yes, the hunters were far worse than the government but she’d been created to be stronger than the hunters and they would regret that she was ever born.

She looked up; the back door opened and a man walked in. He was a lot shorter then Derrick and his face was scarred; his eyes trailed over her body making her skin crawl.

“Jack has the boss on the phone,” He spoke to Derrick but his eyes never left Lexia. He looked at her with a sick, greedy hunger, and for just a second Lexia wanted to beg Derrick not to leave her alone with him.

Derrick got up with a sigh, and headed for the door. The hunter who’d brought the message took a step towards her with a twisted smile on his face. Lexia shuffled back, which only made him laugh, but as his hands bent to touch her Derrick’s head popped back inside.

“Dave, you are to watch her, not touch her! Do. You. Understand?”

"Yes," Dave sighed, stepping away and taking a seat.

Lexia let out the breath she had been holding. For a minute there she'd felt helpless and vulnerable and she didn't like it. She sat in silence, not looking at him, but never once did she feel his eyes leave her. She hoped he'd do as Derrick said.

After a few minutes he pulled his chair close to her, smiling as he pulled a long knife free. The knife was almost as long as a sword, the hilt decorated with red rubies and filigree. Lexia thought the knife was rather feminine but as the blade neared her skin she stopped admiring the weapon and took a deep breath.

"He said I wasn't allowed to touch, but this can." The blade glistened in the light as it travelled toward her chest, the sharp edge sliced through the material of her top.

"Like my knife? I took it off this woman I killed," he smiled at the memory. "She was real pretty...like you."

As the fabric of her top split, the blade sliced her skin; Lexia sucked in a breath at the sharp sting. "Oops, sorry," he said as he continued to lightly cut her, trailing the blade down between her breasts.

Lexia felt sick; fury and revulsion rose up her throat like vomit. Her heart pounded in her chest as the monster kept slicing into her top and exposing her skin for his viewing. She felt dirty and weak; why didn't she do something? But she couldn't get her mind to respond; her body felt frozen, her muscles had locked, and her breath was caught in her throat. She'd never felt so alone…so violated.

He stood above her admiring his work; a slow trickle of blood ran between her cleavage and down to her navel. He'd successfully cut away all the fabric that covered her chest revealing her plump, lace-covered breasts. His hand stretched out to touch her, and Lexia pressed further back into the wall, her skin crawled with revulsion. A little voice in her head kept telling her to do something, not to let this monster taint her, but her body wouldn't respond. Any second his dirty, repulsive hand would touch her.

A single tear slid down her face and his grin grew wide. She looked into his eyes seeing greedy hunger there, and in that second she gave up, accepted that his hands would feel her flesh. His eyes lit up with her defeat and a single finger touched her collarbone making her quiver; he trailed it slowly toward the curve of her breast, savoring the anticipation.

Lexia bit back a cry, tears flowed freely down her face as she shook. She felt so ashamed; she was a hunter, more than a hunter, but right now she was just a frightened girl, lost and alone.

She thought she heard a faint call; hope blossomed and she listened harder. There it was again, the faint, distant call from her panther. Lexia's blood boiled to life; she wasn't alone, she had her panther and he would never leave her. The rope around her legs tore apart and for a split second she sat stunned, looking at the monster that had been touching her moments ago. He lay curled on the floor, groaning and clutching at his groin from the kick she'd given him.

Lexia shuffled over to the blade he'd dropped; she picked it up with her hands still bound behind her back. No matter how hard she pulled they wouldn't come free.

Dave stirred. Lexia scrambled to her feet and walked over to him. The kick to his head knocked him out cold and she ran for the stairs, clutching the knife at her back.

The air was now filled with the cries and growls from the fight outside, she could hear the pounding feet of hunters running towards the back yard; Lexia sent a silent prayer to her panther before heading to Alice.

She'd nearly reached the top of the stairs when a loud gunshot reverberated around the hall. White-hot pain pieced through her thigh causing her to cry out and fall. Someone grabbed at her ankle and with her hands bound at her back, Lexia couldn't stop her head from hitting the step. Her vision blurred as her head bumped each step as she was pulled down.

Lexia still had the knife clutched in her hands and it dug into her flesh as she was flipped over by the hunter that had shot her. She kicked out, hitting him in the gut, but the pain in her thigh weakened the blow and he lashed out, hitting her across the cheek.

She felt dazed and the more she struggled, the more the knife at her back dug into her skin. Yet she didn't stop fighting, she wouldn't give in. Her panther was coming, she just needed to stay alive until he found her. He would come. He'd always come to her rescue. So many things in her life had changed, so many people had lied to her but this one thing, this one belief. It was the foundation of her strength, a truth that ran to her core.

With the panther in her mind's eye, she kicked with her good leg and caught him between the legs. He called out, his eyes watering in pain as he bent over gasping, clutching his crotch. Lexia ran up the stairs, tripping she hit her shoulder against the banister but she gritted her teeth against the pain, reaching the landing as another shot sang into the air.

She felt the bullet graze her arm, the burn of hot metal making contact with her skin. His heavy foot falls pounded up the stairs and as she reached the door to her bedroom, she heard him grunt and fall. The sound of fighting drifted up the stairs, and then a gunshot, leaving behind only silence. A silence that spoke of death, a silence worse than the cries of battle.

Not waiting to find who'd taken him out, Lexia jumped into the door, her shoulder hitting it first. Smashing through, splinters of wood went flying everywhere. Alice's eyes widened in fear but she seemed incapable of speech. Lexia raced to her friend turning and holding the blade down near her feet. "Cut the rope against this, careful of your skin."

Alice obeyed moving her legs up and down against the blade. Lexia could hear footsteps slowly coming up the stairs, each heavy foot fall more deadly than the last. "Hurry," she hissed.

The rope split and Alice began on her hands. The boards creaked on the landing.

"Alice, quick out the window."

"What?" her voice was hoarse with fear.

"Alice, look." Lexia pointed out of the window. "Linc is down there waiting, you need to leave now."

Alice climbed out the window; her hands shook with fear and she looked into her friend's eyes. "What about you, Lex? Your hands, how will you climb?"

"Yes, *Lex*. How will you climb?" Derrick said from the doorway.

"Go now," Lexia ordered. Turning to face Derrick, she heard Alice sob as she climbed down.

"I don't need to climb, I'll jump," she answered Derrick; her voice calm and deadly.

"Really? Even with all those injuries?" He spoke back in the same indifferent tone he always used. "Hmm, you really must be something."

Emotion flashed in his eyes, but before Lexia could work it out they became sad and haunted again.

Lexia took a step back towards the open window, limping with the pain in her leg. She heard Alice calling Lincoln's name and his answering roar.

The pain in her body was a constant hum, her head felt slightly fuzzy but she smiled, Alice was safe and Lincoln would protect her.

"What's so funny?" asked Derrick.

"Are you going to make a move then?" Lexia asked instead.

Derrick took a step forward and Lexia sat on the window sill, for some reason she didn't feel threatened by him. His hand touched his gun in its halter. Lexia swung one leg out the window.

"You're really going to jump?" he asked, not moving.

"Yes, you best shoot me, Derrick." Lexia smiled.

"Not today," he said.

Lexia swung her other leg out dropping towards the ground. The air whipped past her face, twisting her hair in the air. She heard Alice scream her name and then met the ground. The air whooshed out of her body, and she gasped in pain as she met the ground. Her knees buckled, and Lexia fell forward. For a second Lexia laid in stunned silence, then she heard her panther growl, and more gunshots fired.

Everything came into sharp focus. She rolled over seeing Derrick standing in the window, he nodded once, and she jumped to her feet running across the lawn towards Alice and Lincoln.

With each step, pain shot up her body. Limping as she ran, her heart drummed loudly in her ears. She was nearly there, freedom just seconds away. Lincoln took out two more hunters before his eyes rested on her.

"Go!" she screamed at him. He hesitated then turned into the forest, Alice running ahead.

The sound of a car crunching on gravel made Lexia force her body to go faster; the tree line was yards away, she was nearly free.

"Maura baby?" Lexia slowed, she knew that sweet, soothing voice. "Maura, don't go."

Lexia stopped. That was the voice from her dreams, that voice sung her lullabies. *But who's Maura?*

"Maura?" Lexia turned.

There stood a petite woman; she had pale skin and long, straight hair the color of corn fields, and her eyes were gold. She looked so pale and beautiful; she seemed to glow in the moonlight.

"Mom?" Lexia whispered. So many emotions bombarded her mind: confusion, disbelief, hope, fear.

"Yes," she replied, and time stopped.

"But..."

"Maura, my dear, come to your mother."

"But my name's Lexia." Anger flashed across her mother's face and her hands turned into fists before relaxing again.

She felt confused by her reaction, the hunters around her seemed to tense.

Lexia's every nerve felt alert, ready, waiting for someone to make a move.

"Well, I see Jonathon did more than just take you away from me."

"I don't understand," she whispered.

"Did he tell you nothing? How stupid he was to think

hiding you away, and giving you that name would change your fate. I designed your fate, Maura, there is no escaping it."

"Jonathon? What do you mean, changed my name?"

"My dear, sweet, stupid Maura, your father wasn't who you thought he was."

"My father was Mike Granger."

"No, he was Jonathon Michael Burton. Come with me, Maura, and I will tell you everything; I will show you your true destiny."

Lexia looked at the arrogant woman and wondered how she could be her mother. She was small and petite where Lexia was tall and curvy. With her pale skin and blond hair, they looked nothing alike, and yet the way she now fidgeted in impatience and how her eyes blazed with anger seemed so familiar. But there was one thing Lexia was certain of, this woman was surrounded by darkness. As she stood there waiting and her impatience grew, the dark swirls of energy grew stronger; her aura was nothing but blackness.

Lexia was nothing like this woman and she had no interest in the things she had to show her.

"I'm sorry but I'm going to have to decline." Lexia slowly turned to leave, every sense following the dangers around her.

"You dare defy me? You are mine, Maura."

Anger swirled through Lexia's veins. "Yours! I am no one's,

and my name is Lexia." She turned and walked towards the tree line, the hunters around her moved with her but didn't close the distance between them.

"Lexia!" bellowed Lucy.

Lexia froze, suddenly frightened by the anger in her mother's voice. The air around her felt charged with power…with darkness.

"I created you! I created you to be man's destroyer, not man's defender! You are named Maura for the darkness you will bring to this world!"

Silence settled around them, not even a breath could be heard. Her mother trembled with rage; a volcano ready to erupt.

Lexia felt frozen in time, the whole world moving around her while she was stuck in a nightmare where she was created for evil. She saw movement to her right; her heart began to pound louder but still she couldn't move. She watched in horror as a twisted smile crossed her mother's face, and caught the glimpse of black velvet in the tree line.

Her dad's voice spoke into her mind. *Whatever you do, don't trust her,* and the sound of a gunshot broke the silence.

In that moment Lexia realized she'd made the biggest mistake of her life. How silly she was to think a voice from her dreams could be the mother she'd always wanted. For just a split second, Lexia had forgotten what her father had told her, she hadn't wanted to believe she'd been manmade to kill. She wanted a mom who actually loved her; she became the little girl that wanted a family.

Lexia had never realized until that moment how much she'd wanted, needed, a mom.

Lexia watched her panther, her life, collapsing to the ground. Listening to the screams of her best friend; she turned and looked at her mother one last time. Saw the satisfied smile that lit her face; she was a monster and Lexia would never be fooled again. She only hoped that it wasn't too late.

"Lex! Lexia!" Alice's frightened screams blasted through the haze.

She looked around to see the hunter who'd shot Lincoln aim his gun at Alice.

Lexia moved, sprinting towards her; she jumped putting herself between Alice and the gun. She felt the bullet as it tore through the flesh and bone in her shoulder. She hit the ground crying in pain.

She had never felt pain like it. Her body began to shut down; overcome with pain, but she couldn't because the hunter was aiming his gun again, and others circled like vultures.

Lexia forced back the pain and the fog in her head.

"Run!" she screamed at them. She saw Alice trying to help her panther as he collapsed a few paces away.

How she wanted to run with them but there were a dozen

hunters out for blood and only she stood in their way.

Lexia turned, facing them head on. She reached deep inside of herself to find the will to drive her on. The pain became a distant memory as she felt a powerful energy fire through her muscles, giving her strength.

Lexia became a hunter; she became more than a hunter.

The world dropped away and she heard nothing other than the steady rhythm from her heart and the calm rush of her breathing; she craved blood, she craved their deaths.

The cuffs that bound her hands, broke easily apart. The men before her froze in fright. Lexia stepped forward, wielding the ruby-covered knife, hacking it into their flesh.

Cries of pain filled the air; blood ran from Lexia's arms and covered the knife until the red rubies could no longer be seen. Men and women dropped dead around her as she moved with lightning speed, chopping and slicing into their bodies.

Lexia didn't feel any pain as they cut through her skin, or as their fists and feet connected with her body; her blood dripped to the ground, staining the earth. And with every drop of her blood that was spilt, she felt more powerful. Their cries of pain, and fear, only made her want more. Lexia was lost in the fury of her bloodlust, the power that she had within her had taken over, and it drove her on through the pain. She craved to feel the blood of her enemies run through her fingers; the metallic smell of blood filled the air and she loved it. She smiled in triumph, she relished in the kill.

"Lex!" Alice called.

But Lexia didn't hear her friend's call. She wasn't Lexia anymore, she was the hunter her mother had created; she'd become the monster her father had feared.

"Lexia! Stop. Please!" Alice's voice was filled with fear and worry.

A small part of Lexia's mind registered her friend, but as more gunshots were fired, she became lost again. Leaping onto the man holding the gun, he fired a second time, but Lexia had already reached him. Twisting his hand to the sky, she wrenched his arm, ripping it from its socket. He called out in pain, dropping the gun.

Lexia smiled, retrieving the discarded gun, she put it to the hunter's chest. Her heart beat faster, adrenaline coursing in her veins.

"Please…" he begged. She laughed, pulling the trigger, watching the life drain from his eyes.

"Lex! Lincoln needs you. Please, he's dying."

Lincoln?

She moved onto the next Hunter, her hands clenched around his head.

"Lincoln needs help!" Alice screamed "He's dying, Lexia!"

Lincoln is dying, he needs me.

The sickening thought broke the bloodlust; Lexia looked down at the man beneath her and his lifeless eyes stared back.

Turning to run into the forest, her gaze swept across Derrick stood in the doorway of her home; he looked at her with pity and fear. Then she looked upon her mother, at her car, and the look in her eyes chilled Lexia to the bone.

Lucy looked at her daughter in awe, she was everything she hoped she'd become; a killing machine who fought past pain and injuries.

Lucy knew she had to take away all the things that Maura loved. The people who helped her keep the power under control, and then she would be hers to use as she pleased. They would be an unstoppable force.

Maura was everything she had wanted to create; she smiled at her daughter as she ran to her lifeless panther. "Let her go," she called. Yes, her daughter would soon be hers and the panther would soon be dead.

Chapter 30

When Lexia reached Lincoln he was laid limp on the ground, his breathing slow and labored. Lifting him into her arms, she struggled to hold his weight, but somehow found the energy to run through the trees. Alice sobbing behind her.

"Hold on, baby," she repeated continually as they travelled deeper into the forest.

With every step, pain pulsed through her. Lungs burning with every breath, her arms trembled with the strain of holding her heavy cat. Her stride faltered, slowly she felt the power in her veins deserting her. Barely jogging, Lexia focused everything into making one foot step in front of the other. She hurt everywhere; blood ran over every inch of her, making her hands slick, threatening to dislodge Lincoln from her grasp.

"Lexia, where are we going? He needs a hospital, you need a hospital!"

Lexia stopped. *Just a breather.* Laying Lincoln down gently, Lexia panted hard, fighting against the nausea she felt. The urge to give up was almost impossible to ignore. She could let the darkness sweep her under until she felt no more pain, until she felt nothing at all.

"Lex, Lexia? Are you listening to me?"

Lexia focused on Alice. She looked blurry. Swaying, Lexia reached for the nearest tree trunk to keep herself upright.

Alice sunk to the ground, sobbing uncontrollably. She looked at Lexia, her expression saying, 'save us Lex.' Yet Lexia needed someone to save them. She looked down at her panther's body, his breathing so shallow she could barely see his chest moving.

"Lex... please," Alice sobbed

But Lincoln always saves me; what am I going to do? He's dying and I can't carry him to a hospital. How do I explain him being a cat? What am I going to do? God the pain, I wish it would stop. Please, someone make it stop.

Lexia looked around her, staring into the trees. Lincoln moaned at her feet and when she looked down he exploded into light.

Alice gasped.

Lincoln lay in human form at her feet, the bullet had hit him in the side just below his ribs.

Shit, how am I going to carry him now?

"What's that mean?" Alice whispered.

"I don't know. Come on, you will have to help me."

Lexia heaved him up, wrapping his arm around her shoulder and Alice did the same on the other side.

"Hold on, Lincoln," Lexia said sternly.

Both walking as fast as they could manage, they half dragged Lincoln through the forest. His quiet moans, and their clumsy steps the only sound to be heard.

"I can't carry him much further, Lex." *Neither can I,* Lexia thought.

"Just a little further, please," Lexia begged. She couldn't lose him, not her panther.

Alice tripped. Lexia struggled to keep Lincoln up, she cried out in pain as her shoulder was jostled and dropped to her knees.

"Get up! Help me!" Lexia shouted at Alice's crying form.

"But Lex, it's no use, he's too heavy! Look at him, he's dying and we are miles from help, and look at you! You're injured worse than him; how are you still standing? Any min…"

"Alice!" Lexia's voice was like a blade. Alice stood not even daring to breath.

"We're here, help me."

"We're nowhere, Lex," Alice whispered, lifting Lincoln onto her shoulder.

Lexia walked forward and pulled aside the vines that covered the entrance in Lincoln's home. They kept walking towards the center tree.

"But Lexia?"

"Look up," she answered.

She heard Alice gasp as her eyes settled on the huge aerie nestled in the tree. They laid Lincoln gently down and Lexia looked up the tree trunk.

She ran jumping, digging her hands into the bark, pulling her body higher up the trunk but as she reached out with her arm to grasp the lowest branch, pain from her shoulder zapped through her body, stealing her strength. Lexia fell to the ground.

"Damn it," Lexia cried, the pain consuming her every muscle. "I need to get up the tree for the first aid kit!" She collapsed on the ground crying, her body shaking uncontrollably. Everything hurt, her thigh, and shoulder felt like they were on fire. She crawled to Lincoln. "I'm so sorry, Linc, this is all my fault," she sobbed. "I'm just not strong enough, I couldn't save my dad and now I'm going to lose you, Lincoln... Lincoln, I love you."

Lexia pulled off the last bits of her shirt, sobbing, she pressed it against his side. She looked at his deathly pale face as he whimpered in pain.

Lexia kissed him gently on the forehead remembering the words he'd once said to her, 'have faith in yourself.' She wouldn't give up, she'd fight to her last breath.

"Hold this," she said to Alice.

As Lexia stood up, the world tilted. She looked up into the tree, *I have to get up there! I have to save Lincoln.*

Lexia braced to run, when sensed another presence, and Alice gasped. Bending, she pulled the knife from her boot as spun to face the intruder.

The first thing she noticed was his eyes were not gold but green, as green as the forest around them. They glowed in the darkness, and he stopped immediately upon seeing Lexia.

He was as tall as Lincoln with a well-built body, his light brown hair was cut short showing off his sharp, masculine face. His skin was sun-kissed, and he was dressed smartly in a suit, yet it didn't hide the fact that he had a wild edge; there was something about this man, something…not quite human.

Lexia stood her ground, holding the blade towards the man, and slowly moved to cover Alice and Lincoln.

"Alice, keep pressure on his wound," she said as she slipped in front of her. "What are you?" Lexia directed at the green-eyed man.

Her voice was calm and deadly, but in reality Lexia was fading. Her body felt weak and tired, and it took all of her effort to hold the knife steady. She forced every breath from her lungs, keeping her blurred vision on the green-eyed man.

Lexia wanted to surrender to the darkness that was calling her.

"I'm a doctor, my name's Caden. Linc called and left me a message yesterday, saying he needed my help. I came as soon as I got it. Look, I won't harm you, hunter. Let me help you. Let me help Linc."

"I'm no hunter!" Lexia growled, stepping forward.

"Hey, hey. I meant nothing by it... y-your eyes are gold."

"What are you?" she asked again. The darkness claimed her for a second and she felt her legs wobble.

"Leopard," he whispered.

Lexia swayed. The world was drifting away, she could hear buzzing in her ears. She clung to life. She had to protect them.

"Let me help you, please."

Lexia never answered. Her head swam, she called Lincoln's name but nothing left her lips; the pain had become too much for her. It was all-consuming; a raging monster attacking every fiber of her being. She wanted it to stop. She needed it to stop.

The darkness swept her under, and Lexia welcomed it, welcomed the numbness that took over her mind and body. She felt nothing, no pain, no fear.

She never heard Alice cry out as Lincoln's heart stopped beating, or her sobs begging Lexia not to leave her alone.

Lexia lay unconscious and broken on the ground, her blood seeping into the earth around her. She felt peace at last; in the darkness nothing could tear out her heart. She didn't want to leave, no matter how many times she heard her name being called.

She let the darkness claim her.

About the Author

Rachel M Raithby started her writing career in 2013 and hasn't looked back. She draws her inspiration from the many places she has lived and traveled, as well as from her love of the paranormal and thriller movies. She can often be found hiding out with a good book or writing more fast-paced and thrilling stories where love always conquers all. A Brit who has lived in New Zealand, and Australia, she now resides in a small village in NE England.

Keep up to date with Rachel

www.rachelmraithby.com

38361065R00177

Printed in Great Britain
by Amazon